About the author

Writing has always been a passion of mine and I love getting creative. It's very therapeutic for my Asperger's and mental health. Outside of writing, I enjoy football, music, film and reading.

NATURE'S FALL: EVOLUTION

JOSEPH CORNFORTH

NATURE'S FALL: EVOLUTION

Vanguard Press

VANGUARD PAPERBACK

© Copyright 2022
Joseph Cornforth

A CIP catalogue record for this title is
available from the British Library.

ISBN 978 1 80016 304 1

Vanguard Press is an imprint of
Pegasus Elliot MacKenzie Publishers Ltd.
www.pegasuspublishers.com

First Published in 2022

Vanguard Press
Sheraton House Castle Park
Cambridge England

Printed & Bound in Great Britain

Type I — A Tribute

"It is not the strongest of the species that survives, not the most intelligent that survives. It is the one that is the most adaptable to change." — Charles Darwin

Humanity has always been a superior race. History has celebrated the strengths of mankind for a long time and our actions play an important role in shaping our world today. It was a century ago that the human race underwent a significant change — the Type I enhancement.

It all started as visionary scientist and Cox Industries founder, Edward Cox, tried to cure his dying wife, Sandra. The operation was a success, but it didn't just become their success. It became our success. Cox told the *New York Eye*, "I am excited to reach the century year of the Type I enhancement and I am so proud to have achieved human evolution. This is a celebration of our species and it demonstrates that we are the superior race. Being human is no longer a weakness."

On the Type I, Sandra told us, "I was on the brink of death. There were no doctors who could cure my disease. Edward's scientific breakthrough has given me life again. I feel reborn and all because of my loving, doting husband who didn't just save my life, he enhanced it."

However, the Type I enhancement has had its share of controversy. Many believe that the scientific breakthrough is unnatural, and some say that Cox is 'playing God'. For the past century, Christianity had gone into decline due to the significant advances in science and technology, especially since the breakthrough in nanotech and mind-reading technology by HORIZON and the establishment of artificial intelligence by GENESIS Robotics. This also started the theory that the Type I enhancement was promoting an elitist cause and accusing the more privileged people in our society of ignorance towards the less fortunate, including those that had been affected by the rise of unemployment that is happening today. In 2291, an assassination attempt was made on Edward Cox's life, which thankfully he survived as the bullet had just grazed him. This incident has not deterred Cox's work and he still remains more determined than ever to, as he once quoted; "become our own makers".

Its impact on the world has been huge. Edward Cox's company, Cox Industries, became XCS' largest company for two decades, and is now worth trillions of dollars. Edward has also been the subject of the new movie *Cox Enhancement*, starring Ryan Daniels, coming soon to stream on Viewpoint. Cox had won the MASTER (Mastered Art of Scientific Technique and

Evolutionary Research) prize in 2285 for 'Breakthrough of the Year' and 'Saviour of the World'. Edward has already been tipped for a 'Man of the Century' nomination, with the category's inception to take place in 2399. Love him or hate him, Edward Cox is mankind's messiah and our answer to everything.

The Anniversary Party

Was I so wrong to fear greatness?

Or at least their version of it. Greatness was supposed to be great, right? But the Type I enhancement just seemed wrong. I didn't see it as an achievement. I saw it as defiance.

I sat down on the couch with Laura at the anniversary party. Laura was my best friend from school, but she was more than that. I mean, to me anyway. There were no other people my age at the party. It was mainly adults there, but I didn't mind, as long as Laura was there. I didn't have many friends anyway, but Laura was not just my only friend, she was the only friend I needed. She had a smile that would make you feel so warm and at peace inside. She was so intelligent and so beautiful, even if we didn't always agree on everything. She wore glasses and a black dress, which suited her. Laura didn't like wearing glasses, and she hoped that the Type I enhancement would be able to give her perfect vision. I thought she looked so sophisticated with the glasses. I was so shy and embarrassed to tell her that. I was still finding myself, still trying to work out what I was. I was a foster child, so I had always been keen to know who I really was.

The apartment was filled with the gentle sound of soothing jazz music, appreciated by the high society present. There were so many important people at the party. I saw Hollywood star Ryan Daniels, HORIZON founder Don Williams, who was the richest black person in the world and GENESIS founder, Charles Stanson. I had only met them briefly. They seemed nice but I've always found it hard meeting people. There was a holographic banner above the musicians, reading '100 Years of Type I', so brightly lit with multi-coloured letters. The window had a bright and colourful view of New York City. The neon lights intersected the towering skyscrapers of the city and cast a vibrant glow across the skyline. I could also see the lights from the aerocars, aerotaxis and aerobuses. There was hardly any traffic congestion. Ever. The transportation was so efficient as they all had autodrive mode. Living in the big city was sometimes so overwhelming. The buildings I walked alongside were so tall that they reached the sky. I felt so small, as if the buildings were looking down on me.

The men were dressed in tuxedos and the women were dressed in glittering evening gowns. Our android, Christopher, a G-28 model, who was dressed up in a tuxedo, held up a tray of glasses of champagne and refreshments. The G-28 models can be purchased by civilians as servants, unlike the other models, and they had a metallic appearance. Those androids were programmed to be polite to those around them and spoke in traditional upper class British accents. Their vocabulary and response systems were so advanced that, sometimes, it would seem as if you were talking to another person.

"They look so beautiful, don't they?" Laura said, as we admired the women around us. I agreed. I admired them but was also intimidated. They were so mature and sophisticated. I was just a fourteen-year-old girl, as too was Laura. She was way more confident than I was. Laura added, "I mean, they're over a hundred years old, and they're just so stunning. Do you think we'll look this good when we're a hundred?"

I froze. I never thought about undergoing a Type I operation. You had to be twenty-one to have the enhancement. I remembered when I read *Frankenstein*, and Edward was just like Dr Frankenstein, because he performed an experiment that was just so unnatural, and I was so afraid of the consequences. Okay, it may have been just a story, but it just seemed so similar. Was I just paranoid? I had no idea yet. "Yeah, I hope so," I answered Laura blankly, with my mind elsewhere.

"Terra, what's going on? Are you feeling okay?" Laura asked. She knew me so well. She can always sense when I'm feeling troubled. Her intuition was what I loved about her.

"I don't know, it's just... this whole thing is..." I started, but Laura shook her head before she replied.

"Terra, what your father is doing is..."

"He's not my real dad," I answered back sharply. I didn't resent Edward; I was just concerned about what he's doing. He wasn't actually my real dad, so I was just stating a fact.

"Whatever, I mean Edward has done an incredible thing. Didn't you read his interview in the *New York Eye*?"

"I did, but… it all just seems…"

"Terra, greatness doesn't have to be feared," Laura said as she put her arm round me. I stood by my opinion, but the calmness of Laura's arm around me made me feel less tense. She then embraced me, and it made me smile. "Hey, are you hungry?" Laura asked, changing the subject. I nodded.

So, Laura and I got up from the couch and we approached Christopher, who was conversing with my foster mom Sandra. She looked so elegant, with her pale skin, flowing blonde hair and her glittering red dress that shone from afar. I always admired her beauty, but not in the same way I admired Laura though!

"Girls! I thought you might be hungry," Sandra said enthusiastically. "The canapes are just to die for."

"Good evening, ladies," Christopher said. "May I interest you in some refreshments?"

"Yeah, that'd be great," I answered.

"I shall bring you a collection of our cuisine," Christopher said as he walked into the kitchen.

"So, girls, how are you two enjoying this evening?" Sandra asked.

"Oh, it's really good, thank you," Laura answered. I nodded along in agreement. I saw Sandra gesturing to a woman to come over. There was confidence in the way she approached us, and such enthusiasm. I couldn't imagine why. Her smile was widening as she walked over. Maybe it was the champagne. I hadn't drunk alcohol myself, but I knew that it could make people act weird.

"Sandra, this party is just darling!" the woman said with excitement.

"Oh, Catherine, I'm so happy you're having a good time," Sandra replied to the woman. Then Sandra gestured towards me. "This is my daughter, Terra."

"Foster daughter," I corrected her. Again, I wasn't showing any resentment. I was just stating a fact.

"Right," Sandra said in acknowledgement, but I couldn't tell if she was offended by that. "And this is her good friend, Laura. Girls, this is Catherine. She works for the *New York Eye*."

"How do you do?" Laura said politely yet excitedly. She's a reader of the *New York Eye*. "I loved your piece on the last of the tigers. It's so sad that they're no more."

"Oh, my goodness, I know," Catherine said. "It's always sad to see a species of animal go extinct. The tiger was a mighty breed of animal, one that should be celebrated. Sadly, a lot of animals from the old world have died this past century." I never understood why some people referred to the past as the old world. It's still planet Earth. Just that it's a lot different to how things used to be. Hearing people calling the past the old world made the Earth sound like a science fiction story or something. "Isn't it sad, Terra?"

I hesitated. I wasn't sure how to answer. Animals from the past had died because of extreme weather in areas where there was a lot of wildlife, like extreme droughts across the Savannah during the twenty-second century. The Type I enhancement allowed people to control the weather, and that meant third world countries had to endure severe natural disasters. There was a blissful ignorance about the upper class to ignore the effects of how it affected other places which didn't have America's wealth. It seemed that the richer countries got richer, and the poorer countries got poorer. "I agree," I awkwardly answered, trying to avoid any further questions. Sandra then left us to go and see Edward, leaving me and Laura with Catherine.

"You girls go to the same school, right?" Catherine asked. Laura and I nodded. "Tell me, how do you find being at a girls' school?"

"Uh, good, I guess," Laura answered.

"Yeah, I have no problem either," I said.

"I went to a mixed school when I was your age," Catherine said. "There's nothing wrong with same-sex schools obviously. It's just that my parents were so keen for me to engage with boys from a young age. Have you two ever interacted with guys?"

"Not much," I answered.

"I do attend parties like this with my mom where there are boys," Laura said.

"Right," Catherine said. Just as she was about to speak again, Christopher arrived with a tray full of refreshments.

"Thank you, Christopher," I said as he put down plates of rare, luxurious refreshments on a table next to us. The table was small, however, and it didn't seem like all the plates would fit.

"Allow me," Catherine said as she touched the table, and then it extended itself to allow all the plates to fit. On the plates were delicacies such as grilled lobster, poached eggs, caviar, pepper truffles, rice pancakes and kelp. The meat and vegetation were artificially cloned, as good food was rare; they weren't naturally produced. Meat was grown in laboratories because animals were becoming extinct.

"This looks amazing. Thanks, Christopher," Laura said.

"My pleasure, ladies," Christopher said. "Anything to drink?"

"Uh, can I have some kiwano and elderflower juice?" Laura asked.

"And some guava and pitaya juice for me, please?" I asked.

"Right away, madam," Christopher said as he made his way to the kitchen.

"This looks so divine, doesn't it?" Catherine asked excitedly.

"It certainly does," Laura said as she put a spoonful of caviar on her plate. "I've never had caviar before."

"Oh, Laura, you're going to love it!" Catherine said. "It's only catered for New York's finest. Do savour it though."

I put some caviar on my plate, and I took a small spoonful. It was incredible! So incredibly rich in flavour. I was used to the finer things. Even though I was sceptical about Edward's work, I did appreciate my upbringing. There weren't many people in the world who can experience these luxuries, or even just simple things like shelter and food. Since the rise of artificial intelligence, unemployment has grown worldwide, making so many people poor. I knew that I was rather fortunate and privileged in that way. I was never one to brag and boast about it though.

"It's amazing, isn't it, Terra?" Catherine asked me.

"Yes, it's really good," I replied, after I finished my mouthful. I was always around upper-class citizens, so I usually had to be mindful when it came to showing good etiquette. Sandra used to teach me about how to act when around the company that they were keeping. It was important to her and Edward that I try to make a good impression with everyone. In one way, it was intimidating to me as it seemed that I couldn't be myself, but I also thought that maybe they just wanted me to show off my good qualities.

"Tell me, how old are you two again?" Catherine asked.

"Fourteen years old," Laura replied.

"Ah fourteen, such a wonderful age," Catherine recalled. "I had my first kiss at fourteen. Have you two had your first kiss yet?"

"No," Laura giggled. I laughed along with her. It was an incredibly awkward topic. Edward and Sandra were incredibly protective of me, and they had never forbidden me to fall in love, they just didn't encourage it. I was sure they would have to approve of any relationship I had when I got older. Laura was the only person I was attracted to. I guess you could call it love. I couldn't tell anyone that I had an attraction towards girls. Maybe it was just Laura. I didn't know what it was. I was afraid of being judged. There was nothing wrong with homosexuality though. Edward and Sandra have friends who are homosexual and had attended many gay weddings. I was just never keen on being the centre of attention. I was only fourteen, so I was still discovering myself.

"Listen, there is no pressure. You girls have plenty of time," Catherine said reassuringly.

"If we underwent the Type I, then maybe," Laura said. "I can't wait to not wear these glasses any more."

"Honey, that day will soon come," Catherine said. It really saddened me that Laura didn't want to wear glasses any more. They suited her. I wished Catherine could tell her that, but she didn't. "It's just a few more years yet."

I wished I had the confidence to protest against what Catherine said. I was conflicted about what I thought of Catherine. She came across as intelligent and kind, but yet it seemed that she was interrogating us with awkward questions and influencing us to believe that it's okay to not be what we are. Everybody in high society was so preoccupied with their own privileges that they had put their own greed and desires ahead of helping others.

Then I heard three clinks coming from a glass.

"May I have your attention please?" The commanding voice of Edward said as he stood up on a chair. He was a proud man. You could not ignore him. His posture was so upright, being the confident man that he was. He was the complete opposite of me. He thrived on being the centre of attention. Sandra was stood by him. She was such a devoted wife, always standing by Edward, no matter what. He observed the room, making sure that everyone was listening. He was like a king. "This event marks the one hundredth anniversary of the Type I enhancement."

Everybody applauded, including Laura and Catherine. I only applauded to not stand out, though I did so reluctantly.

"There are so many people I wish to thank tonight," Edward continued. "There is one man who invested so much in me. His faith in me has been so inspiring and allowed me to work on one of the most ambitious experiments in the history of science; to make humanity something more. He cannot be here this evening, but Mr Anton Monroe, I thank you. I would also like to acknowledge my beautiful daughter, Terra."

Edward gestured to me, then everybody looked at me. I didn't know how to react. I wasn't used to this sort of attention. I did appreciate the acknowledgement by Edward, but I didn't like him referring to me as his daughter. I was adopted. I also didn't want to be associated with something that was so unnatural.

"And of course," Edward continued, "I want to thank my darling wife, Sandra. It was because of her that this idea took place. It was over a century ago that Sandra had been diagnosed with leukaemia. She had not very long to live. I wanted so badly to eradicate the disease my wife had, so I thought, what if I could fast-track human evolution? What if I could make us immune to disease? With the trust and funding from Anton Monroe, I cured my wife. She was my first patient, and not only did the procedure save my beloved Sandra's life, we have found the key to human evolution, which will make us the dominant race. My company has been founded thanks to this success, and we have become the most valuable company ever. Now, even though we have made trillions of dollars, I tell you this, my friends, the Type I enhancement is just the start. Yes, there have been, let's say, certain radicals who have attempted to tarnish what I have done, but I have never let that tried to stop me. The next phase is the Type II, where not only will you evolve, but your offspring will experience the benefits of human evolution too. This project will see us gain increasing power in our universe, and we will become our own creators. Being human is no longer a weakness. We will become supreme deities and become our own gods!"

There was such a rousing applause when Edward finished his speech. He spoke like one of those great political leaders I learnt about in history class. Edward got down from the chair and went to kiss Sandra after his speech. I looked on in concern. I never found Edward intimidating before, but he had such an appetite for power that I couldn't see him as the caring foster father that he was.

"Wow, that was some speech, wasn't it, Terra?" Catherine asked me. I didn't respond. I didn't know how to. Everybody seemed to be so excited about Edward's speech, but it had made me so uncomfortable.

"Terra?" Laura asked me, pressing for an answer.

"Oh, it was all right," I answered bluntly, unsure of how to answer.

"It doesn't sound like you liked it," Catherine laughed.

"Are you okay, Terra?" Laura asked.

"I don't know," I said awkwardly, as I was about to draw attention to myself, the last thing I wanted. "Doesn't this seem wrong? Isn't this playing with God or…"

"Terra, nobody believes in God any more." Catherine interrupted me as she put her hand on my shoulder. She seemed to be shocked about the mention of God. Religion wasn't illegal, but it was considered insanity and something that to be ashamed of. "Didn't you hear what your father said? We get to become our own creators."

"He's not my real father!" I raised my voice impulsively, which was really unlike me. "And all of this just seems unnatural and wrong! What's wrong with believing in God? What's wrong with liking yourself the way you are?"

Catherine and Laura looked shocked, and everybody at the party looked over at me, including Sandra and Edward. I had never been keen on being the centre of attention, especially not like this. All of New York's high society were gazing in my direction. I was incredibly intimidated and embarrassed. The worst thing was the disappointment on Laura's face. That really upset me most of all. I didn't regret how I felt. Maybe I could have expressed it better. Sandra walked over to me. There was ferocity in the way that she walked. She was clearly very upset.

"Terra, I think you should go to bed," Sandra suggested. Her expression was stern, but she put her arm around my shoulder, maintaining her loving nature. I didn't want to upset anybody, so I just went along with Sandra's suggestion and agreed with her. I wasn't tired, but I thought that maybe I should just hang out in my room and stay out of the way for a while.

"It was nice meeting you, Terra," Catherine said politely. I don't think she was hurt by my outburst. Laura just said "see you tomorrow" but didn't embrace me goodbye. That was quite painful, but I didn't think she was angry with me. I hoped that we would be okay with each other the next day. Sandra went to kiss me on the cheek and embrace me. I then made my way to my room.

The door to my room automatically opened, sensing my presence. I didn't know what the world would be like without the technology from HORIZON. All you had to do was think something and their products would do it. Their sensors were highly advanced. HORIZON was the biggest company in the world. Pretty much all their products had 'Hori' on the first part of their names. It was like their trademark.

I then trod on something. I didn't yell in pain. I just kept it to myself. I hopped to my bed and sat down to discover that it was a cocktail stick. I took the cocktail stick out and the blood that came out of my foot evaporated and my skin healed. I'd seen this happen before, but I couldn't tell anybody about it. Not even Edward, Sandra or Laura. I thought about confiding in Christopher, but I didn't know if G-28s were programmed to keep secrets. I knew they served mankind. I just didn't know how deep a bond they were programmed to have with us. I feared if someone found out that my skin could regenerate like that, I would be persecuted by everybody. The pain eventually subsided, much to my relief. It had to remain a secret. I then got out of my dress and put on my tracksuit and T-shirt and opened up my HoriTab. I used its thought processing tool and commanded 'open HoriBooks' in my mind, and then it opened. I clicked on the 'holo-mode' function, and then the screen opened as a hologram. I tapped on a book about nature in the past (the book had the old world in the title, but I was able to look past that) and read it in order to remind myself of when nature was valued on Earth.

The Symbol Around His Neck

"Good morning, Terra Cox. It is now seven thirty a.m."

I heard the gentle automated wake-up message sound in my room, which was accompanied by mellow music. The lights then switched on and the duvet moved aside and under the bed. The music then faded out. I yawned and then I got out of bed.

I walked into the bathroom. All the rooms in the apartment recognized when we entered by automatically switching on the lights and sometimes greeting us. The bathroom did exactly that. There were two sinks underneath the HoriMirror, which showed the time and date. There were lots of applications on the HoriMirror. I put my hand on it and thought-requested an old piece of music from the rainforest playlist; that kind of music always soothed me. I got out a bottle of strawberry-flavoured AquaDenta from the drawer, and I poured a little bit of it in a glass. AquaDenta wasn't just really strong mouthwash; it had replaced toothpaste as the primary teeth-cleaning tool. They did chocolate, vanilla and strawberry flavours, but each flavour had mint mixed into it. I sipped it and let it flow around my mouth. I did it for just a minute, and then I rinsed my mouth. I was starting to feel more awake.

I then undressed and took a shower. The shower recognized my presence and water came out of the jet. On the far side of the shower, there were two silver buttons with glowing letters reading 'gel' on one and 'shampoo' on the other. I washed myself and then got out of the shower, reaching for a big towel for my body and a smaller towel for my hair. They heated up when I put them round me. I walked back to my room and I got a hairbrush out of my closet to brush my hair.

I then got dressed into my school uniform. I wore a black skirt and blue shirt that had a 'Clifton School for Girls' logo on. I always felt so pressured in my school uniform. It was like my school uniform was heavy, because it represented a huge weight of expectation of me. Clifton School for Girls was a very prestigious school, and I had always been a misfit. I didn't dislike Clifton; I was just so overwhelmed with representing such a prestigious institution. I should be honoured and grateful to be able to attend such a place.

The walk down to the living room was a daunting one. After what happened the night before, I kept thinking about what Sandra and Edward would say to me. I eventually reached the living room, and I could see Sandra and Edward sat down on the couch.

"Terra," Edward said sternly. "A word please?"

I took a deep breath, and then slowly approached Edward and Sandra. My mind was playing through all kinds of hypothetical situations. I took a couple more deep breaths to try and compose myself. I've never really been in trouble for anything, but I've always had to be mindful about my behaviour, especially when very important people were around. Edward wore a suit as usual, which gave such a presence of authority.

"Terra, we need to talk about last night," Edward said to me. I didn't reply. I just let Edward carry on talking. "What you did, Terra, that's not like you. Sandra and I were disappointed about what you did."

"I'm sorry," I said, but I wasn't sure whether I meant it or not. I just said it because that's what I thought Edward and Sandra wanted to hear and I really didn't want to upset them further.

"Terra, if you're ever upset about anything, you can always talk to us about it," Sandra said softly.

"I know, Sandra. I was just..." I said, but then I immediately stopped. I couldn't tell Sandra and Edward how I really felt about the Type I and about the way the world is. I especially couldn't tell them about myself regenerating. "I don't wanna talk about it now."

"Well, whenever you want to talk, just remember that we're here for you," Edward said gently. I was so conflicted. I didn't want to hurt Sandra and Edward, no matter how I felt about Type I. Maybe I was too nice.

Then Christopher approached us. He greeted me before he asked, "Would you care for some breakfast?"

"Oh, absolutely," Edward answered, keen to change the subject. "I think we'll have a selection of fruit and pastries, right, guys?"

Sandra and I nodded in agreement. It was a welcome change of subject by Christopher, but then he made his way to the kitchen.

"You know, there are many people who would give anything to be in your position," Edward lectured me. "It's not easy nowadays to earn the privileges that we are lucky to have. A great apartment, a great education; you're very lucky, Terra. We all are. I know we are not your real family, but that doesn't mean we won't provide you with the best life possible."

Once again, I was conflicted. Of course, Edward and Sandra weren't my real parents. I couldn't blame them for raising me the way they had. The frustrating thing for me was that I just didn't fit in with them and their social circle. All these high-class functions, including the anniversary party last night, were awkward affairs for me. I eventually replied, "I know, I totally understand."

"Great," Edward said with a smile, but it instantly subsided. "Terra. If I may ask, do you believe in God?"

Edward asked me such an awkward, intimidating question. He had run into controversy with religious groups before, and although religion wasn't illegal, it was frowned upon in society. I didn't know how to answer. I froze.

"Look, Terra, it was just after what you said last night, I was just curious about where you stand," Edward said, trying to take the pressure off. I remained silent. Thankfully, Edward followed up with, "Forget it, Terra. I know it's such a strange question."

"Well, I don't personally," I eventually answered. "It's just that I don't understand how believing in God and religion can be so bad. Why should it be mocked? I honestly just don't know."

"Terra, I know some things are so hard to understand," Sandra said softly. "You're welcome to believe in whatever you want. It's just that so much has been achieved through science and technology which makes certain concepts implausible. You will understand one day."

Christopher arrived back with a tray that held plates of fruit and pastries. He put them down on the table in front of us.

"Thank you, Christopher," Edward said. "This looks great."

"My pleasure, sir," Christopher replied. "Anything to drink?"

"Can we have some orange juices, please?" Sandra asked. "Terra, you want some orange juice, right?"

I answered "yes" and Christopher left us once again. I reached across to grab a buttered croissant. The richness of the taste calmed me down, as rich foods brought comfort to me, but not entirely. I was still conflicted and was very mindful of what I would say.

"This is good, right, Terra?" Edward asked me, as he put some melon on a small plate. "Not many people can enjoy good food like this. I hope you do realize how lucky you really are."

Edward lectured me once again. It was like he was trying to make me feel guilty about what happened at the anniversary party. Edward was rather unpredictable and very hard to read. He was caring, but he was a very powerful man, and I was too afraid to protest anything he did. I only did so privately. "I know," I said in reply, then I absent-mindedly added, "I didn't mean to be so ungrateful."

"Oh, Terra, we know you're not ungrateful," Sandra said in her soft tone. She was very motherly, even though she wasn't my real mother, and there was a clear contrast between Sandra and Edward. I felt more comfortable around Sandra. "Edward was just making a point, that's all. We know we're not your real family, but we still brought you up and treated you as one of our own."

Of course, I knew that I was lucky to have the upbringing I had, and I was thankful that Edward and Sandra had given me a privileged upbringing. However, I felt that I was out of place in this environment. Christopher brought the orange juice for all of us, and I washed down the croissant in my mouth.

"So, what classes do you have today?" Sandra asked me, conveniently changing the subject.

"I have history, geography, math and English," I answered.

"English is your favourite subject, right?" Edward asked me. I nodded in agreement. "You remember Catherine from last night? She's really interested in literature and if you have another chance to meet her, she'd love to speak to you about books and culture. She majored in English at Harvard. She's very intelligent, like yourself, and I know you guys would get on great."

I hadn't really thought about Catherine. I knew she was smart, and Laura really loved meeting her. She didn't seem like a bad person, but I was intimidated by her. She had such a desire for knowledge that I felt she would get secrets out of me and then expose me. If I did meet her again, would we get on? I wasn't sure.

"I'm just gonna get my stuff now," I said, escaping the difficult topics brought up by Edward. I went up to my room and put my HoriTab in my bag. It was such an essential item for school as that was how teachers gave us work, through sharing files containing fact sheets and homework on various subjects. I put on my jacket and put my bag over my shoulder. I got down the stairs, said goodbye to Sandra and Edward, and got out the door.

There was a light breeze outside with blue skies up above, even though it was fall. The Type I allowed high society to manipulate the weather outside. It didn't seem right to me, allowing civilians to have such a high power like controlling the climate. This had been happening for a hundred years, so I guess everybody was used to it.

I walked along Madison Avenue, and I could hear the hovering sounds of aerovehicles flying above me and videos playing on the holographic billboards by the roadside. The holoboards, as they were commonly known, weren't actually made by HORIZON, but HALO, who specialized in holographic products. I then came across a holoboard featuring Edward, which grabbed my attention. I stopped to gaze at the holoboard, which had Edward looking onwards.

"My name is Edward Cox," Edward said within the holoboard. "For a hundred years, the Type I enhancement has seen us gain more power on the world than ever before. I have shown that human evolution can be made possible. Being human is no longer a weakness."

'Being human is no longer a weakness' was Edward's signature phrase. He used it very frequently in his articles and speeches at events. The holoboard then showed clips of people speaking about the Type I. Those comments included, "I am literally a new man", "Everything that Edward has done is just incredible", and "There is no doubt that Edward Cox is a great man". I always thought it was weird reading about Edward in articles and seeing him on TV. Then a clip of the US president, Marsha Bergsson, showed on the holoboard. Just as she started to speak, a caption stating 'Marsha Bergsson' and 'President of United States of America' appeared.

"Edward Cox has changed the world," Marsha said defiantly, like the leader that she was. "It is always change that makes history, but this change is like no other; it is a change to our biology. A species has not just been preserved; it's been enhanced. Our world is full of great men who have made significant changes to society and to humanity. Mr Cox is one of those great men. Through the Type I enhancement, we have more freedoms and opportunities available to us. Our society has become more functional and reliable than ever before. I can personally assure all of you that this is a society that you, the people of this great nation, can trust. Thank you, Edward Cox, for giving us the path to becoming a superior race. You have blessed America, and you have blessed the world."

I had never met the president, and it was quite overwhelming to hear her thank Edward for the Type I. The president and Edward were probably the most powerful people on Earth, so they had to be affiliated with each other. I eventually continued my journey to school.

I looked behind me, and I noticed that there was a man dressed all in black not too far behind. I didn't think much of it, but when I looked, he attempted to hide by putting his back against a building. It was a poor attempt to hide, and I was very suspicious of him. I took a deep breath in order to relax myself and continued on my journey. The man was still following me, though, and he was walking faster. I noticed a symbol on a chain necklace he wore. It was one of the cross, like from the Bible. I never read the Bible, but I had heard stories from it, like when Jesus died on the cross for our sins. I remembered Edward saying that religion was a symptom of insanity. I didn't agree with him, but the way the man was following made me nervous. I was fascinated by the symbol, but I was more occupied on trying to get away from him. I walked at a quicker pace, but then the man walked more quickly. I was frantically breathing, terrified. My heart was pounding, and my heartbeat was getting louder. My entire body was pulsing. The man finally caught up with me and pulled me into a vacant alleyway. He put his hand over my mouth, just when I was about to scream for help.

"Please don't scream. Don't make a sound," the man requested assertively but quietly. "I know you're Mr Cox's daughter. My name is Father Thomas, and I believe in a path of faith and hope, and I believe you do too."

He pulled his hand away from my mouth. I had never heard the title of 'Father' before. Not in that sense anyway. I was in shock. A man I didn't know had grabbed me, and I probably should've fled, but then I had sympathy with him. Religion had been ostracized from society and I always thought it was wrong to deem religion as insanity.

"Please forgive me for my hostility, Terra," Thomas said softly after taking a deep breath. "I don't wish to hurt you. I am just in protest of your father's work."

"He's not my real father," I corrected him, unsure of what difference it would have made. He was against the Type I like myself. I then confronted him and asked, "Why were you following me?"

"You're not like everyone else," Thomas answered. "Edward talks about you in interviews. He always says you're very intelligent. I saw the way you looked at that holoboard. You looked like someone who believes in something else."

He was right. It was creepy that he sneaked up behind me and took me aside, and he certainly didn't make a great first impression, but it turned out that I surprisingly had a lot in common with him.

"There is something wrong about this Type I," I said. "It's not natural. I read a lot about how the world used to be. It seemed so simple and in place. Edward has said a lot of bad things about religion, but I disagree with him."

"I'm glad you think so," Thomas said, his tone becoming warmer and calmer.

"But why did you threaten me like that?" I asked, despite becoming more comfortable around him, especially as I was able to tell him stuff, I couldn't tell anybody else.

"Terra, I sincerely apologize once again," Thomas said. "I really didn't mean to frighten you, but I had to get your attention. We do hope to make faith in the Lord part of society once again. We will never lose hope. Terra, if I may…"

Thomas was interrupted by a police android who apprehended him and held him up against a wall. This android was a different model to Christopher, though it still had a metallic appearance like the G-28s. The police androids were a G-75 model, one used by the city for law enforcement. They weren't as polite as the G-28s. They were more aggressive, but not dangerous. They had to be aggressive when it was necessary. They could only be bought by city officials.

"My sensors inform me that dangerous and/or suspicious behaviour is taking place here," the android said in a deep, assertive voice.

"Please, let me go," Thomas pleaded. "It was just a misunderstanding."

"Terra Cox, is this man causing harm to you?" the android asked me. It had face recognition sensors to find out who I was.

"No, it's okay," I said. "He's not causing any trouble."

"Are you sure?" the android asked. "I am only here to protect and serve."

"Yes, I am sure," I said. "Please let him go."

The android took a long look at Thomas before releasing him. It seemed reluctant to do so. "I hope you have a pleasant day," the android said as it walked away.

"Thank you, Terra," Thomas said. "As you can imagine, people like me aren't highly regarded by the hierarchies of today."

I did understand. The way the world saw faith, no wonder there was a sense of desperation in him.

"You know, Edward might be a brilliant man but being a brilliant man doesn't always mean being a good man," Thomas insightfully said. I guess it was true. Edward was an amazing foster father, but his work was against what I truly believed in.

"I'm late for school," I said. I was so absorbed by my encounter with Thomas that I lost track of the time.

"Oh, Terra, I hate to delay you further," Thomas said. "I know you have just met me, but I am holding a prayer meeting at my house tonight. I'd love for you to join us."

I wasn't sure. I had only met Thomas, but I hadn't met someone who was against the Type I before. Even though Laura was normally who I needed whenever I felt alone, there was a warmth to Thomas that meant I didn't fear being exposed.

"I'll try to make it," I said without giving a definitive answer. Maybe it was because I'd just met him, but I was fascinated by this prayer group, and I'd always felt like a misfit when around people, like at the party the night before. "Put your details in here."

I got my HoriPhone out of my bag to give to Thomas and he inputted his contact details. He passed the phone back to me.

"Please, Terra, don't tell anybody about this encounter, and don't tell anyone about the prayer meeting," Thomas pleaded with me, and I agreed to keep it secret. "Have a good day at school," Thomas said as he walked away. I said "goodbye" in return and eventually continued with my journey to school.

I finally arrived at school. There was a metallic sign saying 'Clifton School for Girls' in the schoolyard and there were white pillars along the path to the school building. There was a holographic logo of the school above the main entrance. The logo had the name of the school with words floating around it such as 'excellence', 'brilliance', 'genius', and 'intelligence'. The building was very wide and it had a dome at the centre.

I walked into the school building and I was greeted with a stern, automated voice.

"Terra Cox, you are fourteen minutes thirty-seven seconds late," the school's HoriNoy said to me. It took me by surprise as I was never late for class. I knew about the HoriNoy identifying late students though. It was just that I was never identified as a late student. I *was* late though, of course. It was still such a surprise to hear. "Your history class is located in Room 278."

The school passageway changed colours slowly. There was something so hypnotic about it. I reached a classroom with the holographic sign '278' above it. The door opened as I walked in. The classroom was all white. The walls, ceiling and floor were all the same colour. The desks and chairs were black. Ms Simmons was teaching class, and she looked at me with surprise. The class did too, as I was never late.

"Terra, it's not like you to be late," Ms Simmons said.

"I know, I'm sorry," I said. I went to take my seat. Ms Simmons didn't ask me why I was late. The school system reported my lateness, which would get sent to the principal. A form was sent for me to fill in to explain why I was late. There was a holographic screen up at the front of the class, which had information about the fall of the European monarchy, which occurred in 2153. The class had their HoriTabs upright in front of them. I sat next to Laura, like I did in every class.

"Where were you?" Laura whispered to me, concerned.

"I was held up," I whispered back as I got my HoriTab out of my bag. I tapped on the 'stand' button, and a stand came out from behind the tablet, and it stood up.

"Really? What happened?" Laura whispered again. Ms Simmons looked sternly at Laura, and she stopped whispering. I was glad that Laura was concerned, as it meant that she still cared about me, even after what had happened at the party. However, I couldn't tell her about what happened and me meeting Father Thomas. As much as I liked Laura, I was afraid of being exposed. If Laura and I became a couple, when we were both adults and more sure of ourselves, maybe I could tell her my true feelings, but I couldn't at that moment. I tried to concentrate on class, but I was so tense after meeting Thomas. Was Laura going to get the truth out of me? What would happen if she found out?

The Anonymous Faith

School had finished, and Laura and I walked home, as we usually do. This was the first time that I felt tense around Laura. I had promised Father Thomas not to tell anybody about me meeting him and the meeting that he had invited me to. Laura and I didn't talk much. While I was enjoying her company on the way home, I was very secretive. If Laura tried talking to me about something, even if it was just about class, I would give her a straight answer.

"So, you're not going to tell me what happened on the way to school?" Laura asked me. "Terra, I know something is up. I think I know you pretty well to know that the way you've been acting at school isn't you."

"Look, can't we let this go?" I asked, frustrated that Laura wouldn't drop the matter. I was never uncomfortable around Laura. This was the first time I felt on edge around her. I loved walking home with her but hoped that she would change the subject. There were times when we would walk home together without saying anything, and yet I would still enjoy her company.

"Terra, please. I'm just concerned, that's all," Laura said. I'd always appreciated it when Laura was concerned about me. I just couldn't speak to her about meeting Thomas that day.

"Please, Laura, I just can't talk to you about it," I said, trying to sound calm, but it was difficult because Laura was so concerned about me. I started to get a headache, as so many thoughts swirled around my head.

"Why not?" Laura interrogated me. I frantically inhaled and exhaled as I was having what seemed to be a panic attack. The pressure of not being honest like I would normally like to be with Laura was really making me nervous and stressed in a way I had never experienced before. I hadn't suffered from mental illness, so I can't say whether or not it was a panic attack, but it was incredibly intense. I hated keeping secrets, especially from Laura. If I had said something about meeting Father Thomas, he could end up in prison or be harmed by someone.

"Laura, please!" I raised my voice at Laura, something I never thought I'd do. I guess all friendships have sour moments but didn't think I'd feel sour with Laura. "I cannot tell you what happened, but it was nothing dangerous. I'm fine."

The look on Laura's face was one of shock. She seemed hurt. Even though that was a release, I never meant to hurt her. I felt so bad. I wish I could tell her what had happened, but I was afraid of what her reaction would be. While I trusted her, I couldn't take the chance that she could tell other people, like Sandra and Edward. It was best that I kept it to myself.

"Laura, I really do wish I could tell you everything," I said, trying to comfort Laura. "It's just that sometimes, I feel there are things about me that nobody can understand. I'm not in mortal danger or anything. Maybe one day I may be able to tell you what exactly is going on with me. It's just not today."

I think Laura understood. She didn't bring up the subject again on the walk home. It was still such an awkward walk home though. I couldn't even look at Laura, as much as I wanted to. The silence between Laura and I felt so loud. I tried to distract myself by looking at the holoboards. I saw a trailer for *Cox Enhancement*. I still thought it was weird that they had made a movie about Edward, and it was strange to see a trailer of it. It didn't look that good though. It looked too sophisticated for me. The movie was about Edward and Sandra's relationship and how the operation had saved her life. Ryan Daniels was probably the biggest actor in Hollywood at the time. He had won an Oscar for *The Finest Line* back in 2381. Erin Anderson played Sandra.

I had never really liked Erin Anderson. She seemed so fake and melodramatic in her interviews and seemed to care more about her looks. She wasn't really that good an actress; that's why I suspected that she had never won any awards. *EUPHORIA* magazine often said that she was the most beautiful woman in the world. I think that's all she really cared about. I had only met her briefly. She just seemed so vain and obsessed with herself, especially in those Femme fragrance commercials. She seemed to crave the attention of men, like when I saw her in articles where she wore such bright and sometimes revealing outfits at different events. She was clearly confident as a person, which I guess was admirable, and I remember some of the girls at school would constantly talk about her and how they wished they could be like her. My dislike for her could had been envy that she was way more confident than I was, but I used to be so put off of people who were so full of themselves.

Thankfully, we arrived at my apartment building. I breathed a sigh of relief, as it meant that the awkward tension between Laura and I could be set aside for a while. We embraced each other goodbye, but there was something about Laura's hug that just didn't seem right. I couldn't explain how, but her heart just didn't seem into it. It was complicated.

As Laura walked away, I put my thumb on the touchpad at the side of the door. I reached my apartment and then I heard an automated voice say, "Welcome, Terra Cox." The recognition system installed in the apartment acknowledged my presence. Edward and Sandra were in the living room, sitting on the couch.

"Terra," Edward said sternly, immediately grabbing my attention. His voice was much more assertive than it was that morning. I trembled for a brief moment, and then I reached the couch where Edward and Sandra were sitting. Edward had his arms folded, and he didn't blink. There was a hardened seriousness to him, especially as he was still dressed up in his suit, which left me feeling tense. Did he know about my meeting with Thomas? If so, would he get the truth out of me? "Terra, I have received communication from the police today. They told me that there was an incident involving yourself today."

"Is that true?" Sandra asked, putting her arm around me. Sandra was still motherly like she always was, and it wasn't that Edward was threatening. I had never seen him so stern towards me before.

"Yeah, a man did approach me today," I said, without giving away too much detail.

"Did he hurt you?" Edward swiftly asked. "Please answer me, Terra. Sandra and I really care about you and we'd hate to see something happen to you."

"No, he didn't hurt me at all," I said defensively, which prompted Edward to visibly breathe a sigh of relief. I didn't want to worry Edward and Sandra any further.

"Who was that man?" Edward asked. "What did he say?"

I froze. I didn't know what to say. If I told Edward the truth, I didn't know what he'd do, but I didn't think it would end well. I just stared ahead, blankly, away from Edward and Sandra.

"Terra, please answer me," Edward pleaded.

I was still frozen, but that sense of panic came back to me. I didn't know what to do. Without thinking, I got up off the couch and went towards the stairs.

"Where do you think you're going?" Edward asked with his voice raised. I stopped moving and felt a chill on my back. When Edward demanded your attention, you had no choice but to give it to him.

"I was just going to my room," I said softly, being mindful of how to reply to Edward.

"Terra, I love you," Edward began, trying to approach the matter in a delicate way that would try to comfort me, but all it did was leave me conflicted, because I knew he was still interrogating me and his voice would rise again, "but if there's a chance that you're in danger, I would give my life to stop it from happening. What did that man say to you?"

This was worse than when Laura had asked me. I would have been more likely to tell Laura than Edward and Sandra, as much as I loved them. Laura was my best friend, or maybe more than a friend. Laura requested answers from me, but Edward demanded it.

"He was lost," I said in a panic, not knowing what else to say. I've never been one to be dishonest, but I couldn't tell them the truth. "He was looking was just looking for directions to…"

"Tell me the truth, Terra." Edward demanded, clearly not believing what I said. It was obvious to him and Sandra that I was lying. I just wasn't a good liar that even I couldn't convince myself. I just froze, not knowing what to say. I knew they wanted me to tell the truth, but I just couldn't do it in case they went after Thomas.

"Terra, please answer your father," Sandra said, and referring to Edward as my father angered me. She knew that Edward was not my real father, so how could she say that?

"He's not my father!" I said assertively. I hadn't argued with Edward and Sandra before and was not prepared for an argument between us. This was an impulsive response from me.

"I may not be your real father, but I would give my life to protect you," Edward said as he got up from the couch. "I don't know who your birth parents are, but I bet they would care about you in the same way, so you answer me like you'd answer your own father."

"How do you know what my father is like? Stop pretending you know him!"

"Hey, I care about you, and so does Sandra," Edward said as he walked towards me. "We are genuinely concerned about you and we are demanding answers from you so that you don't get hurt."

"I don't wanna talk about it, okay?"

"Terra, don't you dare talk back to me!" Edward said, his voice getting louder. "We are asking you for your protection, so you better tell me who that fucking man was!"

I ran up the stairs, with tears emerging from my eyes. I reached my room, and I jumped on the bed, holding my face in my hands. Edward curses when he gets angry. Edward wouldn't hurt me, but I was protecting Father Thomas. If Edward found out about him, I believed that he would hurt him or Thomas could end up in jail. I wasn't sure. Edward can get assertive at times, but despite being a powerful man, I didn't believe he would be capable of actually harming anyone. He can be very overprotective of me, and he would do anything to keep me safe. I guess that was a good thing, but I wasn't sure how far Edward would go. I cried, constantly wiping tears from my eyes. I tried not to cry loudly, so I wouldn't draw any more attention to myself. Edward's aggression confirmed why I couldn't tell anybody about my meeting with Thomas that day.

Sometime later, Sandra came into my room. I had calmed down a bit, but I was still pretty upset and really didn't want to speak to anyone, especially not Edward.

"Terra," Sandra said softly. "Are you okay?"

I took some deep breaths to try and calm myself down, and then I answered, "Not really."

"Terra, Edward didn't mean to yell at you," Sandra said as she sat down next to me on my bed. "We are just concerned, honey. If the police call us about you, we will naturally be concerned."

"But why can't you just trust that I'm fine?" I asked. "Honestly, I wasn't in any danger."

"Terra, when you have kids of your own, you'll always be worried," Sandra said. "Look, I'm sorry I said Edward was your father. I know we are not your real parents. I wish we could tell you who they are, but we honestly don't know."

48

"All I want is to belong," I said. "Sometimes I feel so out of place and that I don't belong here."

"It doesn't matter how different you are, you always belong here with us. Now, Terra, are you sure you're not in danger? Are you sure that man didn't hurt you?"

"Yes, I'm sure."

Sandra was reluctant to accept that I was fine, but I think she did eventually.

"Terra, if you ever want to tell us anything, we'll be there. Do you understand?"

"Yes, I do. Thank you, Sandra."

Sandra smiled as she kissed me on the cheek and left my room. I started thinking about the prayer meeting that Thomas had invited me to. I was tempted to go, but I wasn't sure how to get past Edward and Sandra. All my clothes had nanotechnology in them, so they could track me down and see where I was. This was another thing by HORIZON. Clothing could also automatically clean up any stain and dry if it ever got wet, and also heat up in cold weather or cool off in hot weather. Mankind decided the weather though, with the Type I in effect. Again, I was fearing for Thomas' safety. If they knew I was at the prayer group, then Edward could track down where Thomas lived and hurt him. I didn't know what to do. I wasn't sure about it at first because I had just met Thomas, but I was so intrigued by it because I felt like an outcast most of the time, especially at Edward's parties or those we attended.

I decided that I would do it. I would go to that prayer meeting. I wore a plain navy T-shirt, blue jeans, and a beige jacket. Even with my clothes having tracking devices in them, it was worth the risk. I went down the stairs and Edward looked awkwardly in my direction. Christopher greeted me and asked where I was going. Christopher was intelligent enough to notice that I was going out, assuming so because I had my jacket on.

"I'm going to Laura's house to study," I said, almost meekly because even though I'd hidden stuff from people like Edward, Sandra and Laura, I had never really told a lie to anyone. I was an honest person. The lie didn't seem so elaborate and I didn't think it would invite any questions.

"Okay, Terra," Edward said, believing what I had said. "Would you like me to drive you?"

"No, I'm fine," I said. "I'm happy to walk over there."

"Are you sure?" Edward asked, trying not to aggravate me like before. "I'm happy to take you, and you know I just want you to be safe."

"Honestly, I'm fine but thank you," I said politely. Sandra entered the living room and seemed surprised to see that I was ready to go out.

"Terra, are you leaving?" Sandra asked.

"She's going to Laura's house," Edward said.

"Yeah, I'm going there to study," I said, with my pulse still racing.

"Well, have fun, and stay safe," Sandra said as she embraced me.

"Thanks, but we're gonna be studying so we're not really gonna be having fun." I kidded to try and lighten the mood, even though I was still panicking inside. I never liked confrontation and I knew that something bad would happen if Edward and Sandra found out where I was really going. Edward and Sandra laughed in response to my humorous response, which was a relief to me as they seemed to be at ease.

"Terra, if you need a ride home, just call me." Edward said as he got up. "I'll be up all night if you need me."

"Thank you," I said as I embraced Edward. "I'll let you know." Then I left the apartment with a sigh of relief that they believed me.

I reached Jefferson Avenue, the street that Thomas' house was located on, in South Bronx. It was nothing like anywhere in Manhattan. There was a different kind of hustle and bustle there. I saw alleyways that had a fire with homeless people warming their hands on it. I also saw a few people lying on the street in sleeping bags, looking as though they're trying to sleep but the cool breeze was keeping them awake, even though they were dressed in winter clothing. I hadn't encountered anybody poor before. I knew they existed and I went to a charity event with Edward and Sandra, but I had never actually met anyone who were living in poverty. I wasn't sure on the statistics of poverty in America, or anywhere. I could only assume the percentage was pretty high, seeing how South Bronx had plenty of people living on the streets. Manhattan was the wealthier area of New York, and everywhere else was clustered with the poorer citizens of New York. I was nervous, as I didn't know what to expect, but I was also greatly sympathetic with them. Nobody carried cash anymore as stores only took credit cards.

A homeless person along an alleyway then looked at me. She was visibly old and frail and her clothes were torn and dirty as she limped towards me. I wasn't scared, but I didn't know what to do. I had nothing to give her, but I wished I had something to give her, like food or water. When she came up to me, she had a friendly expression on her face. She seemed nervous too and unsure of what to say, but I knew what she was going to ask me.

"I'm sorry, I don't have…" I said. It pained me to finish that sentence as I wished I had something to give her, but she seemed to understand and then walked away. It was upsetting to see her go back into the alleyway and sit down against the wall, covering herself with a blanket. It was depressing for me to realise that the alleyway was her home. She, along with other homeless people, didn't even have a roof over their heads. I knew of homelessness in New York, but I had never seen it first hand, seen the adversity that these people were going through. I then remembered what Edward said about me being lucky compared to what other people are going through. To actually witness what Edward meant was heart-breaking, yet important.

I reached Father Thomas' house, number 1129. He lived in a bungalow that was around a cluster of them, all surrounded by pathways with more homeless people on them. I pressed on the button next to the door, and a voice came from the speaker above it.

"Who's there?" the voice said. It wasn't a warm voice, but one of paranoia. It made me feel more sympathetic rather than unwelcome.

"It's Terra," I said in response.

The door opened and I walked in. The living room was filled with a circle of chairs, occupied by a group of people, with Father Thomas standing up to greet me, and his greeting was followed by the rest of the group. The living room wasn't as vast as the one in my apartment and there were hardly any electronics. The room was filled with religious paintings and Bibles, which seemed strange to me as I had never encountered a room like that before. Most houses and apartments I had been to were filled with electronics. Everybody I knew was so reliant on technology. I was still feeling a little awkward, as I still wasn't sure what to expect, although I felt a sense of warmth when I walked in. I tried not to worry what would happen if Edward tracked me down. I was more worried about what he would do to Thomas than what he would do or say to me.

"Welcome, Terra," Thomas said. "I'm so happy you've decided to come tonight. This is my wife Claire and my daughter Kate."

"Hello, Terra," Claire said, and then Kate waved at me with a smile. There was a chair next to Kate, so I sat next to her.

"Hi, everyone," I said to everybody. "I can't stay late. Edward and Sandra may worry about me."

"Say no more," Thomas said with a smile. "It doesn't matter how long you'll be here. You came, and that's all that matters."

"Is there anybody else here my age?" I asked. I wasn't sure how old Kate was, but she seemed around my age. Everybody else looked older than me. It wasn't intimidating. At parties, I was usually the only child there and I was used to speaking with adults.

"I'm afraid not," Thomas said. "Please don't despair. Kate here is seventeen, but we don't judge on age. In faith, we judge people by their beliefs and values."

"Can I get you some tea, Terra?" Claire offered.

"Oh, is there a G-28 here to get it?" I asked, which drew a chuckle from the group. I had never been served by a person before, so it seemed strange to me.

"No, dear, I'll make it," Claire said with a laugh. I said that I would like some tea. I felt embarrassed, but just a little bit. I didn't feel stupid though. It was just not what I was used to.

"You have always been accustomed to a life of luxury, haven't you, Terra?" a strange-looking man said with a smile. I didn't think he meant anything malicious by that, but he did grab my attention. I couldn't make out what his accent was. It was incredibly distinct. Maybe he was Irish or South African or Australian? I couldn't decide. He had blonde spiky hair and silver chain necklaces with mysterious symbols on them. There were mysterious symbols on his rings too. He wore a fiery-red T-shirt and blue jeans. He had a trendier style in comparison to all the plain-clothed people in the group.

"Okay, let us begin," Thomas said. "I'd like to thank you all for coming this evening, and I would like to welcome Terra Cox to our group this evening."

"Are you Edward Cox's daughter?" a woman asked. She seemed displeased, although I had imagined that the people in the group would be very disapproving of him.

"I am," I answered awkwardly, "but I'm not in favour of the Type I."

"You're not?" the same woman asked, and became very surprised, as well as everyone else in the group.

"I've just always believed that there's something wrong with it," I said, as if I was trying to prove my innocence. "I read a lot about how the world used to be. It seemed so peaceful and actually quite beautiful. Now, everything is just... I don't know, it's just not right, I guess. I know it sounds stupid, but..."

"No, absolutely not," the strange man interrupted me. "It's not stupid to appreciate the old world. The old world was beautiful, and this new one is different."

Claire brought me my tea. I took a sip and the warmth of the tea soothed me.

"As you all know, religion has been dismissed for a long time now," Thomas said. "This, of course, is sad for us here in this circle. Its marginalization is why this meeting is secret. All we can do is pray and retain faith that the following of our Lord can be considered sanity again."

Murmurs of agreement sounded, before Claire said, "If I may, I'd like to talk about these dreams I've been having."

"Of course, sweetheart," Thomas said. "Do tell us."

"Well," Claire said. "I had this dream that one day there will be hope, and that among us, there is a saviour. Someone who could change the world for the better, as if they were the resurrection of Jesus."

"Who is this saviour?" I asked as I took an interest. I had heard a lot about people praying for hope, but the people I'd associated myself with deemed it as a symptom of insanity.

"I don't know," Claire answered. "I don't know the appearance of this saviour, but I pray these dreams come true. I used to believe that it's stupid to have these dreams, but that's just what society wanted me to think."

"I think we should all pray too," the strange man said. "A saviour could come in many forms. We are all hoping for that dream too."

"Thank you, Vagus," Claire said to the strange man, who, as it turned out, had a strange name too.

"I used to believe that I was crazy," I said. "That I was the only one who had the same values you all do. Edward would tell me bad things about religion, but I never believed it. Faith in God is not a bad thing and it shouldn't be ridiculed. However, I was too scared to tell anyone. I was afraid of being deemed insane. Edward said that the Type I can allow you to become your own god, but I think that challenging God and seeking ultimate power can be dangerous."

Nods and murmurs of agreement sounded across the room. I saw for myself that Edward was totally wrong about religion. I saw how it had brought people together and created a perfect little harmony. I couldn't imagine that type of closeness from the class of people I'd been around. I found them all to be more genuine people than the people I usually hang around with. It seemed that people who didn't have very much in terms of wealth actually have more humanity about them. They were all good people who were just looking for hope. What was so wrong about that?

"I feel the same way, Terra." Kate said. "All these scientific advancements just seem dangerous and unnatural to me. We don't need a robotic servant or anything. I find that not using technology can bring us closer together."

"I mean, I can't hate Edward though," I said. "He brought me up and he gave me shelter, an education, so many things. I don't like the Type I, but I can't dislike the man who was a father to me because I have no real family. I know you all despise him, and I can understand that, but he didn't have to raise me and give me a home, but he did."

"Every one of God's creatures have some good in them, even Edward for all his flaws," Thomas said. "Despise is a strong word, and yes, we are all capable of hatred, but for all of man's mistakes, we must learn to forgive. You are not alone. None of you are. God would never make us to be alone." It was a real release that people listened to me about what I really thought and didn't try to correct me in how I should think. I had been nervous when I'd first come to the group, but now a part of me didn't want to leave. Thomas then said, "Why don't we all take a break?"

The circle dispersed, but just for a while. Kate and I stayed sat next to each other.

"I must admit that I had never looked at Edward in that way," Kate said.

"Edward is a good man," I said in his defence, but I sounded passive. I saw sense in what those people were saying. "I know it's hard to believe, but he has done good things as well as bad things."

"Sure, I mean nobody is perfect, right?" Kate said. "I know he is your adopted father and all, but…"

"I know," I said. "I do wish Edward could be more noble, like help all of humanity, not just the elite. I wish I could have the courage to tell him."

Thomas then came over and said, "I do hope you haven't told anyone about this group."

"No, I haven't," I said. "Edward and I kind of had a falling-out. He heard that someone had approached me before school, and I refused to tell him that it was you and what you do."

"Oh good," Thomas said with a sigh of relief. "I'm sorry that you had an argument with Edward, and I'm sorry to impose this secret on you, but society will never understand faith the way we do."

"It's okay, I understand," I said. "Thank you for inviting me here."

"Oh, it's my pleasure, Terra," Thomas said.

"I am truly sorry how you guys are not understood," I said. "I had no idea how underprivileged you guys are. I do feel guilty, however, because…"

"Why? What have you got to feel guilty about?"

"Because I'm from a more privileged background than everyone here and I wish there was more I could do."

"Terra, we welcome those who value the Lord, regardless of their background. We don't judge the backgrounds of others. If they believe in God, then they are welcome here. We don't ask for riches, just respect."

I had never met anybody who didn't desire more money, just something that costs no money at all. I felt more in place at the prayer group than I did at every party I'd been to.

"Terra, I would like you to meet Vagus," Thomas said as Vagus came over. Thomas and Kate then went to Claire.

"Hello, Terra," Vagus said. "I had actually been hoping to meet you."

"Oh?" I said. It was a blunt response, but I didn't know how to respond to that. I didn't think anyone would want to meet me particularly. He must have read about me in the press, but I had always evaded interviews. I had been awkward with Catherine at the anniversary party. I was never great with meeting journalists. Apart from when I was with Laura, I had always kept myself to myself.

"Terra, I really loved what you said," Vagus said. "It was interesting to hear a perspective from the other side."

"You mean from society, right?" I asked, and Vagus nodded with agreement.

"So, you say that you've never really fitted in?" Vagus asked.

"Yeah," I answered. "I mean, at parties that Edward throws or takes me to, I find it quite awkward. My best friend Laura makes me feel comfortable in social events, but even with her, I can't tell anybody my real opinions on the Type I or anything."

"I can imagine how hard that can be," Vagus said, "especially when high society are amongst you."

"Right," I said. "There is so much expectation amongst them. I can never really be me."

"I sympathize with that. Terra, I know you have just met me, but I know who you really are."

I was shocked. How could he know who I really am? He couldn't have known Edward, Sandra or Laura. They knew more about me than anyone. He must have been kidding, I thought. Does he have a really weird sense of humour? I asked, "What do you mean?"

"Terra," Vagus said as he began to whisper in my ear. "I can't explain any more than that right now, but I know *what* you are."

"*What* I am?" I asked. That was more shocking. Did that mean I wasn't human? I had no idea. I didn't know anything about my birth parents, and I had been dying to know for a long time. "I'm sorry, but is this a joke? You're kidding, right?"

"Terra, there is a reason you can regenerate and heal," Vagus said to my astonishment. How did he know about that? I had never told anyone. Vagus didn't seem creepy, but I was intimidated that he knew something incredibly private about me. Maybe he wasn't kidding. "It was I who sent Father Thomas to you. It's too complicated to explain now, but we must speak again."

"When?" I asked eagerly. "Please don't tell anybody! How did you know about that?"

"Let's speak again tomorrow," Vagus said. "After you have school."

"Why not now?" I asked impatiently. Why was he leaving me in suspense?

"Terra, I can't tell you with all these people here," Vagus answered. "I must tell you in private."

I agreed, but I was so impatient. Did that mean that I would finally know who my family really were? All sorts of questions and thoughts were swirling round my head. I couldn't concentrate on anything.

"Okay, let us take our places back now," Thomas said to the group as we all got back in our chairs to resume the meeting. I wished that I could've focused on the rest of the group, but it was so hard. I was full of anticipation and anxiety, and it was impossible to concentrate. Why couldn't Vagus have told me then about my true heritage? Why did it have to be secret? Did Edward and Sandra know? As soon as I thought about them, I got nervous about whether they would discover where I was. I was frustrated, but for whatever reason, I had to be patient. I was finally about to find out the truth.

The Swirling of the Leaves

I had trouble sleeping. I wished Vagus could've told me the truth at the meeting, but for whatever reason, he couldn't. Of course, it was frustrating, but whenever it was going to happen, all I ever wanted was to find out who I really was. I had to get through just one more day of school, and then I would find out the truth. It was going to be such a fateful day. The first that I had ever experienced.

I went into the living room for breakfast as usual. I was incredibly nervous. I was actually a mixture of emotions. I had to hide it though, as nobody could know that I had been at a prayer group. The prayer group made me question everything about the Type I, as I was so sceptical about it before. Was it a good thing or an evil thing? I was hoping that Edward and Sandra wouldn't ask me about the night before. I hoped that they hadn't tracked where I was.

"Terra, are you okay?" Sandra asked me.

"Yeah, I'm fine," I said, trying to calm myself so I didn't sound paranoid.

"How was studying last night?" Edward asked.

"It was good," I answered bluntly to avoid suspicion. I hoped that they wouldn't ask me any more about it.

There was an awkward silence between the three of us. I couldn't show that it was awkward, I just didn't want them to ask me any questions. I was still reeling from the argument I'd had with Edward.

To my relief, Christopher showed up and asked, "May I offer you some breakfast?"

"Yes, please," Edward said. "How about some poached eggs and rye bread?"

"Terra, is that okay with you?" Sandra asked.

"Sure," I answered. I wasn't really hungry, but I said yes to avoid suspicion. If I said that I wasn't hungry, Edward and Sandra would ask questions. I could try to force down some breakfast, I thought.

"Okay, so eggs and rye bread it is, then," Edward said to Christopher, and then he went to prepare our meal. I knew Christopher wasn't human, but he had been our servant for a long time, so he was like a member of the family. I tried not to think about who my real family could be. I had to be patient.

"So, studying last night was fine, then?" Edward asked.

Why did he have to re-ask that question? My heart started racing. Did he suspect something? I couldn't tell. I had to maintain that lie, although I had no idea how. I eventually answered, "Uh, yeah, it was."

"What were you studying for?" Edward asked.

"History," I answered bluntly, still trying to avoid further questions.

"What period?" Edward asked. Was he interrogating me again? I didn't want to argue with him again.

"Twenty-first century monarchy," I answered, with my heartbeat still racing.

"Sounds interesting," Edward said.

"Terra, is there something you want to tell us?" Sandra asked. She may have noticed how agitated I was. I didn't know how to answer. I couldn't tell her or Edward how I was really feeling.

"No, I'm fine," I answered. I obviously wasn't fine, but I had to hide my true feelings away.

Christopher arrived back with three plates of rye bread and poached eggs, which he put onto the table. The plates each had two poached eggs and two slices of rye bread.

"Thank you, Christopher," Edward said enthusiastically.

"You're welcome," Christopher said as he left the living room.

Once again, there was an awkward silence between us as we ate our meals. I didn't have much of an appetite. I pretty much just ate to keep up appearances, but I ate more slowly. Edward and Sandra eventually finished their breakfast, but I couldn't finish all of mine. I just had one poached egg and one bread slice. Christopher came to collect our plates.

"Thank you, Christopher, that was amazing," Edward said.

"My pleasure, sir," Christopher said as he collected Edward's and Sandra's plates. He then looked at mine. "Are you finished, Terra?"

"Yes, I am," I replied. "I couldn't finish it all."

"Oh," Christopher said, surprised. Edward and Sandra were surprised too. "Are you quite sure, Terra?"

"Yes. Thank you, Christopher," I said. Christopher then collected my plate and went to the kitchen. I had to prepare myself for the questions that Edward and Sandra were about to ask me.

"You lost your appetite, Terra?" Edward asked.

"Uh, I wasn't really that hungry," I said.

"Terra, are you okay?" Sandra asked. "Are you sure there isn't something you want to tell us?"

The way Sandra asked me questions wasn't quite as aggressive as Edward's, but I was still uncomfortable. I had to keep hiding my true feelings. "Yeah, I'm totally fine. I better get going now."

I went to my room to get my backpack for school. I wasn't in the right frame of mind. I didn't know how I could focus on the subjects I had that day. Nonetheless, I got my bag and arrived back downstairs.

"Terra," Edward said, "if you ever need to speak to us about anything, we're here, okay. I know I can be a bit aggressive sometimes, but it's just that we care about you. I really do insist that if there is anything that's bothering you, or worrying you, please just the word and we'll be there. Do you understand?"

"Yes," I said, with my heart racing yet again. I eventually said goodbye to Edward and Sandra as I left the apartment.

***

School was finally over. The last bell of the day indicating the end of the last class was such a relief to me. I told Laura that I was going to be in the library after class, so I could avoid her. I was never really a liar. I may have hidden truths from people, but I hardly ever told lies. I just kept myself hidden.

I walked out of the school gates, half an hour after school was finished, and my heart was still beating rapidly, anticipating what could happen. I approached an aerobus depot, which had a computerized timetable and a holographic map. There were other people at the aerobus stop, who were all adults. The map had a satellite view of the city, with all the bus routes on. I paced up and down as I couldn't relax, but I was also cautious not to be spotted by anyone I knew. I kept my head down and tried not to draw any attention to myself.

The aerobus finally arrived. It was yellow, like how buses used to be, and it had motion banners on the side. I got on eagerly and had my travelcard scanned by the scanner next to the android driver. I sat at the back and was relieved to have not been spotted by anybody. I looked out of the window, speculating the possibilities of my visit to Vagus. I saw holoboards advertising various things. They were already advertising for December 25th. They used to call it Christmas a long time ago, but as people had stopped believing in religion, the holiday was renamed. It was still October, and I found it weird that they were advertising December 25th two months before the holiday. Everybody still gave out presents and took the day off work and school though.

Then the holoboards showed a trailer for *The Conversion VI: Crucifix of Doom,* which was an upcoming horror movie sequel about a priest who converts people to a strange religion. *The Conversion* was one of those movie franchises that kept doing sequels for whatever reason. I had never seen any of *The Conversion* movies. I was more into books than movies, even though they were all digitalised. Having been at that prayer group the night before, I realized how ignorant that movie was. Hollywood believed that if you believe in God or some supreme being, you were crazy. The movie looked kind of lame anyway, but it was the message of the movie that made me feel so incensed. The prayer group I went to had been so pleasant, and the people there were all good people, who valued and welcomed everybody; they always saw the best in people, even Edward. The upper class, however, just looked for the worst in people. It brought out that part of me that was glad to be lying to everybody. They couldn't know what I was thinking, how I could regenerate, and my protestation against the standard attitude towards religion.

Eventually, the bus stopped at my destination. I hoped that Edward and Sandra weren't tracking me down, just like how I hoped they weren't tracking me that previous night. I would normally be at the apartment at that time of the day. It was sixteen thirty, and I imagined that they would check my location. I had to do this though. I had to find out the truth. I checked my HoriPhone for directions to Vagus' address and then walked at a fast pace to my destination.

I finally got there. It was like Father Thomas' house, but smaller. I pressed my finger on the touchpad next to the door and took a deep breath. This was it. This was the moment of truth. Vagus answered the door.

"Come in," Vagus said.

"So, who am I?" I asked as I came in. I was impatient and wasn't in the mood for small talk. It was impolite, but my impatience got the better of me.

"You may not have understood why I couldn't tell you last night," Vagus said, "but it's best if I explain to you here. Follow me."

I followed Vagus out of the back door and into a small greenhouse, with my heart beating frantically. The greenhouse had dead plants and leaves all around. I had never seen any kind of plant before. There were very few plants in the world.

"Terra, your background is one of mighty authority," Vagus said.

"What do you mean?" I asked. I wished he hadn't been so ambiguous. I was too impatient. I really wanted to know why I could regenerate. Vagus then picked up a dead flower and gave it to me.

"Terra, this will seem bizarre right now," Vagus said, "but I want you to focus on this plant."

"What?" I asked.

"Terra, I know you can heal," Vagus said. "Heal this plant."

I didn't know what to do. I knew that I could heal myself, but I've never tried healing anyone or anything else. I didn't even know if I could.

"Focus your mind," Vagus said.

I tried to do what he said and focused on the plant. Why would he ask me to do this? Couldn't he just have told me the truth already? For whatever reason, I kept focusing on the plant.

The plant then rose, and a fresh scent came from it, one I had never smelt before. I was shocked. I almost dropped the pot. How had I done this?

"Did I do this?" I asked frantically. "What am I?"

"You are Mother's daughter," Vagus said. Wasn't he just stating the obvious? I knew that I was surely a daughter of a mother, but who was my mother? Or my father? I had to know.

"Who is my mother?" I asked, getting more frantic.

"Mother of all," Vagus said. While I was getting frantic, Vagus was calm. How could he have been so calm while I was going through this? "You are destined for greatness, Terra. I had to tell you here. You wouldn't have believed me last night."

Maybe Vagus had a point. If he had told me that I could heal plants or whatever else, I wouldn't have believed him. I just wished that he hadn't made me go through a day of hysteria.

"Why do you have these things?" I asked, referring to the dead plants.

"In the hope that I would meet you," Vagus said. "I knew that you could bring life to them."

"So, shall I bring all of them to life?" I asked.

"Not now," Vagus said. "I travel a lot, Terra. I am a wanderer and I've been to many places and many worlds."

"What do you mean worlds?" I asked. Did he mean other planets? Or something else?

Then the leaves on the ground lifted up and started swirling around me. They started swirling faster and moved at such a vigorous pace. I was becoming alarmed, unsure of what was going to happen.

"What's happening?" I asked in a panic.

"The leaves are taking you," Vagus said.

"Where?" I asked, still in a panic.

"Your destiny," Vagus said.

I was fully surrounded by the leaves and hardly saw Vagus. My view was getting blocked by the leaves.

I wasn't sure how, like I wasn't sure about everything else that took place in the greenhouse, but the leaves then took me away.

I was no longer in the greenhouse.

I was no longer on planet Earth.

Quercas Alba

The rampant flock of leaves subsided, and I felt a thud on my back, yet I wasn't in any pain. The ground was soft and was full of green grass. I took a moment to feel the grass between my fingers. While I was feeling it, a fresh scent came from it. The smell calmed me down, but only for a moment as I was still trying to understand what was happening. Vagus had been so vague with me, and I was literally in another world. How did I get here? Did those leaves transport me to this place, whatever it was? I looked up, and I found that I was in a forest with trees so high that they almost touched the clear, dark blue sky. I had never seen so many plants before, as there was hardly any natural life on Earth. I was in total disbelief at what I had seen, but I was also in awe too. It looked so beautiful and peaceful. It was actually refreshing to be surrounded by the serenity of trees and plants instead of soulless, tall buildings and loud vehicles.

I got up and walked around the forest of giant trees. I inhaled deeply once again, closing my eyes to embrace it. I had never breathed in air this fresh before. The air satisfied my lungs, relaxing me. There was still a part of me that was confused about where I was, and rather anxious that I was so far away from New York. Would Edward discover where I was? He and Sandra must have been rather worried about me. Could they still track me down even though I was in another world? Then I heard a high-pitched squawk from high up. Given the lack of wildlife on Earth, it gave me a shock. The sound was also unlike any animal I had heard before. The noise came from two flying creatures who were majestically soaring in the sky. I couldn't see what they were exactly, but they had a large wingspan and their feathers were very small and almost invisible, unlike birds. They had incredibly long, slender jaws, short arms and a bony crest on the back of their heads. The two soaring creatures turned out to be a pair of Quetzalcoatlus. I knew a little bit about dinosaurs and prehistoric life, though I wasn't really an expert. I was stunned to see the Quetzalcoatlus flying above me. Were they cloned, like creatures in an old sci-fi movie? I wasn't sure. Everything about this place was incredibly strange to me, though the sight of seeing these creatures soaring freely was rather awe-aspiring. I was both bewildered as to what this strange land was and struck by the beauty of nature, a sight I didn't think I would see back on Earth.

In the large forest, there was one tree that caught my attention. It was a great white oak tree with its bark a light shade of grey and its height reaching about thirty meters, or higher. There were a couple of small holes adjacent to each other within the bark, and a curved mark underneath them. The roots at the bottom of the oak tree stretched out to a great distance. As I went to move closer to the tree, the curved mark moved.

"Why hello, my child," the tree said in a slow, croaky voice, which made me jump and fall over. Eyes emerged into the adjacent holes within the bark, and the tree just simply looked on, without reacting to my shock.

"You can talk?" I asked, which was a dumb question as the tree obviously just spoke. I didn't know what else to say.

"Yes, Terra, I can talk," the tree replied with a smile and a slight laugh. "Fear not of me, my child. I am just a gentle oak tree; wise and old I be."

How did it know my name? The tree speaking was shocking in itself, but for the tree to know my name… this place, whatever it was, just kept getting stranger.

"How…" I began, as my shock caused me to stutter. "How do you know my name?"

"I've known about you for a great number of years," the tree answered. "I know your mother very well."

"You know my mother?" I asked immediately. Who was she? Will I find her?

"Yes, she is the most loving of all," the tree said.

"So how can I heal? Why do I have these abilities?"

"You are Mother's daughter."

There was that phrase again: Mother's daughter. What was the tree saying? I am the daughter of a mother? Either the tree was just being dumb or there could be a meaning beyond what I thought that phrase meant.

"What is your name?" I asked.

"My name is Quercus Alba," the tree answered.

"Where am I?"

"The Upper World, Terra, where Mother and Father reside."

Whose mother and father were Quercus Alba referring to? Did they even have names?

"How did I get here?" I asked.

"You were sent here, child," Quercus Alba answered.

"I know, but I was around these leaves and then…"

"You were brought to the Upper World, child. I know it was Vagus that sent you here."

"How do you know about Vagus?"

"He is an adventurer and an explorer of many surroundings."

"Where is my mother?"

"She is everywhere. Her presence is felt amongst everybody who adores the nature of this land, and of other lands, and she preserves the sacred order of everywhere. She knows you have entered this world and therefore she will find you. I know you must have a lot of questions to ask her."

"Yes, I do. What's in this world?"

"In this world are the creations of Mother and Father."

"What creations?"

"Why, all of this, child. Everything in this world and every other world was created with love by Mother and Father."

"Who is my mother?"

Quercus Alba exhaled and then, to my frustration, it stood still.

"Quercus Alba?" I tried to get an answer out of the tree, but it was unresponsive. I was so frustrated that I didn't get the answers I needed. Just when it seemed that I was going to be told what I needed to know, I just kept getting weird replies that didn't make any sense to me.

I then felt the ground rumble. The rumbling grew, causing me to get up. I followed the rumbling, and as I grew closer to the source of the sound, the noise was followed by a gentle bellow. It was a sound that I had never heard before, and while it wasn't intimidating, it did make me very curious. I also heard the sound of thumping footsteps, which shook the ground and my heart kept pounding rapidly. I was nervous and anxious of the sound, but also intrigued, so I walked slowly and carefully. I could vaguely see giant shapes in front of me, which was where the noises were coming from. I didn't know what it was I saw exactly, and I became much more intrigued, and just as anxious as I was before. The shapes became clearer as soon as I got closer and the bellowing became louder. I struggled to balance myself every time the ground shook. I would stumble over occasionally, but eventually I managed to get used to the shaking ground and eventually maintain my balance. The bellows were gentle, so I wasn't afraid to get up close.

I eventually stepped out of the forest, and saw a beautiful, lush valley with a giant sparkling lake and green ferns. There were mountains surrounding the valley. I was so overwhelmed by the sight of huge bodies surrounding me, and the huge bodies were accompanied by long tails and long necks. They were giant creatures, but they were gentle. They were Alamosaurs. An Alamosaurus saw me and came closer. The giant creature gently bellowed. I was intimidated at first, as I had never seen one before, but the creature gazed at me in fascination and put its head up against me. Its head alone was taller than I was, which made me nervous, but the creature wasn't harmful at all. I didn't know what to do, so I reached up and stroked the top of its head, as if it was a pet, even if it seemed taller than my apartment.

My apartment. Home. At least I thought that it was my home. Edward and Sandra must be desperately looking for me. I checked my HoriPhone to see if they had contacted me. There was no signal. I also thought about Laura. She must be worried too. If I couldn't get any signal, would that mean that I was untraceable?

Meanwhile, the Alamosaurus exhaled with satisfaction and put its head back up, and marched on majestically, with its body walking over me. A flock of Quetzalcoatlus then flew by and landed next to the lake, dipping their mouths into the water as they had a drink. A couple more Alamosaurs drank some water.

I walked on past the lake. I saw a crested dinosaur bellow loudly from the top of the mountain. The noise sounded like a horn, and all the creatures by the lake looked up at where the loud trumpeting sound was coming from. The loud noise came from a Parasaurolophus, and after bellowing, it got down on all fours and walked away from the top of the mountain. I walked further along the valley, and I saw many more dinosaurs. I saw a couple of Pachyrhinosaurs, a herd of Euoplocephalus and a herd of Camptosaurs marching towards the lake. They drank from the lake too and, similarly to the Alamosaurs, communicated with each other.

I eventually left the valley and walked back into the forested area. After walking past giant bushes and shrubs, I came across a swamp, which wasn't as lush and as beautiful as the valley. There were dark green water lilies on the water, and there were trees growing out of the swamp, which were nowhere near as giant as the trees in the forest. The trees had no leaves on them, and their branches were dark. Those trees didn't appear as majestic as those in the forest, and they looked very creepy. The water didn't sparkle like the lake in the valley. It was dark, and there were insects flying around it. The grass around the swamp was dark too, which created an atmosphere that made me feel intense.

I saw a sail emerge from the swamp. The sail was then followed by a head and its mouth displayed sharp teeth. My heart was beating harder and I was even too tense to breathe. I stumbled as I saw the emerging creature was a Dimetrodon. The Dimetrodon glared at me, which made me paralyzed with fear, and let out a subtle growl. It was so nimble in its movement and it had razor-sharp teeth, displaying a fierce pose as it readied itself. I got up and ran through the forest, and the Dimetrodon chased after me. I ran as fast as I could, but the Dimetrodon was gaining on me. I tripped over a rock while I was running, but I quickly got back up and ran. I was getting out of breath as I sprinted away from the Dimetrodon. I stopped and leaned back against a tree, but the Dimetrodon was squaring up to me. I stood and stared at the Dimetrodon, anticipating an attack. This was it. I thought that I was going to die. As the Dimetrodon ran up to me, an arrow struck the creature and it fell onto its side, wailing in pain as it lay dying. I jumped at the arrow striking the Dimetrodon, though I was so relieved and finally able to breathe.

A woman who was barely dressed approached. She was wearing a mini dress made of flowers and had a tiara around her head that was made of vines. She carried a bow and arrow on her shoulder. She was taller than anybody I knew back in New York. She seemed to be about seven feet tall. She stopped at the Dimetrodon, as it died.

"Foul creature, you shall perish for harming she known as Terra," the woman said. Another stranger knew my name. Was I famous up here or something?

"You know my name too?" I asked uneasily. The woman looked at me, warmly smiled and approached me.

"Yes, Terra, I know who you are," the woman, who placed her hand on my shoulder, said. "This foul, rogue creature knows not of royalty. Everybody here in this land knows of your arrival."

"I've been told that I am Mother's daughter," I said confused, referring to what others had said about me, though I still had no idea what they meant. "Am I... a celebrity?"

"You are royalty, my dear." The woman nodded.

"What is your name?" I asked, beginning to warm to the woman.

"My name is Mulieris," the woman answered warmly.

"What are all those dinosaurs doing here?" I asked, looking around me.

"You must mean the giant creatures that surround us. That must be what they are deemed as in the world of men, but we give them the title of tanniyn, mighty creatures made to accommodate this world."

"What do you mean accommodate this world?"

"Water that must be drunk and leaves that must be eaten. It is the natural order that takes place in all worlds."

"Mulieris!" A male voice cried from afar, which was followed by the sound of running footsteps. I was anxious, as I was in a strange place, but Mulieris stood calmly and happily, as she recognized the voice.

"Hominem!" Mulieris shouted back. A man emerged from the forest and approached Mulieris, and then they embraced and kissed each other. The man was wearing a sleeveless toga made of dark green leaves, which covered him down to his calves. Mulieris said to the man excitedly, "Hominem, Mother's daughter has returned."

"I knew it was true," Hominem said happily before looking at me.

"Terra, this is my husband, my love, Hominem," Mulieris said.

"It is your mother who has gifted us this happiness." Hominem smiled at me. "Mother and Father have blessed us with love and an eternal paradise."

"Terra, we must take you to Mother. She requests your presence," Hominem said, offering his hand for me to take. I was overwhelmed. This was the moment I had been waiting for, to meet my real mother, so I took Hominem's hand. I took a deep breath, bracing myself for what was to come. There were many thoughts running through my head. Mulieris took my other hand and we strolled on through the forest.

Mother

I walked further into the forest, led by Mulieris and Hominem. I took deep breaths as I walked along this alien world, embracing the fresh air that was so rare back in New York; I didn't miss the pollution back home. I was a bit of a misfit back home, and coming to an all-new world I had no idea existed, I did feel like a misfit again, but there was something about this world that made me feel that I belonged there. It was the lack of technology in the Upper World that brought a sense of tranquillity to the place. Back in New York, technology was pretty much everywhere and it was so noisy. I didn't mind it so much though, as it was pretty much normal in New York, but when I experienced the contrast in the Upper World, I found that I didn't miss the noise. I walked along in confusion and anticipation.

"You need not be afraid, child," Mulieris said to me calmly as she sensed my anxiety.

I closely observed the forest, as it was like nothing I had ever seen before. It was such an intriguing yet beautiful sight. I looked down at the grass that swayed with the gentle, cool breeze. I looked upwards and saw a flock of Quetzalcoatlus flying above, screeching towards each other as they flew.

"They are magnificent creatures," Mulieris said. "Don't you think, Terra?"

"Yes, they are," I said as she continued gazing into the sky. "Where are they flying to?"

"Mother," Hominem answered.

I looked around me and heard a rustling. It was then followed by a growl and then footsteps, which made me feel tense and I stood very closely next to Mulieris. I was starting to develop a bond with her and felt confident that she could protect me. I saw feet with vicious claws through shrubs and bushes, making me gasp with horror. The feet were followed by long, slender hind legs and arms with killer claws on their hands too. At the end of its emerging long neck was its long, flat head which had wide, bright eyes on the side of its face, and then I held Mulieris' hand tightly, intimidated by the emerging figure, especially having been chased by that Dimetrodon. The figure turned out to be a Troodon, and it approached us. I was paralyzed with fear and reluctant to make any movement, but Mulieris and Hominem were calm. Should I have been calm too? The manner of the Troodon's approach seemed threatening at first, as it let out a loud screech, but the slender dinosaur calmed itself in its movement, and it appeared to bow before me. I was confused and wasn't sure what to do about the Troodon's gentle approach.

"What's it doing?" I asked Mulieris, terrified and confused.

"It knows you, Terra," Mulieris said calmly. "It knows that you are Mother's daughter."

I stared at the Troodon, and the dinosaur looked back in a friendly way.

"What must I do?" I asked Mulieris, still engaged in eye contact with the Troodon.

"Affection, Terra," Mulieris answered. "You have Mother in you."

Mother in me? That doesn't sound right.

I was unsure of what to do at first, if not more unsure of anything since I first arrived in the Upper World, but then I had an impulse to reach out my hand and touch the Troodon on its head. The Troodon seemed to purr as it embraced the affection I showed. The dinosaur then screeched several times and a pack of Troodon emerged from the forest and surrounded me. Mulieris stepped aside making space for the Troodon. I didn't sense any hostility and I embraced being surrounded by the Troodon. Mulieris and Hominem looked on, and they looked at each other and smiled.

"Terra," a voice from afar called in a gentle, breathy manner. Mulieris, Hominem and I looked towards the direction of the voice, while the Troodon stepped away and looked in the same direction as us. A bright white light shone strongly, and I squinted my eyes. Mulieris and Hominem weren't affected by the light and they gazed on, along with the Troodon. The light subsided and a Tyrannosaurus emerged, and it was accompanying a woman dressed in a long white dress.

She had her arms spread out, as if she was orchestrating something, and she had long blonde hair which was let down, and then she glanced at me.

The woman was embracing the air around her and she had a gracious presence as she started to approach me. She was taller than Hominem and Mulieris, about nine foot tall. The Tyrannosaurus followed her. Its appearance was fearful and intimidating, but it had no harmful intentions. As the woman approached me, Hominem and Mulieris kneeled before her, and the pack of Troodon bowed to the woman too. The woman was right in front of me, and I looked up at her. The woman's skin was pale and so smooth, and her hands were placed on my shoulders. She was beautiful and mysterious, but she had a warm presence to her as well as a gracious one.

"Terra," said the woman calmly. "It's been long, my little one."

"Mother?" I asked awkwardly. How could you just go up to someone and ask if they were your mother? It was such a big thing to ask.

"Yes, Terra," the woman said gently to my relief. If she'd said no, I would have looked really stupid. "I am she who you seek. I am your mother."

I gasped in disbelief and exhilaration. I had finally found her, my real mother. Mother embraced me and stroked my hair.

"Mother, I can't believe… I just…" I said tearfully, lost for words in that moment.

"I know, Terra," Mother said gently. "It has been quite a journey for you, but now I am gratified by your arrival."

Those words brought great warmth and comfort to me, and Mother felt warmth from me embracing her. A bond between Mother and I had been immediately established, as though I had found what I had been looking for and everything about me made sense.

"I know you must have a lot of questions for me, Terra," Mother said, and she had a gentleness in her voice. That made me feel so close to her, even though I had only just met her.

"I do, Mother," I said. "I had wondered where I really belonged. I'm not like most of the people on Earth."

"You are here, little one. This where you belong now." Mother smiled at me and I smiled back. Mother then turned to Hominem and Mulieris. "Hominem, Mulieris, I give you my gratitude for bringing my dearest Terra to me."

"We accept your gratitude, Mother," Hominem said gratefully, as he and Mulieris left us. They held hands and jogged back the way they had come. The pack of Troodon left too, scattering in different directions. Mother then turned to the Tyrannosaurus.

"Oh, mighty trecarun, I give you my thanks for accompanying me here," Mother said with gratitude. "You may go now, my trecarun, and take my gratitude with you as a gift from I."

The Tyrannosaurus kneeled before Mother and she stroked the front of its face, in-between its nostrils. I watched in amazement as I witnessed the bond between the two. It stood up and walked through the forest, and its footsteps made a loud thumping noise. I had gotten used to the thumping footsteps I had come across in this world.

"The tanniyn are very friendly creatures," Mother stated. "They may appear fearsome, and mighty in stature, but they worship their queen and they worship you too, little one."

"Why?" I asked.

"Because you're my daughter," Mother reminded me, and it felt so good to hear her reiterate that. "And therefore, you are royalty in this world."

I wasn't sure how to react. I guess I should've been honoured. I was unfamiliar with the concept of royalty, although I had been learning about monarchy in school. My lifestyle as Edward and Sandra's adopted daughter seemed close to royalty. Then I asked myself, why was I on Earth in the first place? Should I just go ahead and ask her? Or let Mother explain it to me when the time was right?

"Come, Terra, there are many who are awaiting your arrival," Mother said.

"Where are we going?" I asked.

"To the Caelum Palatium," Mother said as she held my hand and we made our way through the forest. I felt so much safer now that I was with Mother, my real mother. I was startled when I saw an Anatotitan being attacked by a Carcharodontosaurus. The Anatotitan tried to fend off the Carcharodontosaurus, struggling away by shoving it with its duck-like bill, but the Carcharodontosaurus demonstrated its strength and fatally bit into the Anatotitan's skin and took the herbivore down with its foot, biting and eating its flesh. I clutched tightly onto Mother's hand.

"I thought they were friendly!" I cried as I stopped walking and was startled by the sight of the attack.

"These creatures must feast on others," Mother told me. "That is the natural balance of life, Terra. There are some beasts whose diets are not plant based."

"Yes, I know, but..." I stopped, unsure of what to say as I was confused once again.

"Terra, my duty as queen is to preserve the natural order," Mother said. "I cannot corrupt nature, Terra. The Order is sacred and must be honoured by all. This sight might be ghastly, but it is the natural order of this world, and there are creatures that must sacrifice their lives to provide food for others. I assure you, Terra, none of these creatures are killed for sport or hatred. They exist to provide nutrition for others."

I reluctantly accepted what Mother said. We walked on, and then we came out of the forest and into the valley, where dinosaurs kneeled before us. Dinosaurs were drinking the water that was all around the valley. A herd of Argentinosaurs was drinking the water from one of the lakes and got on their knees when they saw Mother and I walking through. Their footsteps made such a loud thumping noise, but I had learned not to jump from the sound. A family of Giganotosaurs kneeled too, and even though they were surrounded by herbivores, they weren't hunting. There were many more dinosaurs across the valley, in a variety of sizes. Some of them had mysterious crests on their heads, some had solid bone on the top of their heads and others had very large claws that looked bigger than my arm.

"So, do you have a first name?" I asked Mother. "Or are you just 'Mother'?"

"I am mother of all, Terra," Mother answered. "I mother everything in this world and others. The tanniyn, the people, the plants; they are creations of Father and I."

Mother and I eventually reached the end of the valley, and we reached a log bridge. It was surprisingly stable for a bridge made out of wood, but I wasn't too nervous about crossing it, especially as I was holding Mother's hand. We both crossed the bridge and reached a pathway that was surrounded by giant plants. I saw large green tree ferns growing alongside the pathway, as well as huge cycads and rafflesias. The surroundings looked so beautiful and exotic, but I didn't stop to gaze at them.

We then approached a village, in which we saw dinosaurs and angels; the latter wore white togas and had large, feathered wings tucked behind them. They were pretty much what you'd expect angels to look like, but I was still so surprised to see them. I didn't think that in my wildest dreams that I would see an angel, or a dinosaur, a talking tree and a powerful deity like Mother. Religion was so minimal on Earth that I never knew much about them, but the word 'angel' was used on Earth to describe someone who was good. The village was on a hill and the buildings were made of stones. As soon as they caught a glimpse of me walking alongside Mother, the angels and dinosaurs kneeled. The angels quietly said, "Mother's daughter." I was the centre of attention, which I wasn't sure how to handle. Mother didn't look fazed by the attention she got. She seemed so used to it. I then saw a giant castle that was made of stone, and it was decorated with vines all over. The path led to a wooden bridge over a moat, and the castle door was guarded by a Styracosaurus and a Pentaceratops standing to one side of a giant door.

"We're here, Terra," Mother said. "We're at the Caelum Palatium."

Mother and I crossed the bridge that led to the door and the Styracosaurus and Pentaceratops recognized both of us and they kneeled. Mother released my hand and spread her arms out, which caused the door to open. Mother began walking towards the doorway.

"Come, my little one," Mother said to me as we walked through. We were greeted by a couple of Maiasaurs. They kneeled to Mother and me, and Mother gently stroked their faces.

"Dear creatures of the Heavens, my daughter has come," Mother said as she stroked the Maiasaurs. I gazed at them, and one of the Maiasaurs approached me. I was reluctant to make any movements in front of the dinosaur, though they didn't look as dangerous as the Troodon or the Carcharodontosaurs.

"It recognizes our royalty, Terra," said Mother. "The bonacter wants your affection."

I reluctantly put my arm out and touched the Maiasaur. The dinosaur responded happily as it stroked my cheek with its cheek. The two dinosaurs then stepped backwards and made way for Mother and me to move forward.

I witnessed a horde of servants who were dressed in material made of plants. They all greeted and welcomed me. I was overwhelmed by the welcome we received, as the servants all surrounded me and bowed to me. The palace was decorated with sticks and leaves on the walls, which were all made of stone. The floor was made of stone too, and there was a window at the end of the hall. This place was so grand and I guess it made me proud to be a part of it. As I had discovered, this place was where I belonged. Eventually Mother led me away from the servants and took me up some stairs and into a room which contained a long table and a throne at the end. At each side of the throne were two windows overlooking the view. There was a man looking out of one of the windows. He wore a white toga that covered all of his body. He had long black hair that went down to his shoulders.

"Father, Terra has come," Mother said to the man at the window. Was he her father? Or was it just a name for him, like Mother? He turned around and smiled at me.

"Hello, Terra," Father said gently. He had a soft, deep voice, which was warm, yet assertive. He was like a gentler version of Edward.

"Are you my father?" I asked awkwardly, as I was making another big assumption. I may have been right about Mother, but I was hoping I wasn't wrong and was afraid of being embarrassed.

"I am father of all, Terra, just like Mother is mother of all," Father answered.

"So, are you, like, God?" I asked, again awkwardly. Asking someone who you've just met if they're your father is a big question, but just how can you possibly ask someone whether they are God the Almighty?

"The world of men, your world, have many different terms for what I am," Father said. "A god, I am, Terra. Create all, I did. Mother sprinkled my creation with love and life."

"So, am I like Mother?" I asked.

"Of course, you are, Terra," Father said, putting his hand on my shoulder.

"What you bear, Terra, is a gift," Mother said. "A gift that the world of men could never understand. This is your home, Terra. Your real home."

"It looks so beautiful," I said as she walked towards the window. I was enticed by the view of beautiful forests, plantations and dinosaurs grazing the grass and drinking from lakes peacefully.

"Beautiful it is, Terra," Mother said as she walked over to the window to be beside me. Father looked on, smiling.

"So why was I on Earth?" I asked as I turned to Mother.

"Terra, there are some things that you would have been unable to understand," Mother said. "But a young mind like yours bears curiosity, and it constantly seeks answers. This world is a peaceful one, but there are other worlds that seek war with our world. There is one world, the Underworld, whose ruler bears tyranny and seeks vengeance against Father."

"Why?" I asked.

"He bore greed and sin," Father said assertively. "His name was Lucifer, an angel that I created. He was not just a servant to me, but he was a son. I gave him my trust, but he betrayed it and waged a war against me and my kind. It was with much might and power that we defeated Lucifer and his army, and it was therefore my duty to cast them all into the Underworld, never to escape. Lucifer's resentment towards me was too great, and therefore we had to put you on Earth for your protection, as there was a great risk that Lucifer would escape, but such risk has not materialized. Any child would not have been safe here, which was why they had to grow up in other worlds."

My face was in shock when Father was talking about Lucifer. Not only did God turn out to be real, although he was known as Father, but maybe the Devil, the very symbol of evil, might be real too. I felt numb for a moment, then I leaned against the window.

"You needn't fear, Terra. We in this world are here to protect you," Father said reassuringly, and Mother nodded and placed her hand on my shoulder. I smiled slightly as she felt rather reassured. "We must have a celebration of your return, Terra."

"Indeed, we must," Mother said, and my smile grew. "Tonight, we shall gather everybody and feast on the finest foods this world has to offer."

I started to feel enthusiastic as I embraced Mother and went on to embrace Father. I guess Mother and Father were similar to Sandra and Edward. Like Sandra, Mother was motherly and caring and Father was protective and stern, just like Edward. My concerns about being away from New York, from Sandra, Edward and Laura, were finally cast aside. I was also no longer worried about the concern that everybody in New York must had been feeling.

I was finally where I belonged, with my real family.

I was finally home.

The Underworld

The Underworld was nothing like the Upper World.

It was a wasteland, with no plants and not much water. The ground was full of rocks and sand, and there were lakes of molten lava. Dust flew in the air, and the cries of dead spirits could be heard from the sky, which was as red as blood. The dead spirits were vaguely seen, as their appearance transparent and cloudy. The atmosphere was just full of death, as there was a lot of poison and hostility in the air.

A shadowy figure emerged from the flying dust. The figure was agile in the way it moved, gliding at a fast pace. The figure was female, but not human. She wore a torn red knee-length dress. She had scaly skin, long blonde hair lying beyond her shoulders and claws on the ends of her hands and feet. She blinked sideways as she had a third eyelid.

She approached an elderly man who was standing at the edge of a rowing boat sitting on a red stream. The old man was holding a long dark wooden oar and he was very bony, his skeleton visible through his wrinkly skin. He had one eye open and the other eye was scarred. His head was bald and scarred. He had very few teeth and they were all yellow, and he had a pale, grey beard which grew down to his waist.

"Ah, Femos, how wonderful to see you again," the old man said.

"Palia, my friend, it's nice to see you too," Femos said to her in turn.

"I believe that you have been summoned by the Lord," Palia said.

"That I have, and therefore I shall be requiring your assistance."

"Of course, Femos," Palia said as he bowed. "How may I assist you?"

"Take me to Him," Femos said bluntly. "For I cannot glide above the river."

"That I shall," said Palia fearfully as Femos boarded the boat. The man who Femos was referring to brought fear into Palia and was a feared figure in the Underworld. As soon as Femos sat in the boat, Palia rowed with his oars. "You have news for the Mighty One?"

"Important news," Femos replied.

"Ah, of course," Palia said intriguingly. "Should the master take satisfaction in your news?"

"Let's hope so," Femos said in a much more relaxed manner than Palia.

"The lord Satan bears a heart of black," Palia said. "Bringer of fear and dark, he be. The deathly souls that are all around us dread our lord. The floating spirits that fly around bear much regret for the sins committed in their existence. It is because of their sins that they are here in the Underworld, and they are punished by the Gods in the Upper World by being cast into the Underworld. Just like the lord Satan was long ago, along with many of us."

"That I do know, but I don't fear our lord," Femos said casually as she looked up at the sky to see the spirits floating around quickly. As the spirits were wailing, Femos grinned, sadistically enjoying the sight and the sound of the wailing spirits.

"You are a brave soul, my dear Femos," Palia said. "You don't fear the very symbol of fear itself. That makes you one of a kind."

"I suppose it does," Femos said, feeling rather proud of herself. "After all, in this world there is nothing but fear and dread. The air around us, this breeze of aeria, is suffocating to us who inhale it. We endure this aeria as we have lived in the Underworld for an eternity."

"This be true, my good friend. Very true," Palia nodded in agreement. "There is much in the Underworld that I have endured, but we do live in hope, for one day we shall reclaim our rightful place in paradise."

"Paradise, Palia?" Femos said.

"The Upper World, of course," Palia answered, surprised that Femos didn't know what he meant. "We bear much resentment towards Father for casting us here, and one day paradise shall be within our reach. I have hoped for so long, and I don't intend to give up."

"I admire your determination, Palia," Femos said. "Hope and determination are usually lost causes in this place, but let's hope that your optimism is rewarded."

Palia steered the boat sideways and stopped at the end of the stream.

"We be here, Femos," Palia said.

"Excellent," Femos said with a grin. "Many thanks to you, my friend."

"My pleasure, friend," Palia said. "Farewell to you!"

"Farewell," Femos said as Palia rowed the boat back the way they had come

The shadowy girl glided along a pathway that led to a village. The village had houses made of stone bricks, which all appeared to be in ruins. The inhabitants of the village were all human-shaped figures made of stone, bound together with lava. The village was also occupied by skinny, heavily wrinkly old people, who were all moaning and wailing in agony. They were all slaving away, while Femos glided through the village casually. She wasn't stopped by any of the villagers as they all ignored her, and they all continued slaving away.

Femos came out of the village and approached a very steep mountain. The mountain had a spiral pathway which led to a tower at the top. The isolated tower was made of stone, like the Caelem Palatium, but similarly to the houses in the village, it was in ruins. The tower was so high that it almost touched the flying spirits in the sky. The mountain looked very dark and grim. Dust was flying off the stones of the mountain. Femos glided along the pathway, unaffected by the dust and the view down from the mountain, which would've looked so overwhelming to anybody else, and the closer she got to the tower, the more she could hear growling coming from the top. The growling made Femos smile, as she sensed that it was her master awaiting her. Femos kept gliding along the spiral pathway until she eventually reached the tower. The tower appeared vacant with hardly any light showing, and there was nothing but a staircase to the top inside.

"Femos!" a menacing voice cried from top of the tower. Femos glided up the staircase to the top. At the top of the tower was the intimidating figure of Satan, who was looking out across the Underworld. He turned at Femos' arrival. He wore torn black short trousers and he had wings to enable him to fly. Satan had a muscular build and stood at nine feet tall. His head was bald, and his skin was part white, part red, and his bright, yellow eyes had no irises and pupils. The top of the tower consisted of a throne made of spikes.

"Femos, my dear apprentice, it is of great pleasure to see you again," Satan said.

"Thank you, my Lord," Femos said. "I bring news of importance."

"I have sensed your urgent visit," Satan said. "Is it in regard to the girl? Mother's daughter?"

"Yes," Femos answered enthusiastically. "She has arrived."

"I knew it!" Satan replied, sharing Femos' enthusiasm. He cackled loudly, his laughter echoing across the Underworld. "She is very special. They call her the bearer of life."

"Soon, we shall take back our place in paradise," Femos said, enthusiastic once again. "And we shall have our vengeance on Father."

Satan screamed the loudest scream, which echoed just like his cackle.

"His name pains me," Satan growled. "Cast me in this world, he did, and I will always detest him."

"As will I, my Lord," Femos said in agreement.

"Ah, Femos," Satan smiled as he put his hands on Femos' cheeks. "I have taught you well, my beautiful apprentice. I remember when I found you as a child, and I have raised you to believe what I believe. I feel nothing but pride when I think of you. An eternity I have spent with you, and an eternity more I shall cherish."

Femos smiled along with Satan, who took his hands away from her cheeks and went to the edge of the tower to look out at the view. He leaned his hands on the stone wall in front of him.

"When do we start our rebellion?" Femos asked.

"Patience, my dear Femos," Satan replied calmly. "Our war shall begin, but in good time. The girl is very important to us. The best plans bear subtlety and the attacks come in instalments. A strategy is required to fool they that not be so easily fooled, even if that strategy be ever so complex. An opponent must never be underestimated."

"Yes, my Lord," Femos said as she glided over to Satan and stood next to him. Femos then looked upwards. "I've always wondered about those spirits in the sky."

"Culprits of sin, they are," Satan said, looking upwards as well. "This world is one of sin, as you know, my beauty, and therefore they are one of us."

"So those mortal lives are reminded of their sins for an eternity?" Femos asked.

"That is so, Femos," Satan answered. "They are then to become one of us. Come, Femos."

Satan walked down the staircase with Femos gliding behind him, and then they both went down the spiral pathway on the mountain. They then entered the village, and the villagers were slaving away as before, doing various tasks.

"Kneel before me, subjects!" Satan demanded assertively, and the villagers immediately stopped what they were doing and kneeled. Satan looked around the village and was pleased to see that his authority was respected. "Pilgrims, I have received news that a girl, Mother's daughter, has entered the Upper World."

The villagers cheered loudly and held up their tools in joy.

"You always knew she would return up there, didn't you, Master?" asked one of the bony villagers.

"I had faith that she would," Satan said. "And fate has repaid my faith! You may all slave away and begin the first phase of our plan. Chalyba Drakos!"

The villagers cheered and held their tools up once again as Satan spread his arms and wings out with pride. Femos looked up at Satan and grinned, excited by Satan's plan. Satan looked on at everyone's excitement and he shared that excitement with a sadistic, joyous laugh. It wasn't one of those cheesy, evil laughs you see in the movies, however, but it was high-pitched and maniacal.

Missing: Terra Cox

Terra Cox, the daughter of Cox Industries founder and inventor of the Type I enhancement, Edward Cox, has somehow gone missing, and due to an error in the nanotechnology in her clothing, her location is unknown. Terra Cox is a schoolgirl from New York, who attends the prestigious Clifton School for Girls, and has an interest in history and literature.

No such malfunction has occurred on any of HORIZON Technology's products before, and why this malfunction has occurred on the nano-clothing is a mystery. Don Williams said, "Our thoughts and sympathies are with Edward and Sandra Cox, who are very dear friends of mine. This is a very unusual error, but I can reassure you that we are reviewing our nano-clothing products so we can protect the children of America."

Edward and Sandra Cox have chosen not to give a statement due to the high amount of distress they're going through. Nano-clothing was launched in 2295 and had always been a very reliable tracking device so friends and families can track the location of their loved ones in the NClo app on the HoriPhone. Nano-clothing can also automatically remove any stains and dry any spills that have fallen onto their clothing.

Parents have voiced their concerns to Horizon due to their malfunction and the company understandably want to ensure that the current nano-clothing products will be able to protect their children. Edward and Sandra Cox have received many messages of sympathy and reassurances from high-profile figures such as President Marsha Bergsson hoping for the safe return of Terra, as are we at *US Observe*. We wish Sandra and Edward well during this difficult time.

Anton Monroe

It was the night that I had left Earth, and Edward was pacing up and down the living room with his hands behind his back. I was usually pretty reliable and was hardly ever late. Edward and Sandra couldn't track me down through my nano-clothing made them even more anxious and stricken with panic. Sandra was sitting on the sofa with her head down.

"Did Terra tell you if she was going somewhere after school?" Edward asked.

"No, she didn't," Sandra answered nervously. "I got in touch with Kim and she's on her way here."

"Does she know anything about Terra?" Edward asked.

"No, dear," Sandra replied. "Laura doesn't know either."

"Is she on her way here too?" Edward asked nervously.

"Yes, dear." Sandra nodded.

"Hopefully Laura will have a better idea of where Terra is," Edward said, feeling slightly optimistic.

"I hope so too." Sandra said, even though she was just saying what she thought Edward would want to hear. She didn't know what to say. "I mean, we should be able to track Terra's location from her HoriPhone and nanotechnology in her clothes, even if she's…"

"Don't say it, Sandra!" Edward interrupted assertively. "Please, honey. I can't even imagine it."

Christopher then emerged from the kitchen and entered the living room.

"May I get you some water in this time of despair?" Christopher asked.

"Please," Edward replied bluntly. "Christopher, could you get four glasses of water? We are expecting a couple of guests."

"Of course, sir," Christopher replied as he went to the kitchen.

Edward sat down on the sofa next to Sandra with his head in his hands. Sandra put her hand on Edward's back in an attempt to comfort him. There was a silence between the couple, and in a weird way, that silence was deafening. They were both scared and unsure of what to think. Edward was always so decisive and he always had an answer for everything, but this was so unprecedented and they both did all they could to stop themselves from imagining the worst, even if it was on the back of their minds. Edward kept looking down with his face in his hands and Sandra rubbed his back with her hand. Christopher entered the living room again carrying a tray with four glasses of water. He put the glasses on the table.

"Thank you, Christopher," Edward said, finally lifting his head and sitting up straight.

"You're welcome, sir," Christopher said. There was a buzzing sound coming from the doorway.

"That will be them. Please answer the door, Christopher," Edward said, getting close to tears.

"Yes, sir," Christopher replied. Edward reached for a glass of water and took a sip. Christopher went to the doorway and pressed a blue button, which was below a speaker built into the wall.

"Yes? May I ask who's calling?" Christopher asked into the speaker.

"It's Kim and Laura. Please open up." The voice of Kim, Laura's mother, could be heard from the speaker.

"Of course, madam," Christopher said as he pressed a red button below the speaker, which made a high-pitched buzzing sound.

"Was that Kim?" Sandra asked Christopher.

"Yes, madam. They are making their way up now," Christopher said. Sandra exhaled a sigh of relief. Edward was still tense. A doorbell sounded. "Shall I get that, madam?"

"Please," Sandra said. Christopher went to the door and placed his hand on a touchpad. The door slid horizontally open and Kim and Laura were there. They greeted Christopher and made their way into the living room.

"Sandra, Edward, how are you two holding up?" Kim asked as she and Laura sat on the sofa.

"We're just trying to cope," Sandra said.

"I'm so sorry that Terra has gone," Kim said sympathetically. "I wish we knew where she was. It's so strange that we cannot track her down."

"I last saw her today at school," Laura said. "I didn't see where she went after school had finished."

"I see," Edward said. "What did you and Terra get up to last night?"

"What do you mean?" Laura asked after hesitating, shaking her head in confusion.

"She was with you last night, right?" Edward asked, getting even more nervous than before.

"No, she wasn't," Laura said, confused again. I had never lied to Edward and Sandra before, so it was a real shock to them that I actually hadn't told them the truth the night before I left Earth.

"Terra told us that she was going to see you last night," Sandra said.

"Well, she didn't," Laura said, still confused. Edward rapidly inhaled and exhaled, and Sandra was shocked too. "I don't know what to…"

"Why would Terra say that she was going to meet Laura and then not go?" Kim asked.

"I don't know," Edward said, shaking his head while he got up to pace up and down again.

"I'm just really confused," Laura said, as she took off her glasses and tears started to roll down her face.

"Me too," Sandra said.

"Can I get a tissue or something?" Laura asked.

"Here, take this." Edward said as he gave Laura his handkerchief out of his pocket. "Don't worry, it's dried up."

Laura took the handkerchief to dry up her tearful face. This would have been such an awful sight; to see them all so saddened like this about me. As happy as I was to be reunited with my family, I never imagined how much pain that would cause the people I knew back on Earth.

"Was Terra okay when you last saw her?" Kim asked.

"I think so," Sandra answered.

Edward's HoriPhone rang. The name 'Anton Monroe' appeared on the phone, but there was no image, just a blank background with a green answer button and a red decline button. Edward walked over to the device and touched the green button.

"Anton," Edward said as he picked up the phone.

"Edward, I heard about your daughter's disappearance," Anton said. "I am so sorry. I know you and Sandra must be going through a difficult time right now."

"Yes, Anton, it's really difficult to take," said Edward.

"I understand," Anton said. "Listen, why don't you come over to my house? We can talk about this. I really want to help if I can."

"Sure, I'll be right over," Edward said.

"Good, I shall see you soon," Anton said. Edward pressed the red button on the phone and put it in his pocket.

"I shall be going now," Edward said to the ladies sitting on the sofa.

"Are you going over to Anton's house?" Sandra asked.

"Yes, Sandra, I will be back later," Edward said.

"Okay, dear, I will see you later." Sandra bid her husband farewell as they kissed and embraced. Edward then went out.

"Laura and I are happy to stay here and keep you company," said Kim. Laura nodded in agreement with Kim.

"Oh, thank you so much. I would really appreciate that," Sandra said gratefully. "I need to phone the police and inform them about the situation."

Edward's aerocar drove in a hurried manner, but not frantically. Aerocars were able to drive themselves automatically, but you had to drive manually if you wanted to reach full speed. You had to enter the location and it would drive you to your destination. You had to be over 18 to operate one, so I hadn't driven one. The car flew so quickly that its headlights appeared to blur. There was severe rain pouring down from the night sky, but that didn't stop the car from driving in such a rush, and it was still able to see where it was going as the windscreen wipers wiped away the rain.

Edward arrived at a pair of large gates. He reached his arm out of the car window and pressed a button below the speaker at the side of the gates.

"Hello?" a polite voice said through the speaker. "May I ask who's calling at this hour?"

"It's Edward Cox," he replied.

"Come right in," the voice said. The gates opened and Edward walked up to the door. The doors were large too, almost three times Edward's height. The doors opened and a G-28 android answered.

"Good evening, Mr Cox," the android said in a polite manner.

"Evening, Andrew," Edward replied. "I have come to see Mr Monroe."

"Of course," Andrew said. "My master has been expecting you."

Andrew led Edward along a corridor. Along the walls were paintings, and while some of the paintings were beautiful, most of them were very disturbing and displayed symbols of suffering, torture, and death. Edward stared at the paintings as he followed Andrew, and gasped with his mouth wide open, absorbed by the paintings, though he had seen them before. They were just fresh in his memory.

"Through this door, sir," Andrew said to Edward.

The room that Edward walked into was huge. At one end of the room was a series of giant paintings, with similar themes to the ones in the corridor, and at the other end was a couch along with a couple of armchairs in front of a fireplace with a roaring fire, this the room's only source of light. This was not like other rooms on Earth as there wasn't much technology seen anywhere. Between both ends of the room were bookshelves against the wall. The figure of Anton Monroe was in the armchair behind Edward. As he entered the room, Anton stood up.

"Edward," Anton said, and the face of Satan was revealed, unbeknownst to Edward. Satan wasn't anything like he was in the Underworld. He looked more human and healthier, yet less muscular, and his height was around six feet tall as opposed to his form in the Underworld. He had dark blonde hair combed to the side. He was wearing black trousers and a dressing gown that was dark red. Anton was a very polite, calming figure, unlike Satan's usual state of anger and resentment.

"Anton," Edward began. "Thank you for agreeing to see me."

"It's a pleasure," replied Anton. "You seemed very aggrieved when we spoke."

Edward hesitated for a moment, and then spoke. "Aggrieved is surely an understatement, isn't it? It's about Terra."

"I know," Anton said. "You told me."

Edward laughed reluctantly but was very quick to withdraw his laughter. Anton approached Edward.

"Edward," Anton began, "I am sure she will be fine, okay. I know she's untraceable right now, and it's all really frantic and strange, but I promise you, she will be fine. I know that she is a very smart girl. Please sit down by the fire. You must be cold from the weather outside."

Edward and Anton both took their seats in front of the fire. While Anton was feeling relaxed with a glass of scotch in his hand, Edward wasn't. He sat right on the edge of the armchair.

"Would you care for a drink?" Anton asked.

"I'm all right, thank you," Edward said.

"I know how difficult a situation this must be for you," Anton began to reassure Edward. "But as I said, Terra is a very smart girl and I promise you that she will be fine."

"How could you make a promise like that?" Edward asked. "Don't kid around with me like me"

"Of course, I'm really sorry." Anton said. "I just remember that she's always done well at school and is very intelligent. How old is she now?"

"Fourteen," Edward replied.

"At fourteen she can take care of herself. She's growing up, now that she's a teenager, almost an adult. I know you love Terra and I hope for your sake, well everybody's sake really, that she will be safe."

"I hope so too," Edward said. "But let me ask you this, am I a bad father?"

Anton looked baffled. "How could you ask that?"

"I think she may have run away," Edward said, his voice breaking.

"Why would she do that?" Anton asked.

"I-I honestly don't know," Edward said in response.

"I see," Anton replied. "Will you excuse me if I just leave the room for a moment?"

"Of course," Edward said bluntly.

Anton got up from his armchair and left the room. Edward sat for a moment, with his head looking down. After a couple of deep breaths, Edward walked around the living room. He approached the bookshelves and had a browse. Edward looked slowly at the spines of books and discovered many classic works of literature. Edward picked up one of the books from one of the lower shelves. The front cover revealed that it was *Frankenstein* by Mary Shelley. Edward lingered at the cover, drawing up memories from the story. Anton walked in through the doorway and approached Edward, who put the book back on the shelf.

"I was just admiring your collection of books," Edward said.

"Well, I am glad that you admire them," Anton gladly said. "I have always been into literature. Classic literature to be precise. I never read tablets or any technological devices. I prefer the real thing. I know this sounds very strange and old-fashioned, but there is nothing that is greater than the feel of reading an actual book."

"I had never properly seen your book collection before," Edward said. "I've glanced at it, sure, but never looked at the books themselves."

"Edward, you need to read an actual book," Anton said. "Not a story on your tablet, I mean an actual book."

"Why?" Edward asked.

"Why?" Anton asked in disbelief. "Edward, it's the feel of it. This feels so authentic and it helps you connect to the story. Believe me, Edward, this is the way to read stories. These books are my treasures. You may notice that I don't have much in the way of electronics and gadgets. I know it's a fad nowadays to read from the HoriPad, but that's because I prefer treasures from the old world. Its authenticity is just beautiful. Anyway Edward, make sure you read a real book."

"Well, I shall give it a try," Edward said. "I mean, I have a lot of things on my mind now, you know with Terra and..."

"I understand, Edward," Anton said, putting his arm around Edward's shoulder to comfort him. "Anyway, you should give it a try one day. I mean, this will help you through the grief of losing Terra, but I am sure that she will be fine. Why don't I give you a book from my collection?"

"Uh, maybe," Edward said. "I'll think about it."

"No problem," Anton said. "I saw you admiring *Frankenstein*, so I thought I'd ask."

"Thank you, Anton, I really appreciate it," Edward said. "So, do you have a favourite book?"

"Me? I have quite a few favourites," Anton laughed. "I've always been more into fantasy. New worlds, fascinating adventures. Edward, with what we do, are we not looking to create our own fantasy stories? Our own science fiction stories, too? Showing the world something beyond human imagination."

"Yes, you're right, Anton," Edward said, nodding in agreement. "You're a very smart man."

"Come on, don't flatter me," Anton joked. "Anyway, about Terra, have you contacted the authorities yet?"

"No, not yet," answered Edward. "I believe Sandra will contact them."

"I'm sure she will," Anton said. "I know Sandra really cares about Terra too. They can help track Terra down."

"Good," Edward said. His phone rang.

"Do you mind if I answer my phone?" he said.

"Oh, please do," Anton said. Edward answered his HoriPhone.

"Hello?" Edward spoke.

"It's Sandra. Just to inform you that I spoke to the police and they will begin searching for Terra."

"That's great, thank you, Sandra," Edward said in a relieved manner, though he wasn't completely relieved. Edward said goodbye to Sandra and hung up.

"Did Sandra call the police?" Anton asked.

"Yes, she did," Edward said.

"Good, that's a start at least," Anton said smiling. "Edward, do you fancy a drink now?"

"I could do with a glass of water," Edward said.

"Sure. Andrew!" Anton called out. Andrew entered the living room. "Could you fetch Edward a glass of water please?"

"Of course, sir," Andrew said as he left to go into the kitchen.

"Listen, Edward, I'm thinking of having a special dinner soon," Anton said. "I wasn't present at the anniversary party. I don't like attending big parties. I prefer to stay out of the limelight of the media and make you the celebrity of the Type I program. Anyway, would you care to attend?"

"That sounds nice Anton," Edward said. "But as you can imagine, I don't really fancy a party right now."

"I understand," Anton replied. Edward loved social events, but this was one of those rare moments where Edward was just not in the mood for a party, but Anton wasn't disappointed. "I'd love if you and Sandra can come, of course, but I know this whole situation with Terra must be devastating you both."

"It is," Edward said. "I try not to think what's happened to Terra because that's when I imagine her…" Edward broke into tears, but Anton knew what Edward's next word was going to be.

"It's okay." Anton said. "I was also going to invite Marsha Bergsson along, and hopefully she could do something to help you guys out with finding Terra."

"That would be great, actually." Edward said, and then Andrew walked in carrying a glass of water and gave it to Edward. "Thank you, Andrew."

"You're welcome," Andrew said. "Can I get you anything else?"

"I'm fine, thank you," Anton said. "Edward, have you had any dinner? Andrew can prepare you something to eat."

"Oh, I already ate, thank you," Edward said.

"Okay, then no, Andrew, we're fine," Anton said. Andrew left the room. "Anyway, if you and Sandra can't stay for the whole party, which I will totally understand, do come and at least meet Marsha, even if it is for ten minutes. With all that you've done, I'm sure she can do something to help."

"Okay, I'll see if we can make it." Edward said. "It might not be for very long, but if Marsha is coming and if Terra is still not found, then hopefully she can help. Who else are you planning on inviting?"

"Just some close friends of mine who would be very happy to meet you," Anton said. "No pressure, of course. Cox bless this dinner party!"

"Oh, don't use my name as a pun!" Edward said, blushing and letting out laughter reluctantly.

"Hey, blame the media," Anton said. "You're the one who makes the front pages after all."

"Right. Well, I better get going now," Edward said. "Better try and get some sleep after Terra disappearing."

"Sure, of course," Anton said. "Please do get some rest, however hard it might be right now. Let me walk you to the door."

Anton walked with Edward along the corridor, where the paintings were. Edward stared at the paintings again, once again gasping with his mouth wide open.

"Hey, I've always wondered, what's with the paintings?" Edward asked.

"They represent fear," Anton said. "Fear is what makes us stronger, and our desire to become something more. I don't believe fear holds you back, it makes you determined to conquer everything."

Anton opened the door for Edward.

"Edward, you know I'm always here for you, right?" Anton asked in an attempt to reassure him.

"Of course, I do," Edward answered.

"I'll open the gate for you, but I will be in touch," Anton said. "Have a good night."

"Good night," Edward said in reply. He got into his car and Anton closed the door. The gate opened for Edward to operate his car out and he set off back home.

Skywhales

I woke up from a queen-sized bed in the palace bedroom. The bedroom carpet was made of grass and was so soft that it practically massaged my feet when I stepped on it. The bed had a white duvet, white pillows, and white bedsheets. The bedding was made of silk and there were silky ribbons surrounding the bed. There was a white crown at the end of the bed. The frame of the bed was made of sticks and twigs, but it was strong and solid. There were sticks and twigs on the ceiling too, and there were some leaves on the ceiling as well.

The room looked so beautiful and more peaceful than my bedroom in New York. I would often wake up to the sound of aerocars and other transportation in the city, as people tried to get to work and to school, but instead here I woke up to the sound of animals (dinosaurs, that is) just communicating with each other. I had never really been around nature until that point, and it was nice. It was weird at first, because I had never known real peace and tranquillity on Earth, but it was really pleasant. I stretched and yawned. I was reluctant to get out of bed however, as the material was so comfortable and just like when I arrived in the Upper World, I was embracing the air that was coming through the window.

I wore a long white dress that covered most of my body, similar to the dress Mother wore. Back on Earth, it wasn't cool to wear the same clothes as your parents, but I didn't mind. I wasn't on Earth after all.

Then a Maiasaura arrived at the doorway, which surprised me. Even though I had met the Maiasaura the day before, it was just such a strange sight to see when I woke up. I had an alarm to wake me up in New York, but I didn't think anybody had a dinosaur trying to wake them up, not even in the movies. The Maiasaura wasn't aggressive, however, and I felt no intimidation from the dinosaur. It made a low-pitched call and then walked out, and then I followed it. I walked out of the door and down a spiral staircase, which was where the Maiasaura walked. The staircase was also covered in sticks, twigs and leaves. The staircase led to the main hall, where there was a long table with different fruits, nuts and bread laid out in wooden bowls and plates. The Maiasaura walked away from the table, but there were more Maiasaurs carrying bowls and plates to the table in their mouths.

Hominem, Mulieris, Mother and Father were among those sitting at the long table, and to my surprise, Vagus was there too. He was wearing the same eccentric clothing he had been wearing at the prayer group. He was eating from a bunch of grapes and had a wooden grail-like cup of wine. I stared at Vagus, unsure as to why he was here, but I wasn't disappointed to see him. Everybody at the table, including Vagus, all turned to me, which was kind of overwhelming, but I had calmed down since I met Mother. They all greeted me, which was weird as I had never experienced a welcome like that on Earth. I always felt so awkward at the parties I went to with Edward and Sandra, but I was okay at parties when Laura was there. This was the first social gathering without Laura where I didn't feel lonely and awkward.

"How did you sleep, little one?" Mother asked.

"I slept great, thanks," I replied as I embraced Mother. I never usually embraced anyone when I woke up. It wasn't that I didn't love Sandra or Edward. I just never felt the need to hug them or anything. I guess I don't get affectionate so easily.

"I am glad," Mother said. "Please sit, Terra, and join us in this feast."

I sat down next to Mother. I reached across for a slice of bread and an apple from one of the bowls. I started eating the apple and I exchanged a smile with Mother, nothing like what I did on Earth. It seemed I had picked up some new habits since meeting Mother. I was where I belonged. I then looked across at Vagus, who made eye contact with me.

"How is the fruit, Terra?" he asked.

"It's delicious," I answered after I finished my mouthful. The fruit was fresher and juicier here than back on Earth, and I ate rare fruits from foreign countries. I guess it was because they were freshly grown in the Upper World and not artificially cloned like the fruit on Earth.

"There was a time on Earth where fresh fruit and crops were ever-present all over the world," Vagus said. "It is so rare to see such nourishment nowadays. The natural world has changed so much, and I fear that we could see an end to nature."

"You may be fearful, Vagus, but I will not stop believing in my creation," Father said defiantly. "All I can do is hope. Man will prevail. I am sure of it."

"I admire your faith, Father," Vagus said. "Even if man have stopped believing in you. There are still good people on Earth who will always admire all that you've done, but…"

"If man is to have faith in me, I must have faith in man," Father said defiantly, and then ate a grape from its stem. A young man appeared from the doorway behind the spiral staircase. He had black hair which went down to his shoulders. He had bare feet and wore white trousers and a white shirt. Father stood and approached him.

"Son," Father addressed him.

"Father," Son addressed Father in return, and they embraced. They then walked over to the table and Son sat next to Father. I guess the gods in this world didn't have first names like me or Vagus, or anybody on Earth. They were just named for what they were.

"Terra, I would like you to meet my son," Father said to me.

"Hello," I greeted Son. I should have felt weird calling him Son because he wasn't my son. I wondered what everybody other than Mother or Father would call him.

"Greetings, Terra," Son said in response. "I had heard word of your return here. How are you finding this reunion?"

"It's been good," I replied. "I mean, I guess it is quite overwhelming."

Everybody turned to me, as it seemed that they were shocked by what I said. My heart started racing. Was it the anniversary party all over again?

"I'm sorry, dear," Mother said softly as she touched my cheek. I smiled, because I wasn't being sent up to my room this time, and it didn't seem like everybody was mad at me. I truly did belong here.

"No, not in a bad way," I clarified. "It's just that all my life I have not known who I really am and where I came from. I knew that I was adopted, but I didn't know my true background. I never thought I'd ever know, because Edward and Sandra didn't know."

"Who are Edward and Sandra?" Son asked.

"They're my foster parents," I answered. "Anyway, when I went to see Vagus, he told me that I was Mother's daughter, but I wasn't sure what that meant. Then I discovered that I had this... power, I guess. I managed to resurrect this plant, but even now, I'm not sure how I did that. Then there were these leaves around me, and then I was here, and then I met my mother, and all of you. It's not bad, I mean of course it's not bad at all, but it's just so unexpected."

"I can understand, Terra," Mother said, with her hand again placed on my cheek. "It is not easy to adjust to a new world and discover a destiny you never knew."

"This atmosphere must be so different to what you have experienced on Earth," Vagus said.

"Of course," I said. "I've never known air like this, it's so…"

"Fresh?" Vagus smiled, playfully finishing my sentence.

"Yes," I said. "It's just so different to what I have experienced."

"Man's violation of the laws of nature, becoming those that made them, could result in negative implications across the other planets they are dominating," Vagus explained.

"But is there hope that men can redeem themselves?" I asked.

"I'd like to believe so," Father said. "When I created your foster world, it was perfect. It was paradise, bliss. Then the more that men thought for themselves, the greater their desires were, and the greater the cost that Earth will have to endure."

"Thankfully not all planets are like that," Vagus said.

"What do you mean?" I asked.

"I don't know if anybody has told you this, Terra," Vagus began. "But there are many different planets in this universe, inhabited by different races."

"Really?" I asked with extreme fascination. "I'd like to explore them."

"They are very far away, Terra," Mother said. "I know that when you become royalty it is important to educate yourself in the way of the universe below. While I am Mother of all, I hold extra concern for you, and I would not want to be apart from you again."

"I'll be fine, honest!" I begged. Laura and I once talked about traveling the world together before or after university, maybe taking a flight to space like those only the rich could afford. I was always so curious about other cultures. I hadn't been to many countries, only India, France, Russia and Japan. The idea of going to another *world* was so exciting, and I wasn't thinking about any potential dangers there may be.

"Terra, I am not issuing a refusal," Mother clarified. "When you are a mother, you become a protector. Of course, reservations will be held, while I maintain my duty as Mother of the skies."

"If I may explain to you, Mother," Vagus said. "I've received word of a distress call from Aurelia. You know this world well, Mother, as do you, Father."

"Yes, it is a noble planet," Father said.

"They embrace their world," Mother said, before she said to me, "Aurelia is a planet that worships us, and while Father is the creator of worlds, the angels here or the Krygurra answer to their distress calls to help citizens through troubled times."

"Anyway, there has been disharmony there which requires a visit from one of us," Vagus said. "I know that normally an angel must meet with the people of Aurelia, but the king has specifically requested that Terra attends before him."

"Why do they need me?" I asked. I was excited about visiting another world, but was curious to know why a planet would need me when I didn't think anybody knew me there, or anywhere outside of New York (let alone Earth).

"But Terra is too young," Mother protested. "Did the king say why?"

"He didn't, but he just said it was imperative that Terra enters Aurelia," Vagus said.

Mother seemed confused, as was I. Why would another planet *need* me? Mother got up, as did Father, and they conferred with each other, suspicious about the request from Aurelia. Father then turned to Vagus.

"You'll keep Terra safe, will you?" Father asked Vagus.

"As long as she is with me, she will be safe," Vagus reassured Father. "Please place your trust and faith in me to keep your daughter safe."

"Of course," Mother said. "Terra, you should go with Vagus, as long as he can promise your safety."

"You have my word," Vagus said reassuringly.

I embraced Mother, and I got up along with Vagus and we left the Caelem Palatium together.

"Stay safe, little one," Mother said as she elegantly waved goodbye. Father waved too.

"May the stars guide you, Terra," Father said while waving.

Vagus and I walked out of the castle door, and Mother looked on with a reluctant smile. Having been so overjoyed to be reunited with me once again, part of her felt disappointment to see me gone so soon, and she was still suspicious about Aurelia's request. However, she understood that this would be for mine and Aurelia's benefit and she trusted Vagus to be a reliable informant. It was within her caring nature to worry about my safety, especially as she was mother of all. A Maiasaura approached Mother, and then she put both her hands on the Maiasaura's cheeks.

"I thank you for serving this wonderful feast, my sweets," Mother said kindly as she kissed the Maiasaura on the head.

Vagus and I walked past the guarding Styracosaurus and Pentaceratops and down the pathway to the Caelum Palatium. My walk was much more confident than it had been when I originally came up to the Caelum Palatium, but part of me was braced for the unexpected. After what I had encountered in the Upper World, I guess I was ready for more shocks with Vagus. I was ready for adventure. Then I thought of Laura and our dream to travel the world together. How would she feel traveling to another *world*? Would I ever see her again? I guess I missed her, but I was still so euphoric about being with my real family. She must have been so worried about me going missing. Maybe one day I might return to Earth, just to tell Laura, Sandra, and Edward that I was okay.

"Terra, what do you know of the universe?" Vagus asked.

"I only know Earth, but nothing else," I answered awkwardly. "I mean, I have studied outer space at school. Earth is where I've always lived. I don't even know where I am now."

"We are now above the universe," Vagus said. I didn't know there was anything above the universe, although the prayer group believed in an afterlife that was somewhere outside the universe.

"So how do we get down to the universe?" I asked, although I was still trying to comprehend the fact that I was above the universe.

"We ride, Terra," Vagus replied.

"Ride what?" I asked.

"Follow me," Vagus answered vaguely as he walked on and I followed. Vagus frustrated me again by being so vague. Maybe I should have called him Vague-s as a joke, though that would sound like Vegas. We both walked across the log bridge and reached the valley. There were many different dinosaurs drinking water and grazing grass, and Vagus and I walked past them. I gazed at the dinosaurs as we walked past, trying

130

to get another glimpse of them as I was still fascinated to be in the presence of dinosaurs.

Vagus and I both reached the other end of the valley and approached a giant patch of flowers; there were also mushrooms, pines, cycads and weeds. There was a pathway within the patch and Vagus and I walked down it. I heard the loud sound of gushing water. I was fascinated by the sound, as I had never encountered this amount of rushing water before. I had been to the coast before, but never came across a gush of water so loud before. When I visited the coast, the sea was always so calm, soothing and beautiful. I felt lucky to have seen the sea, no matter how dumb it sounds, as it was one of the few places on Earth that still had true beauty to it. The sounds of the water that I heard in the Upper World felt powerful, like it was commanding something. Vagus stopped at the end of the pathway and I stopped with him, and we gazed down at a series of giant waterfalls falling into a lake.

"Down there, Terra, is where all the good souls from mortal bodies lie," Vagus said.

"So, this is where the dead live?" I asked.

"Aye, Terra," Vagus answered. "But mind, this is not a haunted place. These spirits are peaceful and are grateful for the lives that Father has provided for them."

"So, are we... dead?" I asked awkwardly. Was *this* the afterlife that the prayer group mentioned? I was getting confused all over again.

"No, Terra, we're still alive," Vagus answered with a laugh, which brought a laugh out of me too, as my nerves had eased.

"Are we going to jump down?" I asked nervously.

"No, Terra, of course not," Vagus replied, laughing once again. "We have reached our ride."

"Have we?" I asked. I couldn't see any transportation down below, or anything mechanical up here. I was so confused. "What are we supposed to be riding?"

Vagus stepped forward and bellowed loudly. What was that? Why did he make that noise? I didn't know if Vagus was doing something extraordinary or just being annoying. Then, a gentle, bellowed responding call came from the sky and two large floating figures emerged. There were small spikes on their backs and on the side of their giant bodies were large wings reminiscent of large fins. They approached Vagus and I quickly, but they weren't intimidating. They were gentle and harmless, despite their large size. I stared at them. I didn't think they were dinosaurs. I had never seen them before, not even in stories.

"I call them skywhales," Vagus said as he gently put his hand on a skywhale's snout and stroked it. They responded happily and calmly to his affection. "They're gentle, Terra."

I hesitated before I stroked the other skywhale on the snout and it was clearly taken with me as it emitted a calm bellow, which brought a laugh from me. They were actually really sweet, even though they were huge.

"Are we going to be riding them?" I asked.

"Yes, Terra," Vagus answered as he climbed onto the skywhale and sat on its back, holding onto a vine that was tied onto one of its spikes. He then tied the vine around his waist. I'd never ridden on anything that wasn't transportation. Not even animals because there weren't many left around on Earth. What would happen if I got onto the skywhale? Would it flick me off? Eventually, I did what Vagus did and climbed onto the other skywhale and tied the vine around my waist. I was relieved as soon as I sat on top of the creature, and then Vagus asked, "Are you ready, Terra?"

"Yes," I answered, although it sounded more like a question. I didn't know what the ride would be like, and I started thinking that maybe going with Vagus was a mistake. Maybe I was going to die and go to the afterlife for real. This was going to be the roughest ride of my life. I remembered when Laura and I once went on this simulator called Space Mission at Disney Galaxy Amusement Park in Florida. On the ride, our seats shook as we viewed a giant screen that showed a journey through space. Planets and stuff came flying out of the screen to make it seem more real. I did enjoy it, but this was not going to be a simulator.

Vagus pressed onto the skywhale's back and it flew, and the other skywhale followed. I clutched onto the skywhale's spike tightly as it flew downwards and through the waterfall. My skywhale followed Vagus' skywhale as we flew through a dark cave. My mount was so quick that I just closed my eyes and let out a scream. I just had to keep telling myself that this was the Space Mission simulator, and myself and Laura were just enjoying the ride like before, and when the ride was over, Laura and I would laugh and say how amazing that ride was, and be aching to go on it again.

But it kept crossing my mind.

This was no simulator.

"This is a mistake," I told myself repeatedly.

"Hold on tight, Terra!" Vagus raised his voice.

Then the speed changed. The skywhale started moving at a steadier pace, and I could open my eyes.

We were in outer space, just like in the simulator.

Once again, this was no simulator. This was real. I blinked my eyes hundreds of times to make sure that I was seeing this right.

Then I realized something: there was no air in space, yet I was still breathing.

"How am I breathing?" I asked Vagus, who was still ahead of me, so I had to raise my voice. "Shouldn't I be suffocating or something?"

"You can breathe everywhere, Terra," Vagus shouted out in response. "You have Mother's lungs."

So, it turned out being Mother's daughter (the term still felt weird to me) meant that I could breathe anywhere, even in space. As the skywhale was going at a steady pace, I could just sit and look all around at the stars and nebulas. The nebulas were bright yellow, pink, blue, and green. My eyes widened at the beauty of the bright lights the dust clouds produced.

"How are you enjoying the view, Terra?" Vagus asked.

"It's beautiful," I replied, maintaining eye contact with the nebulas. "Are we near Earth?"

"We're in a galaxy far away to the solar system you know, Terra," Vagus replied.

So, we were in a galaxy far, far away. It reminded me of this four-hundred-year-old movie about Jedis and stormtroopers I'd seen on Viewpoint. I didn't like it though. Even though I was living in a world with artificial intelligence and human beings with an extended lifespan, I thought the movie was pretty silly.

"Hold on tight, Terra, because we are nearly there," Vagus told me. "We're almost at Aurelia."

The skywhales moved quickly once again, so I held on to my skywhale's spike tightly, and we started to approach a light blue sphere.

Aurelia

The skywhales gracefully entered Aurelia and passed through a series of streamlined clouds, which were white but had light shades of pink all over them. Vagus leaned forward on his skywhale, with his head upright, looking ahead at the view. I looked around in astonishment, as I had never been to another planet before. The Upper World wasn't a planet, though. It was just something else; the sky was of a lighter shade of red with clouds that were light green. Vagus' skywhale flew past a mountain that had blue rocks and patches of yellow grass and my skywhale followed closely behind. I inhaled and the air was different than the air in the Upper World. I couldn't describe it, but the scent was similar to a swimming pool I went to with Edward, Sandra and Laura. It was in Knotsberry Ocean Park, which was the biggest water park in America, and the smell of chlorine was weird at first, but I got used to it. That was what the air in Aurelia was like. However, it was a heightened scent from what I had experienced, and I started to feel dizzy. While in a daze, I leaned to my right, and came very close to falling off the skywhale. I was still tied up on the vine, however, but when I noticed how close I came to falling off, I gasped and let out a scream. The skywhale flung its fin-like wing backwards to put me back up on its back. The skywhale had formed a bond with me, it turned out, and ensured that I wouldn't come to any harm on the ride over, despite my fear when the skywhale sped up at first. To my relief, the ride was over, as the skywhale lowered its body onto the ground.

The grass was light green with a shade of blue, and the trees close to me had dark purple bark and yellow leaves. Vagus and I both got off our skywhales and jumped onto the grass. I was starting to get used to the air in Aurelia, after feeling so dizzy from inhaling it. The skywhales then flew away, and on their way out of Aurelia, they fed upon floating seaweed that was drifting in the air.

"Where are they going?" I asked.

"They're flying for food," Vagus said. "They usually eat aeroplankton, and there is so much of it in the air here."

I looked back at the skywhales as they flew away and then looked at all that was around me, witnessing creatures that I had never seen before on Earth, although there weren't many creatures left there. I saw a flock of small pink hummingbird-like creatures fly towards the trees. They had four eyes above their green beaks, three webbed feet and a multicoloured feathered tail, the shape of which was similar to a lion's. I also saw a family of small bullfrog-like creatures leaping along the grass. They had two small yellow eyes with no pupil and bird-like feet. Also trotting along the grass were a herd of two-headed deer-like creatures with scaly skin and reptile-like feet.

"What are those things?" I asked Vagus, maintaining eye contact with the weird animals.

"This is the blessed wildlife of Aurelia," Vagus said, after taking a deep breath of the Aurelia air.

"Did you ever feel weird from breathing this air?" I asked.

"I've breathed all airs, Terra," Vagus said. "Of course, it takes time to accustom yourself to different atmospheres. It took me time to get accustomed to this planet."

I continued to gaze at everything in Aurelia. It was all so strange, but ever since I had arrived in the Upper World, pretty much everything surprised me. I had seen dinosaurs, flown through outer space, met God himself (Father) and discovered that my real mother was an all-powerful deity. I probably should have been more open-minded considering what I had witnessed. Aurelia was beautiful, even if it was incredibly mystifying.

"This way, Terra," Vagus said, as we walked in the direction of a forest.

Further into the forest, I saw even more fascinating alien-like creatures, as well as the ones I saw earlier. I saw something resembling a moth, but it had eight eyes and fangs with sharp teeth, and it was feeding on the plants on the ground. I also saw feathered monkeys with six arms and two tails and foxes with scaly, snake-like skin. The plant life in Aurelia was also incredibly weird. Aside from the grass and the trees, they were all floating, multicoloured flowers and orange and purple lilies. I looked around in all directions, in order to stay alert. As amazed as I was about this place, I was wary of any potential threats. I stayed close to Vagus, as he was more familiar with Aurelia than I was. I didn't fully trust him yet, but despite how dangerous being on this planet and away from Mother once again may be, this was an opportunity for me to travel and explore new places, even though I had always imagined it would have been with Laura. Would Laura have dared enter another planet, no matter how exotic and fascinating it seemed? Visiting the last rainforest in the world in Brazil would have been safer, and one of the places I had always wanted to visit.

We reached the end of the forest and saw a lawn made of turf-like green grass. I recognized that it was like turf because Edward took me to sports events, though I was never really into sports. I had seen more turf than real grass back on Earth. Beyond the lawn was a palace made of stone and gravel. Its roof was shaped like a dome and the building was very long, but not very tall. Its height was no taller than the mountains behind the palace. I saw some strange creatures on the lawn. They were half-man, half-horse and they were of different colours, with their human and horse-like bodies interchanging colours. They were like centaurs, which I had learned about in a mythology class, but they all had some sort of antenna on the top of their heads and their tails were not like a horse. One centaur had a wolf-like tail, another had spikes on the top, another had a club on the tip, another was scaly and the tip was similar to a whip. All the centaurs wore no clothing, but they all had no nipples on their breasts.

The centaurs were walking along the lawn in pairs, with the male strolling along with the female. A part of me thought it was romantic, but another part made me feel uneasy as there were no same-sex couples, especially considering how I felt about Laura. Were same-sex relationships forbidden in Aurelia? I didn't know, but maybe I was reading too much into it. All of them saw Vagus and I as we started to walk up the lawn.

"Greetings, Vagus," greeted one of the centaurs warmly in a projecting, deep voice. I was surprised that he spoke English, as I thought he would have spoken some alien language like in the movies. He was blue, with his human body of a darker shade than his horse-like lower body. He had a beard and small horns at the top of his head.

"Ah, Ohlakan, my friend, so nice to see you again," Vagus replied as he embraced the centaur.

"Goodness me, how long has it been since we last saw sight of each other?" Ohlakan asked.

"It has been too long, my friend," Vagus said.

A pink female centaur with long blonde hair walked towards Vagus and I and stood by Ohlakan.

"You remember my love, Uhla, don't you, Vagus?"

"Hello, Vagus," Uhla said.

"Oh, Uhla, lovely to see you too," Vagus said as he kissed Uhla's hand. "I bring with me Mother's daughter."

The centaurs all chattered with excitement. Turned out that I was famous in Aurelia too.

"Oh, the daughter of the skies! This must be Terra," Ohlakan said.

I stepped forward slowly, unsure of how to greet them. They may have all spoken my language, but I wondered how much else they understood. Did they know of Earth and its culture and stuff? Maybe I was as weird to them as they were to me.

"Hi, I'm… Terra," I said, needlessly introducing myself. I wasn't really sure of what to say. When I first met people, the first thing I would say is "Hi, I'm Terra." I guess it was a reflex.

"We know who you are, dear," Uhla said in a friendly manner.

"These people here worship Mother and Father of the sky, of the Upper World," Vagus said to me. "They are the parents of all that is around in the universe."

"Do all the worlds out there, worship Mother and Father?" I asked.

"While I have been to many worlds, I however do not have great knowledge of the belief systems of all these other worlds," Vagus said. "I know Earth did, at one time."

"What of this Earth?" Ohlakan asked. "They no longer have the faith for Mother and Father?"

"There was a time when they collectively believed," Vagus said. "Now they choose to believe in something else entirely. It's now only a minority who believe."

"This planet has seen some bad times," Ohlakan said with a more serious tone. "Members of our kind have disappeared."

"What, just vanished?" I asked.

"We believe that it was the monster of the mountains," Uhla said, gesturing towards the mountains behind the palace. "We think he comes at night, and preys on us one by one."

"How did you hear about this monster?" I asked.

"The king told us," Uhla said. "The monster took his brother away. He was king of Aurelia before. He is presumed dead, and the monster may have killed others too."

"Many of us have gone into hiding," a green centaur said. The centaur had short, curly hair and claws on its hooves.

"I'm so sorry, Lathi," Vagus said.

"Terra is what this land needs," Lathi said. "Let us escort you into the Opraso."

All the centaurs walked in two by two, with the male and female centaurs alongside their companions, and Vagus and I walked up a curving path with golden sand on it, and then walked along a bridge that was over a moat with running indigo water which led to the giant door of the Opraso and into the kingdom.

Inside the Opraso, the kingdom had checked black and white tiles on the floor, and in the centre of the kingdom, there was a water fountain, in which water shot upwards. There were human children who had elf-like ears and were wearing white togas. They were running around, playing and laughing. The adult humans, who also had elf-like ears and were wearing togas, were chattering away with each other, with the occasional laugh entering the conversation.

At the very back of the room was a throne and sat on that throne was a man with black hair and a black beard. He held a glass of wine in his hand, wore a diamond crown on his head, a necklace and rings on his fingers that were made entirely of jewels, and looked on with a stern expression. He wasn't intimidating, but he looked very sincere. Sat next to him on the velvet carpet was a woman in a brown, ragged dress. She was skinny and had curly blonde hair and her eyes were all white, with no pupils to be seen. That was very disturbing to see, but maybe she had a condition or something. I wasn't sure. She also moved in a weird way, like maybe she was drunk. I had a fairly good idea of what drunk people were like, having been to parties with Edward and Sandra. I never really engaged with them, as I usually avoided them. It wasn't really because I was afraid of drunk people; I was sure that I'd get to drink alcohol one day as an adult; I just never knew how to interact with people when they were intoxicated.

Vagus and I followed the centaurs into the kingdom and walked across the velvet carpet that was laid out from the door to the throne. Upon seeing me, everyone in the room gasped with excitement and applauded and cheered. I'd had this reaction when I first came into the Upper World, so I should've been used to it, but I still wasn't at that moment. Back on Earth, I always tried to avoid being the centre of attention.

The man on the throne saw Vagus and I walking towards him, and looked with interest, although his facial expression didn't really change. He stood up when Vagus and I reached him. Vagus kneeled before him, although I just still stood. I had never met royalty before, so I wasn't really sure about how to address a king. Was it similar to the way they were addressed in those period British dramas? Were they going to be really Shakespearean? Everyone looked at me with shock, as I just stood, completely unaware of what to do.

"You're familiar with the ways of royalty, are you, Terra?" the man said, sounding as serious as he looked.

"I'm sorry, not really," I said. "We don't really have kings and queens back on Earth. We used to, but that was centuries ago."

"Well, I am King Deorege," he said. "And it is tradition to kneel before a king."

I looked at Vagus, and then I kneeled with him to appease King Deorege.

"Of course, Terra, you are royalty yourself, being Mother's daughter," King Deorege said. "And for this, you shall now stand, and it is I, and this kingdom, that shall kneel before you."

I stood and King Deorege kneeled, along with everybody in the room. This was now getting really weird. Why did he make me feel bad for not kneeling before him? Why even kneel at all? I'd met important people on Earth and I never had to kneel to them. I just greeted them with a handshake or whatever. Eventually, everybody stood.

"Terra, my dear girl, I welcome you to Aurelia," King Deorege said warmly. "And Vagus, old friend, it is so nice of you to grace us with your presence."

"I know, it's been a long time, Your Highness," Vagus said. Did I have to call him stuff like 'sire' and 'Your Highness'? Back on Earth, I knew that 'sir' was a polite way to address a man.

"And I must give you my thanks for bringing Terra to us," King Deorege said.

"I accept your gratitude, sire," Vagus said.

"Terra, I'm sure you've heard of the dangers here," King Deorege said. "Have you heard of the monster of the mountains?"

"Yes, it was mentioned to me," I said.

"There have been too many tragedies here," King Deorege said with his head down. "The monster took my brother and my wife away from me."

"I'm so sorry," I said with sympathy.

"Thank you," King Deorege said tearfully. After he dried his tears, he gestured to the strange woman and said, "Terra, this is my sister, Gemilin."

"Oh, Terra, I have always dreamed of meeting you," Gemilin said as she stood up and kissed my hand. I'd never had somebody kiss my hand before, and I had never seen a woman kiss another woman's hand.

"Vagus, Terra, may we escort you into the palace?" King Deorege asked as he gestured towards a doorway at the back of the room.

"Of course," Vagus said as he, King Deorege, Gemilin and I walked towards the back doorway.

We walked through a corridor which had shiny silver tiles laid out on the floor, a wall with paintings which consisted of the centaurs like those Vagus and I had met, and alien wildlife that were in the forest that Vagus and I had walked through. The roof was glass and therefore had a view of the sky and tall trees that grew around the palace. Also along the corridor were statues of different creatures, including centaurs. They looked just like some of the ones that I had met earlier with Vagus. I stopped to look at the centaur statues. Soon, Vagus and King Deorege noticed that I had stopped.

"These are tributes," King Deorege said. "We had these made to remember the fallen."

"But they only disappeared, right? You said that a monster took them, not killed them. I mean, we don't know if they're dead," I said, which drew a very stern look from King Deorege. Gemilin and Vagus appeared surprised that I answered back. I didn't know what compelled me to say that, especially at what seemed like a really inappropriate time.

"Terra, a monster took them," King Deorege said assertively. "A monster doesn't pamper the people it takes. It's a beast, a fiend! My brother is gone because of this beast, and as king of Aurelia, I ask that you show some respect."

"But I wasn't being disrespectful," I said, completely taken aback by King Deorege. I thought that I was pointing out a technicality, but maybe I should've known better than to say what I did and used common sense. He was just a man who was grieving. "Again, I'm sorry for what happened to your brother, but we don't know if it killed others."

"You *really* don't know how to address royalty, Terra," King Deorege said once again, shaking his head with disappointment.

We moved on and then reached the end of the corridor, and it eventually led to a garden, and King Deorege and Gemilin led Vagus and I to a large fountain which had a diamond statue of King Deorege on the top.

"You remember this statue, don't you, Vagus?" King Deorege said. "This was to celebrate ten years of my reign."

147

"Of course, sire," Vagus replied. "A fine work of art if I may say so."

"Thank you for your compliments," King Deorege said with his hand graciously on Vagus' shoulder.

I just stared at the statue. It was beautiful, but I chose not to compliment King Deorege. I didn't know why I chose not to speak. I wasn't afraid or anything. I just kept quiet, even when King Deorege looked at me, anticipating a compliment. It never came.

"Terra, if I may request something of you," King Deorege said as he gestured towards a floating multicoloured flower bed which had wilting, dying flowers. "I have a bundle of dying flowers in that bed over there. I hear that you're the bringer of life. I request that you make these flowers beautiful again."

"I don't know," I answered. I still doubted that I was this bearer of life or however everybody phrased it, and I felt uncomfortable at that request.

"It's okay, Terra," Vagus said encouragingly. "I've witnessed what you can do with my own eyes. I know you have these powers."

I walked over to the flower bed and the flowers floated down to me. I had to try and remember what happened when I saw those dying plants in Vagus' greenhouse. I picked up one of the dying flowers and, to my absolute shock, a light emerged around it. The flower grew back up again, along with the rest of the flowers. Gemilin gasped and she embraced me, and then King Deorege kissed my hand.

"I offer you my eternal gratitude, Terra," King Deorege said, but I was still in shock, even though I had brought plants back to life before, so I just replied with "uh huh", completely unsure of pretty much everything. This was still incredibly weird to me, and I wondered what else I might be capable of. I could heal, but what can else could I do?

I walked over to a part of the garden which had a view of the dark mountain where this monster lived. The peaks looked sharp and jagged, and the pathway looked very dark too. Whatever plants were there looked dead. I always seemed to be coming across dead plants wherever I went. The mountains looked lifeless and gloomy.

"Has anybody actually been up there?" I asked. "I mean, to find this monster?"

"Travel into the mountains is forbidden," King Deorege said. "This is for everybody's safety. I must warn all of Aurelia not to enter those parts, and I must warn you, girl."

"I beg you, Terra, please don't go up there!" Gemilin pleaded. "Only a fool would risk her life entering those parts."

"Yes, I've heard many terrors about what's up there," Vagus said.

"Aren't you going to send people there though?" I asked. "To kill this beast or whatever?"

"We have a strategy, I assure you," King Deorege said. "We must be patient, however. As long as we stay clear of the mountains, there may be no more lives lost."

"Please listen to my brother, little girl," Gemilin said. I found it condescending to be called a 'little girl'. I was fourteen! "Those who have dared enter have never returned. You are a curious one, yes, but curiosity can be a dangerous thing. You wander the wrong parts, you die."

"That goes for you too, Vagus," King Deorege said to Vagus. "I know you are a wanderer, but even you must have your limits, and I present to you your limits of Aurelia."

"Right," Vagus said, though I wasn't sure if he took that warning seriously. Vagus did like to take risks and he always made his own rules. Changing the subject, he said, "Thank you for your hospitality, Your Highness."

"Vagus, my friend, it is always so nice to see you," King Deorege said as he embraced Vagus. "And, Terra, my dear, we would like for you to stay here a bit longer."

"What, here? Without Vagus?" I asked, unsure of what was happening.

"Terra, we have really enjoyed your company," Gemilin said as she put her arm around my shoulder. I was so confused and uncomfortable.

"I can't stay," I said reluctantly, as I didn't want to hurt anybody's feelings.

"She must go with me," Vagus said.

"You answer for Terra, do you, Vagus?" King Deorege asked.

"No, I really have to leave," I said.

"I see," King Deorege said, disappointed. Gemilin had her head down in disappointment too.

"You must visit, Terra," Gemilin said. "Promise me, you'll visit."

"Uh, maybe," I said hesitantly, though I had made up my mind that these people were really weird. Maybe that was why there were no more kings and queens back on Earth; they were just really strange people. I then said, "It was nice to meet you... sire."

King Deorege and Gemilin reluctantly lead Vagus and I back through the corridor and back into the kingdom, where the adults and children remained. Vagus and I walked along the velvet carpet leading out of the door.

"Terra, my dear, are you quite sure you won't stay?" Gemilin asked as she grabbed my arm."

"Uh, I can't," I said as I got my arm out of Gemilin's grasp, and then Vagus and I left the Opraso. Back outside, the centaurs were strolling along two by two, just like before.

"Have you ever tried go up that mountain?" I asked Vagus quietly, in the hope that nobody would overhear us.

"Terra?" Vagus asked in surprise. "His royal Highness said..."

"I know, but his royal... whatever, is weird," I argued. "I don't know, none of this makes sense to me. Maybe we should go up there?"

Vagus thought for a moment. I knew that King Deorege had mentioned the monster, but I had that adventurous streak in me. I may have been shy and socially awkward before, but Vagus and I had something in common — we were both curious and keen to explore. I wasn't sure if there really was a monster. Part of me wanted to get out of Aurelia as soon as possible, but I thought about the good centaurs I met and the distress that they were going through. Something wasn't right.

"Listen, Terra, there is a conflict in this world," said Vagus. "Yes, blissful it may look, but something is not as it should be. I love to wander as you know, but at what cost, Terra?"

"If I am Mother's daughter and I can heal and stuff, then can I really die out here?" I asked. "Wish I had my HoriPhone with me, though I don't know if I could get a signal. Maybe I could meet you in an hour or..."

"I'll go with you. I suppose you're a wanderer like me now," Vagus said, which drew a smile from me. Vagus then looked in the direction of Ohlakan and Uhla, who were strolling across the lawn together. Vagus then called out, "Ohlakan!"

Ohlakan trotted towards Vagus and me. "Vagus, my friend," he said.

"Ohlakan, my friend," Vagus said, "I need you to keep a secret."

"A secret?" Ohlakan said, knowing that Vagus was not one for secrecy.

"Ohlakan, please, nobody must ever know," Vagus pleaded. "You cannot spread word of this to anyone. Not even Uhla."

Ohlakan looked back at Uhla, who smiled at him in return. He took a deep breath and reluctantly said to Vagus, "What is it?"

"We must go up that mountain," Vagus said. "There are answers that we must seek. Balance must be restored."

"But those parts are dangerous," Ohlakan warned. "Vagus, please, I beg you, you are a wanderer yes, but death awaits up there."

"It was my idea," I said. "I said that something didn't seem right about this monster stuff, and maybe we should do something."

"As long as I have Mother's daughter by my side, nothing can harm us," Vagus said defiantly, although I felt pressured once again.

After sighing deeply, Ohlakan said, "You must take that dark path. It's a long trek, but it will take you where you need to go."

"Thank you," Vagus said.

"Please, the both of you, be careful," Ohlakan said as he embraced the both of us. "You might take His

Majesty's warning for granted, but we of Aurelia don't wish for another death in that zone."

"Don't worry, we will be fine," Vagus reassured Ohlakan, although Ohlakan was still nervous, almost close to tears.

Vagus and I started to walk along a gravel path which was full of dark stones and dirt. Dust flew along the path, although it didn't go above mine and Vagus' ankles.

"I really admire you, Terra," Vagus complimented me. It was the first nice thing he said to me, and the first time that I felt a bond with him. "This world believes in harmony and natural order, and they have great faith in Mother of all and Father of all. The king may be keeping something up there that has corrupted the harmony that Aurelia once had."

Me and Vagus continued our journey along the path leading to the forbidden mountains.

I had met a king for the first time in my life and I was about to defy him.

Even if this was the most foolish thing that I had ever done, a part of me felt rebellious and cool.

Viewing our journey, however, was King Deorege and Gemilin, who were standing on a balcony. Their view was distant, so they weren't at first noticeable to Vagus and I, but Vagus looked through a golden telescope covered with jewels. King Deorege was dressed in dark red silk pyajamas and Gemilin was wearing a green silk nightdress. They were each wearing blonde slippers made of cotton.

"A wanderer Vagus may be," King Deorege said. "But a fool he is."

"He will see things that must be seen and hear things that must not be heard," Gemilin said.

"So, it's true what they say: it was curiosity that killed the cat." An American accent came from the bedroom; the voice turned out to belong to Anton. He was smartly dressed: black trousers, white shirt unbuttoned at the top, and a black blazer. Anton approached King Deorege and Gemilin on the balcony. "You probably never heard that saying before, right?"

"We've never heard these strange tales before, my Lord," Gemilin said.

"They're not tales, they're just sayings," Anton said. "Whatever, it's not important. At least the girl remains."

"We tried to keep her," King Deorege said, "but Vagus took her away."

"Of course, he did, he was always an obstacle," Anton said. "This is not a bad view actually. I mean, the other side is better, but still."

"True," King Deorege said as he, Gemilin, and Anton walked back into the bedroom. The bedroom floor was covered with a silver fur carpet and there were curtains for the windows, balcony doorway and the bed that were made of scaly skin. There were portraits of King Deorege and Gemilin around the bedroom walls.

"You will bring me the girl, won't you?" Anton asked.

"Of course, my Lord," Gemilin said. "We shall do as we promised you."

"And do what you must with Vagus," Anton said.

"Dear brother, what must you do to those that seek your secret?" Gemilin asked worryingly.

"Do not worry, sister," King Deorege said as he put his hands on Gemilin's cheeks. "There is a penalty in place to those who defy the king of Aurelia."

"Keep Terra alive," Anton ordered. "Kill Vagus if necessary, but the girl must remain alive. I need her for something important."

"Of course, oh summoned one," Gemilin said.

"You can just call me Anton," Anton said. "Forget the 'my Lord' and 'summoned one' bullshit, that's just weird."

"Of course, Anton," Gemilin said, to which Anton smiled. He then turned to King Deorege and said, "Brother, the girl arouses me so. What she did and what she can do…"

"She is special," King Deorege said, and Anton nodded.

King Deorege and Gemilin then passionately kissed each other on the lips. Gemilin touched King Deorege's cheeks in return and then both put their hands down each other's back, reaching for their buttocks and expressed their lust for each other.

I knew Gemilin and King Deorege were weird, but this was just vile and repulsive.

They weren't just brother and sister.

They were lovers.

"What penalty will you prepare for Vagus?" Gemilin asked, once she stopped kissing King Deorege.

"Death," King Deorege answered bluntly and coldly, and once Anton left the room, Gemilin lay down on the bed and then King Deorege put his head between her thighs to pleasure her.

To Venture Beyond

Hominem and Mulieris strolled through the forest, both carrying their bow and arrows. The atmosphere was warm and calm, and the mellow breeze graced their faces. They walked past a circle of nests, with the eggs unhatched. The nests were covered with sticks and leaves, presumably to keep the eggs warm up until the point of hatching. A Coelophysis approached the circle of nests, and it inspected one of them. Having seen that the eggs were unhatched, the dinosaur ran away and joined up with its pack, who were waiting for the Coelophysis a few trees away. Hominem started to climb one of the trees, enthused and full of energy. Mulieris didn't climb along with Hominem. She sat down against the tree, looking around her. Her energy levels weren't as high as Hominem's and she looked so downbeat. Noticing her sitting down as opposed to climbing, Hominem climbed back down, and jumped down when he reached the first branch from the ground.

"Mulieris, my love, you look troubled," Hominem said gently.

Mulieris didn't respond at first. She looked up at Hominem who was stood in front of her. She hesitated further before she vaguely replied with, "What is there?"

"My love?" Hominem asked in confusion at Mulieris' question.

"We have spent an eternity in this world, with no knowledge of what is outside," Mulieris said. "A paradise this place is, my knowledge is not fulfilled, and…"

"Mulieris, you must not think such things," Hominem interrupted with his hands on Mulieris' shoulders. "We were made to bless this world, this paradise, this utopia. Thoughts of the outside are dangerous."

"Are you content with a life of confinement?" Mulieris asked as she stood up, somewhat disappointed with what Hominem was implying. "Why can't we venture with our minds? Why can't we be fascinated with the outside?"

"We are not gods like Mother and Father," Hominem said sternly. "Please, my sweet, we can't handle this new knowledge that would be bestowed upon us."

Mulieris wandered off, disappointed, with her head down. Hominem looked on, unsure of what he could say.

"There are many dangers out there," Hominem said as he followed Mulieris. "This world is where we can live for an eternity. To live is just too precious a gift to squander."

Mulieris stopped, and Hominem caught up with her. Mulieris turned around and looked at him, and then Hominem held onto her hand. Mulieris embraced Hominem and cried on his shoulder. Hominem held on to her tightly and stroked her hair and Mulieris felt his love and empathy. Her body was much more relaxed now than it had been before. A family of Dryosaurs approached them, and the mother of the family stroked her cheek lovingly on Mulieris' bare leg, and the young Dryosaurus followed the mother's lead and did the same. Mulieris looked down at the Dryosaurs, and was hesitant before she smiled, and the family of small dinosaurs looked back at Mulieris in return. The Dryosaurs eventually dispersed from Hominem and Mulieris and trotted onward.

"Oh, my dear Hominem," Mulieris began tearfully. "I can't help but think of where we can go. When you've spent an eternity so long in one place, don't you have these feelings?"

"Oh, my love, I am just blessed to be here," Hominem said with enthusiasm. "Why can't we appreciate this paradise, this gift, this blessing? Why must you think so dangerously?"

"Must you control my thoughts?" Mulieris replied assertively. "You are not Father. Why can I be free to think however I wish?"

Hominem was left speechless. He had no idea what to say and didn't want to risk upsetting Mulieris further.

"I think I need guidance," Mulieris conceded. "I need to find purpose to my existence, our existence. I cannot face Father with what I seek."

"Then we must speak with Quercus Alba," Hominem concluded.

"Or the great Sapillien," Mulieris said, almost reluctantly.

"You know she can't be found," Hominem said sceptically. "She cannot be found by any mortal or immortal soul. She's untraceable, my love. She only comes to you."

"Of course, my dearest one," Mulieris said, disappointed. "I just need direction from the wisest of souls and spirits."

"But you know what the answers are," Hominem said. "They will only give you the same guidance as Father would."

Mulieris felt more unsure and insecure than before, as if doubt and diffidence made her a sinful being in Heaven, and feared that if Mother or Father knew of her insecurities, she would be cast into the depths of the Underworld.

"Let's speak with the wise tree," Mulieris said, referring to Quercus Alba. She was reluctant now as she felt that he may not be as helpful and as she had initially hoped, but the old oak tree was arguably the best option for her at this moment.

"Yes, my love," Hominem said, sensing her despair.

They slowly walked over to where Quercus Alba was rooted. Mulieris still seemed reluctant and was worried that their visit to Quercus Alba would be an ineffectual one. Hominem wasn't as reluctant as Mulieris, but his only motivation for visiting Quercus Alba was that it was what Mulieris said she wanted and felt that she needed right now. Mulieris embraced the feeling of the grass on her feet, and it had a calming effect on her. She also spent some time listening to the noises of the dinosaurs around her. Some were soothing, some were fearsome. Despite her discontent at remaining in the Upper World, there was a calming atmosphere about the place.

They eventually reached Quercus Alba. The tree was rooted until Hominem and Mulieris walked right up in front of him, and then Quercus Alba slowly awoke, making a low, yawning sound as soon as he started moving.

"Mulieris, child," the slow voice of Quercus Alba said. "You have come to me."

"Yes, wisest tree," Mulieris replied. "Hominem and I stand here before you. I need you because…"

"You've come to me for direction," Quercus Alba interrupted, finishing Mulieris' sentence. "Even with eternal life, you still seek answers."

"What have I done? Am I of sin?" Mulieris asked.

"Curiosity is what keeps us alive," Quercus Alba stated calmly. "We all have fascination with life's possibilities. Without an inquiring nature, we have no purpose. You are of eternal youth, and you're still so young in nature and wisdom."

"So, what am I to do, oh wise one?" Mulieris asked.

"You have come to me for answers, yet you know of the answers I have to give," Quercus Alba said. "Remaining in the Upper World is not confinement. It is complete safety. Father is not all fearing. He has concern and care for all his children. You know of the war of long ago?"

"Yes, we know of it," Hominem said. "It was the war of greed and temptation."

"All war is formed by greed and temptation," Quercus Alba said. "It is discontent and these dark sensations that turn you to the most desperate of measure and the evilest of deeds."

"So…" Mulieris began. "Must I be content to avert from desperation and evil?"

"My child, I cannot ask you to be at ease," Quercus Alba said. "Nobody can order you to feel amity, and you cannot educate yourself to experience a feeling. All Father asks is that you follow His commandments, and you bring good onto the souls you meet. He is all powerful, yet all loving. You are His finest creations."

Quercus Alba began to stop moving and his face faded away from the bark. Hominem and Mulieris were puzzled as to why he had stopped moving so suddenly. Then they heard footsteps along the grass. They assumed it was Father, who they thought would come to them based on Mulieris' discontentment. In fact, it turned out to be Son, accompanied by a sole Polacanthus. Son's presence was much more calming in comparison to Father. Son walked gracefully along the grass, and it drew relief from Mulieris.

"Hominem, Mulieris, why must you fear?" Son asked.

"Oh, I thought..." Mulieris said, unsure of how to finish her sentence. She then pleaded to Son desperately. "Oh please, I cannot say. I don't wish to delude Father. I don't want judgement passed onto me."

"Please, Mulieris," Son said calmly. "Even the most eternal of us can make mistakes. All Father wants is your safety. You venture beyond the Upper World, it could spell danger for you."

"Do you mean that if we ventured beyond, we could die?" Mulieris asked.

"Worse, there are many temptations beyond these lands," Son warned. "Many of which will make you live lives you won't want to live. Everything you believe in will change. A poison will be brought onto your conscience."

"Then I will abide by Father's wishes," Mulieris stated, almost reluctantly but yet in realization of what she must do.

"We must avoid these dangers," Hominem said to Mulieris. "You underestimate the dangers there are on the outside."

"Please, don't tell Father of my insecurities," Mulieris requested of Son. "I am only lost within my heart and my soul."

Son nodded subtly, although he didn't indicate whether he would honour Mulieris' request. He gestured farewell to Hominem and Mulieris and along with the Polacanthus, walked back in the direction he had come from. Mulieris was anxious, as she wasn't sure whether or not Son would speak to Father regarding what he knew.

Son walked gracefully through the forest. The Polacanthus who accompanied him saw the mother of its family with its young, seemingly settling them down to sleep. Son saw the family of the Polacanthus too.

"Go, mighty steed. Tend to those that need you most," Son said to the Polacanthus as he stroked its armoured head. Son bowed to the Polacanthus, and in return the armoured dinosaur bowed its head to Son. It then walked off to join its family.

Son looked on and subtly yet elegantly smiled at the family of Polacanthus. Son continued to walk through the forest. He was gently breathing the air and feeling the grass on his feet. Son reached the great valley of dinosaurs. All the dinosaurs bowed their heads as they saw Son walking through. He eventually reached the Caelum Palatium and he was greeted and embraced by Father.

"You know something, Son," Father said.

"I have spoken with them, Father," Son said, referring to Hominem and Mulieris. They walked through the palace and up the stairs.

"Mulieris has always been a curious one," Father said. "Her sense of wonder is something I fear may lead to danger. I created Mulieris and Hominem to be all loving and all abiding. Mulieris has a strong mind, and that has a dangerous potential."

"I have faith, Father," Son said, as they reached Son's bedroom. "She is not one to betray you. Her nature is the symbol of this world that you have intended it to be."

"I had faith once, too," Father said, almost in grief. "No matter what good I do, there are those who succumb to greed and temptation. Even as Father of all, I cannot be sure if I will be defied. The war was started because there are those who wish to take my throne."

Mother approached Son and Father, upon hearing the conversation between the two of them.

"The nature of those in Heaven is something that we, as Mother and Father of all, cannot control," she said. "Sin cannot be controlled. It is spontaneous. It can reach a mortal and immortal soul at any moment."

"You remember what I told you of Lucifer, don't you, Son?" Father said. "He wasn't satisfied with serving me. He wanted more. He wanted to rule. When a soul within Heaven becomes disillusioned and wants more than what they have, it spells danger for them, and for us. I love Mulieris like how I love all my children, but I cannot have my will defied again."

"I know Mulieris and Hominem will abide with you no matter the cause," Son said.

"I know them to be good too," Mother concurred. "But sin is spontaneous and can strike anywhere."

"To have faith requires great care," Father said. "You can believe in so much, but defiance can take a spirit to the realms of the unknown, to death."

"So, what of Mulieris?" Son asked.

"For now, she is as good as I believed she was," Father said. "But she must be watched, and I must not be afraid to act when she does. I've cast a creation of mine to the land of everlasting fire before, and if Mulieris chooses a path of defiance and greed, she too will suffer the penalty of expulsion."

Satan's Analepsis

In an open, dusty field of dirt in the Underworld, the bony villagers were digging through the ground with various metal digging instruments such as spades, shovels, digging bars and clamshell diggers. The villagers were hard at work, not conversing with each other while working, as they were being struck with a long black whip. Satan was responsible for whipping the villagers, but groans weren't made by the villagers when they were struck. Just a slight grunt as torture was very common in the Underworld and it was practically natural to all the citizens in the world of death. They just continued on with their work. Femos stood alongside Satan.

"To work, my puny subjects!" Satan shouted as he stretched his arm back to strike the villagers really hard. He then turned to Femos, who looked at the working villagers with satisfaction. "There was a time, my young apprentice, when it was I who served."

"Oh yes, an eternity ago it was," Femos said. "I remember the stories you told me. The stories of being a servant in paradise."

"True, my friend," Satan said, who then started to snarl slightly. "But a place where I served was no paradise. It was nothing but an abyss of inferiority and nothingness. Ambition and aspiration were a sin in the world I slaved in. Here, I was given freedom. I was given a reign of superiority, power that I never thought I could embrace."

"You are the Underworld's finest ruler, oh Mighty Lord," Femos complimented, which drew a slight smile from Satan, but he remained focused on whipping the villagers with sheer force and brutality.

Palia, who was one of the villagers, approached Satan with fear, as he was the most feared being in the Underworld. Satan, with his bright yellow eyes, glared at Palia, as he was standing before him.

"Please, sire, I beg you," Palia began, "we have worked every second you ask of us. I request of you, oh frightful Lord, if we can retire ourselves to our humble abodes?"

"You wish to defy me, do you?" Satan asked in a threatening manner.

"Oh no, please, Lord, it was only but a simple request," Palia begged.

"You will stop work when I say you can stop work," Satan said in a quietly menacing way.

Satan, continuing glaring at Palia, widened his eyes and ground his sharp teeth. The villagers, carrying on working, looked in Satan's direction with fear and intrigue. Femos had respect for Palia, and she was anxious of what Satan's course of action was going to be. As Satan's eyes widened, Palia heard a high-pitched, piercing noise. He then kneeled on his bony legs, covering his ears and screaming. Being an old man, his scream was croaky and not so loud, but his agony was clearly visible to see. Palia cried tears of blood and scars began to emerge on his bald head. Satan widened his mouth, putting his energy into torturing Palia. The more Satan's mouth was widened, the more the pain intensified for Palia. Still kneeling, he was frantic as the piercing sound became higher in tone. Palia eventually lay on his side, with his eyes and face scrunched up, and the rest of his body tensed as his agony increased.

"Master," Femos said as she touched Satan on his arm, "let him go. They have worked enough."

Satan reluctantly calmed and the piercing noise faded away. Although Satan had a close bond with Femos, he was clearly unsatisfied with having to end Palia's torture and angrily turned his back on the villagers. Palia looked at Femos and nodded with gratitude. Palia approached Satan to thank him for relieving him of his torture, but Femos stopped him, indicating that it wouldn't be a good idea.

Palia, along with the rest of the villagers, stopped working as they saw Satan's back being turned — an indication that they were free to retire to their homes. Satan looked at Femos, calming down by taking a deep breath in the toxic air.

"There is no greater feeling of superiority in being the source of someone's pain," Satan said. "It is by being the source of pain that you command esteem from your subjects."

"I had to stop you, Master," Femos insisted. "Me and Palia, we have a mutual understanding, and I mustn't see him get hurt."

"Please, Femos, I am not a trustworthy being," said Satan in a gentle tone, although Femos wasn't sure what vibe he was giving. "Even being outcast an eternity ago, I still have no assurances of anything, and I have turned to baneful measures to assert my authority. I have mentored you and tailored you for when the moment you will wear a crown. You are the only soul I can trust here."

"I welcome your compliments, sire," Femos said as she bowed before Satan.

"Femos, do you remember the stories I told you about the world of men?" Satan asked. "You remember the power of kausark?"

"Why yes, sire," Femos answered.

"With kausark, I can gain an understanding of the world of men that Father never could," Satan said. "I can give men hope, the way neither Mother nor Father could."

"How?" Femos asked.

"Men are creatures of sin," Satan said. "Mankind have desires and are easily allured. They are like me. They have ambition and aspirations, something Father never affirmed. Men want to become the greater race. With kausark, I enter a mortal soul. I become one of them and strive to improve them. I've even called upon favours with this power."

"Favours, my Lord?" Femos asked.

"The girl, Terra," Satan said. "People not of Earth, but somewhere else, I trust will perform the crucial deed."

Then it was nightfall in the Underworld. Everyone in the Underworld were all sleeping in their homes. The atmosphere in the Underworld was much calmer during the night, as even Satan was asleep at the top of his tower. Satan was lying on his side, his head resting on his hands. His wings were tucked into his back and his legs were laid down straight. Satan inhaled and exhaled frantically. He began to make light grunting noises and his face tensed up. His wings began to move behind his back. Satan was having a dream. However, it was not a dream that took him into the realms of the fantastical and hypothetical. It was a memory.

Within the memory, Satan was in the Upper World. His appearance was much different to his form in the Underworld. Here his form was angelic. He had long blonde hair, his skin was pale, and his wings were white and feathered. Satan was armed with a bow and arrows and carried a sword. He, accompanied by other rogue angels, charged towards the Caelum Palatium.

They were flying, with the dinosaurs fighting each other in the valley. Some of the carnivorous dinosaurs were eating each other, some herbivorous dinosaurs brutally injured their own young, and some of the other carnivorous dinosaurs ate their own young. The war was having an adverse effect on all the dinosaurs as they were blinded with rage. As a result of the dinosaurs' conflict, some of the trees in the forest were knocked down, and Quercus Alba looked around in fear.

The Caelum Palatium was protected by another horde of angels, who, like Satan and his army, were armed. They charged at each other with sheer force and gusto, without any regard to what was around them. Arrows were fired in all directions. Angels on both sides were struck with arrows and lay wounded on the ground. Some arrows struck trees in the forest, and some even struck the Caelum Palatium itself. As the conflict grew, bolts of lightning came crashing down from the sky. Eventually, one of the bolts struck Satan and he fell down to the ground really hard.

"Lucifer!" Father shouted as he emerged from the Caelum Palatium. As soon as Father emerged, everybody, including the dinosaurs, stopped fighting with each other. Father was accompanied by Mother. Both of them stormed through the valley and approached Satan. "Lucifer, explain your deeds."

"You restrict me to being your servant," Satan said with resentment. "I was destined for greatness. The spirits of the forest told me…"

"What pseudo prophecy did they bestow upon you?" Mother asked angrily.

"That I would no longer be your servant," Satan answered assertively. "That I will be more than just your angel."

Father and Mother were insulted. It was clear that Satan, or Lucifer as he was known in the Upper World, had no regard or respect for the values that all in Heaven had, especially as it was he, who prompted the war in the first place.

"I created you," Father said, betrayed. "I gave you the gift of paradise, safety and eternal life, and you repay me with brutality and hatred. You're a threat to everyone in this peaceful place."

"What will you do, oh so loving Father?" Satan challenged.

"You are not welcome here any more," Father answered, ignoring Satan's taunt. "You are not worthy of this blessed world. I will cast you out to the world of death."

Father spread out His arms and opened His hand, stretching out His fingers. Satan felt a barrier pushing him outwards. Father followed Satan as he was moving backwards. Satan moved beyond the valley and moved towards a very steep slope, with a mist at the bottom.

"You will not be Lord of lords forever," Satan threatened Father. "Your crown will be taken."

Father ignored Satan's threats and He forced Satan down into the slope. Satan fell down the slope, almost at lightning speed, and through the mist.

Satan immediately woke up from his dream, briefly letting out a muffled scream and gasping rapidly. Satan eventually exhaled with relief that his dream was over. It was still nightfall, therefore there was nobody outside. Satan came down the tower and strolled through the field and reached a valley of molten lava. He crouched down and touched the molten lava, not feeling any pain. It felt pleasant to him, as it brought back memories of entering the Underworld and becoming its ruler. Those memories were much more pleasant to Satan in comparison to the hatred and resentment he felt in Heaven. Satan stood back up and looked upwards at the amber sky.

"I will come for you, Father," Satan said threateningly yet quietly. "Your rank of king of kings will belong to me."

The Dinner Party

Edward and Sandra arrived in their flying car at the gates of Anton's mansion. The front yard was full of cars and all the windows of the mansion were lit; guests could be seen within socializing. Edward pressed the button by the speaker, which was right next to the gate.

"May I ask who's calling?" the polite voice of Andrew said.

"Edward and Sandra Cox," Edward stated in the speaker.

"Do come through the gate." The voice of Andrew spoke once again as the gate opened. The car glided through and it parked automatically right inside the magnetic parking lines.

As the car came to a halt, the doors opened vertically, and Edward and Sandra jumped out. As soon as the doors closed, the car automatically locked, having sensed that there were no passengers inside. Even before going into the mansion, the atmosphere was vibrant, which was a rarity at Anton's home. There was chattering and laughing coming through the front door. Edward and Sandra felt awkward, as I had been missing for two weeks and they had no idea where she was. They went through all kinds of different thoughts and emotions, and they kept debating whether they should attend the party at Anton's mansion.

Edward and Sandra entered the mansion. There were men in tuxedos and women in sparkling ball gowns holding glasses of champagne and looking at the paintings adorning the walls. Even though the paintings were of torture and violence, the guests didn't respond with disgust but fascination. Having met them before, they greeted Edward and Sandra as they walked in. At the end of the corridor, Anton and Marsha Bergsson were seen conversing with each other. Anton was nodding in agreement with what Marsha was saying. Anton was a sincere man and even when socializing with the President of the United States of America, Anton hardly drew a smile on his face. Anton looked to his right and saw Edward and Sandra walking towards him.

"Edward, Sandra. I am so glad that you made it." Anton greeted Edward and Sandra. He embraced Edward and kissed Sandra on the hand.

"Good evening, Anton," Edward and Sandra both replied half-heartedly.

"Look, once again, I give you my sympathies concerning Terra," Anton said kindly. "I am so glad that you were able to make it this evening."

"Well, thank you for the invitation, Anton," Edward replied, half-heartedly once again.

"So lovely to see you both again," Marsha said as she embraced Sandra and Edward. "And I'm truly sorry about Terra's disappearance."

"Thank you, Mrs Bergsson," Edward said as he wiped his forehead with his handkerchief.

"Please, Edward, I've told you before, you call me Marsha now!" Marsha said warmly to Edward as she put her hand on his shoulder. "Anton, do you know where my husband went?"

"I believe he's with the ladies by the stairwell," Anton said as he gestured towards the passage leading to the stairwell.

"He's always been a ladies' man," Marsha joked. "Well, why don't the two of you just meet my husband quickly, then we can discuss what's going on, okay?"

"That'd be nice, thank you," Edward said with a slight, reassured smile.

"Please, the pleasure is all mine," Marsha said warmly. "Anton, Edward, Sandra and I will be going over there."

"Of course, that's fine," Anton said warmly. "I will talk with you later."

"Thanks, and once again, this is a lovely party," Marsha said.

Marsha escorted Edward and Sandra towards the stairwell. After them leaving, Anton decided not to socialize with any of the other guests and went inside his living room, which wasn't as crowded as the other areas of the mansion. He went to one of the bookshelves and poured a glass of scotch, and then went to sit in his armchair.

Beside the stairwell, there was a circle of women, along with a man, with champagne and small plates of canapés in their hands. They were all chatting away and laughing. Marsha approached them along with Edward and Sandra. Marsha tapped the man on the shoulder.

"Oh Marsha, darling!" the man said enthusiastically.

"George, dear, I do hope you and the ladies are having a pleasant conversation," Marsha said as she kissed and embraced her husband. "You remember Edward and Sandra, don't you?"

"Oh, my goodness, yes. Hello!" George said as he embraced and kissed Sandra on the cheek and shook Edward's hand. "Listen, Marsha told me about the situation with Terra and I really am genuinely sorry. I hope the two of you are okay."

"Yes, Anton told me about Terra being missing and it's an awful situation, really," Marsha said sympathetically.

"And she cannot be tracked down either?" George said with astonishment, while the ladies who George had been speaking with gestured their sorrow for Edward and Sandra. "I truly have sympathy with you both. So glad you're both here this evening."

"And of course, my sympathies for you both too," Marsha said, then turned around, facing the rest of the guests. "Ladies and gentlemen, let's hear it for Edward Cox, the greatest man alive!"

The guests cheered and applauded. Anton emerged from his living room and subtly applauded too, followed by a wry smile.

"I hope you're still used to all the fanfare, Edward," George laughed.

"Well, I try," Edward said as he laughed half-heartedly.

"He should be," Marsha said before placing her arm round Edward. "After all, this man is the greatest man alive. The man who gave us life! If we can't appreciate all that you've done, what does that make us?"

"Democrats," George said.

Marsha and George laughed. Sandra and Edward laughed a little, but not as much. They didn't appear as enthusiastic as Marsha and George and were reluctant to express their true emotions. Anton, remaining in the doorway of the living room, looked on at them with concern.

"Come, let's go outside," Marsha said to Edward and Sandra as she gestured towards the back door. "George, I'll let you carry on with your conversation."

"Oh right, thanks, dear," said George before he turned to Edward and Sandra. "Nice to see you both again."

Edward and Sandra subtly waved farewell to George as the latter turned back to the circle of ladies, chatting away once again. Marsha, Edward, and Sandra made their way to the back door. Anton, meanwhile, went back into the living room. He approached Charles and Catherine, who were at one of the bookshelves admiring a photograph within a silver frame. The photo was a black and white picture of a young brunette woman smiling. The photograph was just of her face and upper body, and she was wearing a black strapped dress.

"Ah, Anton, can I just say, this is a truly terrific party," Charles said gladly.

"I must repeat Charles' compliments, Anton," Catherine said. "The food and drink are truly amazing. Thank you so much for having us."

"Well, I am glad you could come," Anton said. "I am saddened that I couldn't come to Edward's function last Wednesday evening."

"Oh, come now, Anton," Charles said as he put his arm around Anton's shoulders. "I know you were occupied that night, and Edward knows that too. This is a truly wonderful evening, so you needn't worry yourself."

"Anton, Charles and I were admiring this photograph here," Catherine said. "Who is this lady? I must say she is *so* beautiful!"

"That lady there," Anton began hesitantly, "is Mary. I met her while I was studying for my degree at university."

"Ah, which university is that then?" Charles said. "Harvard or Princeton?"

"Actually, I went to the University of St Andrews in Scotland," Anton answered. "I like to think of myself as a man of the world. Sure, I did consider Princeton and Harvard, but I have a love for traveling and seeing the world, and, of course, the school was attended by members of the British royal family."

"Wow, that's impressive," Charles said, stunned.

"Yes, yes, it is quite impressive," Anton said. "Anyway, I met Mary in the university book club. I studied art history and she was an English major. The way she looked and smiled at me; she was so beautiful. An amazing woman she was. After we graduated, we got married, and bought a lovely house in Edinburgh."

"That is so romantic," Catherine said in a daze.

"But sadly, the love we shared didn't last forever," Anton recalled. "She got sick and died in hospital. I was by her bedside during her final moments. Of course, my heart remains broken and I have always loved her."

"Oh Anton, that is just tragic," Catherine said as she sympathetically put her hand on Anton's chest.

"Yes, but that is why I'm doing what I'm doing," Anton said. "Nothing is worse than seeing the death of a loved one. Nobody should have to go through that."

"Agreed," Catherine and Charles said as they clinked their champagne glasses in agreement. Anton then looked away with a cold, blank expression on his face, as if he was hiding something, and was afraid of being exposed.

Marsha, Edward and Sandra were in Anton's back garden. The garden was so vast, and it was arguably the only outdoor space on Earth that could be considered paradise. The grass and hedges surrounding the garden were green and the trees all had green leaves on. There was a fountain with a statue of an angel shooting water out of its mouth vertically. There were guests along the patio and walking around the garden holding glasses of champagne and small plates of canapés.

"Listen, have you tried any of the refreshments yet?" Marsha asked Edward and Sandra. "I can assure you they're incredibly sumptuous."

"Oh, we're not hungry," Edward said.

"Well look, I know what you two are going through, and I don't blame you for your lack of appetite," Marsha said sympathetically. "Now, I'd like to talk about Terra. Had she been acting differently in any way?"

"Well, Laura, her best friend from school," Edward began, "said that she was late for class last Thursday, the day before she disappeared, and she was acting strangely on their walk home."

"And then that evening," Sandra said, continuing Edward's story, "Terra said she was going to Laura's house to study, and it turns out that Terra wasn't there. Now, we can't track her. The nanotechnology in her clothes wasn't working and the police have said that they can't do anything. Now we literally don't know where our daughter is."

"That is truly awful," Marsha said as she took out a handkerchief and gave it to Sandra as she was crying. "It must be terrible to not know where Terra is at this moment."

"You have no idea," Edward sighed. "Listen, Marsha, my wife and I would never ask for anything from you, but…"

"Edward, please, let me speak," Marsha interrupted. "I know you're not a man who asks for anything from anyone, but I'll personally put in a request to the crime and investigations unit. They take care of the G-75 models across cities here in America, and they'll look out for any encounter with Terra."

"Wow, thank you," Sandra sighed with relief.

"Rest assured, Mrs Cox, I will personally see to it that your daughter is found, and I will do everything in my power as President of United States of America," Marsha promised, which slightly relieved Edward and Sandra.

"Listen, Marsha, I don't think I can possibly…" Edward said with gratitude.

"Please. For the man who gave mankind hope, I owe you a debt," Marsha said. "So, I will give you my personal number at the end of the evening and I will keep you updated whenever I can."

"Marsha, this is incredible," Edward said, elated. "You know I'm not a man who always asks for favours."

"Of course not," Marsha said. "I never imagined you to be, but for the greatest man alive, it is the very least I can offer to do."

Edward and Sandra smiled with relief and gratitude, and they, along with Marsha, looked onwards at the garden.

"I must say the view is just stunning," Marsha said.

"I know," Edward said. "It's so rare to see paradise like this. Must be the last paradise left on Earth."

"I know, honey," Sandra said as she held hands with Edward. "It must be such a romantic place."

"Quite," Marsha agreed. "Now what do you say we get ourselves some of those wonderful refreshments, huh?"

Edward and Sandra nodded, and they went back inside. The corridors were still filled with guests conversing with each other and admiring the artwork on the walls. Andrew approached them along the corridor. He was holding a perfectly balanced silver tray full of canapés and glasses of champagne.

"Good evening, Mrs Bergsson," the polite android greeted.

"Andrew, just the man I want to see," Marsha said with charm and charisma.

"But I am not a man," Andrew said. "I am a robot." Marsha, Edward and Sandra laughed before Andrew went on to say, "And Mr and Mrs Cox. So delighted to see you both."

"And lovely to see you too, Andrew," Edward said.

"Anyway, I couldn't help but notice the fine food and drink on offer this evening," Marsha said.

"Oh, please, by all means," Andrew said, holding up the tray to Marsha.

"Don't mind if I do," Marsha said, taking a glass of champagne.

"For you, Mr and Mrs Cox?" Andrew said, holding up the tray to Edward and Sandra.

"Sure, that'd be nice," Edward said as he and Sandra took a glass of champagne and a plateful of caviar and smoked salmon on a small pancake.

Andrew made his way back to the kitchen. As Andrew was doing so, Charles and Catherine, followed by Anton, approached them. Each of them was holding a glass of champagne.

"Edward. Sandra," Charles said as he embraced Edward and kissed Sandra's hand. "Can't believe we missed you both. How are you?"

"Yes, we're ever so sorry to hear about Terra. How are you both doing?" Catherine said sympathetically.

"We're both doing just fine," Edward answered.

"We managed to talk about it all outside," Marsha said. "And I will personally do all I can to help."

"That's wonderful news," Anton said. "I am genuinely happy for you both."

"As too are we both," Charles said, referring to himself and Catherine. "I know Terra will be fine."

"Anton here was talking to us about Scotland," Catherine said.

"Yes, my studies in Scotland," Anton said. "You remember, Edward, how I've mentioned attending university at Scotland?"

"Yes. St Andrew's, right?" Edward asked, which Anton answered with a nod.

"So how are you enjoying the food?" Charles asked.

"Amazing," Sandra said after she finished her mouthful. "The salmon is just so delicately flavoured."

"I have to agree with my wife. Such a beautiful delicacy," Edward said, before carrying on eating.

"Well, I say we head back outside and enjoy the refreshments before the beautiful view," Marsha said and they all agreed and started to walk towards the back door, except Anton who walked towards the stairs.

"Anton!" Marsha said, noticing that he wasn't beside them. "You're not retiring early, are you?"

"No, Marsha," Anton answered with a hearty laugh. "I'm just attending to something upstairs. Please go, enjoy the view, the last paradise on Earth. I will join you in a moment."

Marsha nodded and went outside with Edward, Sandra, Charles and Catherine. Anton looked on before going up the stairs. The upstairs corridors also had paintings on the walls and, just like the paintings downstairs, they revolved around the theme of pain and torture. Anton walked into his bedroom at the end of the corridor. His bedroom was spacious, with a king-sized bed at the back, a small wooden bookshelf that had only two shelves, with only a handful of books up on it, a desk with a supercomputer that was only thirty-two inches wide and a projector in a hole in the wall behind his bed. The walls around his bedroom had paintings similar to the ones he had up on his corridors, and on the ceiling, there was the 'touch of God' painting, which managed to spread and fit across the whole room. Anton looked up at the painted ceiling.

"No matter which life I live, you are always here above me," said Anton, whose tone was pleasant at first, before, while pacing up and down his room, he began to get aggressive and snarled, "You just couldn't help but take it all from me. Paradise, love, Mary. Faith in God is a disease here and those radicals must be eradicated. I have a desire for greatness. Men here will do anything for power. I have led them on a better path than you ever would. AND YOU STILL CAST ME OUT! I will regain paradise again. It is I who is the true ruler."

Andrew entered the bedroom urgently.

"Master Anton, I sensed a commotion from you. Are you all right?" Andrew asked with concern.

Anton looked away from the ceiling and made eye contact with Andrew.

"Oh sorry. Everything's fine, Andrew. I'm just coming back down," Anton said, breaking away into a much more pleasant tone.

Andrew went out of the bedroom and Anton followed him, after having one final look at the ceiling.

"Paradise shall be mine again," Anton said as he left the bedroom and went back downstairs.

Malomira

The night sky fell in Aurelia as Vagus and I walked up the forbidden mountains. The sky was black and even the streamlined clouds were black, but of a lighter shade. There were stars up in the sky which were of a darker shade of yellow. I shivered as the cold air blew towards Vagus and I while we searched for this monster that everybody kept talking about. The pathway up the mountains wasn't too steep, so Vagus and I managed to keep our balance and didn't fall. However, there was a large drop beside the pathway and there was no barrier to prevent us from falling. I tried hard not to look down, but I couldn't help but notice the drop. All I could do was keep walking.

"Was the king always this crazy?" I asked, almost out of breath as I kept walking.

"When you've been to as many places as I, everybody is odd in this way," Vagus replied, who also had trouble catching his breath. "I never thought that he was a liar though."

"Something just doesn't make sense," I said.

"Aye, so hopefully we might find the answers that we want," Vagus said as we eventually reached the top of the pathway and stood before a cave.

A deep groaning noise could be heard from the very back of the cave, which startled me. Maybe that was the monster? There were also very high-pitched screeching sounds too, which made me cover my ears. Along with the screeching noises were flapping sounds too. Vagus and I couldn't see what was inside the cave as it was pitch black. I tugged Vagus' top.

"Is that the monster?" I whispered urgently.

"Honestly, Terra, I know not of these parts," Vagus said.

"How can we even see what's inside?" I asked anxiously.

Vagus got out a flashlight, which was so small and thin that it was about the size of a small stick. The flashlight was made by HALO, but it didn't really sell as there was a flashlight app on the HoriPhone. The light wasn't too blinding, but as soon as the flashlight lit, the groaning noise came again, louder this time, which shocked me, but I was still curious.

The inside of the cave was surrounded by shiny rocks of a variety of colours, but mainly black and grey, in which myself and Vagus could see our reflections. The ground was covered with white and silver sand and the surface was flat and smooth to walk on. There were small winged creatures hanging from the top of the cave. They resembled vampire bats, but they had no eyes, camouflaged wings and two scaly tails. They made quiet, yet long hissing sounds but remained still.

Vagus and I slowly began to walk inside the cave. Once we walked past the flock of winged creatures, the deep groaning noise sounded yet again, which made me suddenly stop.

"Who comes here?" the deep voice groaned.

"Please don't fear us," Vagus said calmly.

A figure began to walk into the glow of the flashlight. It wore ragged, torn-up clothes, had six toes on each of its bare feet and a disfigured face. It had a jagged chin, one working eye, with the other blocked out by excess skin, no nose, flappy ears and a big, bald head which looked as inflated as a balloon. The figure revealed itself to be a man. Was that the monster? Or was it something else? And how could he speak?

"Why you come? Who are you?" the figure asked aggressively. "And how the glow?"

"I am Vagus, and this is Terra, Mother's daughter," Vagus answered calmly.

"And you know not of who I am?" the figure asked in a much calmer tone. "What has he told you?"

"Do you mean the king? King Deorege?" I asked, trying not to look at the figure.

"Yes," the figure answered. Maybe it wasn't a monster, but I wasn't totally sure yet.

"He said that there was a monster here," I answered. "He also said that it took his brother."

The figure laughed, and then cried and started punching its own face. After a while, it said, "Please, get away from me."

"You're not a monster, are you?" I asked awkwardly. The figure appeared upset, and I didn't want to start accusing it of being a monster. I then said, "I'm sorry I asked, it's just that I heard…"

"No, it's okay," the figure said, still in tears. "My name is Malomira. I *am* the king's brother."

Vagus and I gasped. It turned out that there really was no monster, and it was all a lie. Why would the king have lied? How could he have told those rumours about his own brother? It was such a revelation that it only brought on more questions than answers.

"So why are you here?" Vagus asked.

"It pains me to say," Malomira said. "Please, let me not say."

"But you're in despair," I said as I reached out to touch Malomira's face sympathetically, but Malomira backed away. "Are you afraid?"

"You know not of all I've suffered," Malomira said. "Why should I speak to they who side with the king?"

"We're not with the king," I said. "He's weird."

Malomira laughed.

"That's not the worst of him," Malomira said as he stopped laughing.

"What did he do?" Vagus asked.

Malomira looked away from Vagus and I, as he sheltered himself from speaking the truth. He then sat down against a wall of the cave, huddled up.

"All I ask for are the facts from you," Vagus pleaded gently. "I sensed something wrong with the king. An unbalance seems present in the air."

Malomira looked at Vagus and I before getting up. I think he started to warm up to us, having been unable to trust anybody for years.

"It pains me to say his name or to think of his face, after all I have endured," said Malomira reluctantly. "All we are bound by is blood. We grew up together, we fought together, we saw all together. We shared so much together, but we both desired one thing: the heart of Incurtea. She was the most beautiful woman in all of Aurelia. She married my brother and became queen of all the land. Somehow sitting on the throne made Incurtea more beautiful than ever before. Incurtea and I had passion for each other, and therefore we shared each other. From our affair came two children; a boy and a girl. My brother presumed the first child, my daughter, was his own, a secret we kept until the second child was born. My sister…"

"Gemilin?" I asked, interrupting Malomira.

"Yes, she," Malomira answered. "She suspected deceit from Incurtea and I, and therefore that knowledge transposed to Deorege."

"What did he do?" Vagus asked boldly.

"He took everything," Malomira said with a broken voice. "He struck my beloved Incurtea with a blade, right in her heart, and he exiled my two children. I know not where they are, or if they're alive or dead. My sister and brother stripped me naked and bathed me in poison. My hideous form forced myself to be outcast from this land. They abused me and now I'm a monster to all of this world. My place now is in this cavern of darkness."

"That bastard!" I said with anger, then I awkwardly asked, "So, you haven't taken anybody from Aurelia, have you?"

"Of course not!" Malomira replied angrily yet tearfully. "I haven't known of anybody disappearing. Are they dead?"

"We don't know," said Vagus. "I've always known Aurelia to be a place of peace. A God-abiding world that stood by Father's commandments, even if one of their own had committed... adultery."

"I was her true love," Malomira said defensively yet calmly. I would have been judgemental like Vagus was too, but Malomira just seemed so traumatised by what Deorege did to him. "She only loved my brother for his riches and power. Incurtea and I shared a true, passionate love. My brother was nothing but a brute, and my sister was nothing but a common harlot. I have no family. All the loves I've had are gone."

"That's awful," I said. "I always knew that the king and his sister were strange, but now I know that they're horrible."

"So, you really are Mother's daughter?" Malomira asked, to which I nodded. He reached out his hand to touch my face. "Please don't be frightened. I have sinned in my past, but all I ask is the kindness and affection from the dynasty of the skies."

I walked closer to Malomira. He was clearly no monster, just a man in pain. I embraced him.

"It's okay, Malomira," I said as I touched his cheek. "I will never hurt you in the way Deorege did."

"I won't either," Vagus said with a smile.

Malomira felt loved for the first time since Incurtea was murdered.

"Can I ask a favour?" Malomira asked.

"What?" I asked.

"Can you please find my children?" Malomira asked. "I don't wish to beg from any of you, but all I ask is their safety."

"I don't know," I said. "I mean, do you have a picture of them?"

Malomira shook his head sadly and then sighed.

"What are their names?" Vagus asked.

Before Malomira could answer, the flapping noises that Vagus and I heard before occurred again. Vagus and I looked back as we wondered what could have caused the creatures to move. Malomira was startled, as not many people had dared enter this place before. The high-pitched screeches sounded again, and I didn't cover my ears this time, though I did jump slightly. Footsteps were then heard and just when I saw figures emerging, yellow vines were thrown towards Vagus and I, wrapping us tightly as soon as they touched us. Vagus and I struggled to break free, but it was no use. An army of men approached us, and one threw balls at Malomira, releasing spores that caused him to feel dizzy and faint. The army of men were bald and faceless and were all dressed in black. I was too preoccupied with trying to break free from the vines to get freaked out by them. They had no eyes, no nose, no ears and no mouth, although one of them began to speak.

"We are the polifara," one of the faceless men said. "You must come see the king. He requests your presence immediately."

"No, I am Mother's daughter!" I said, hoping that it would mean something to them. They didn't respond, however.

"You can't do this," Vagus said, struggling to breathe just like me as the vines squeezed his torso. "This is an injustice, and you cannot capture Mother's daughter."

"We ask not for your opinion," the polifara leader said again. "You have defied his Royal Highness by going out of bounds. For this, there will be a penalty."

The polifara pulled the vines away, dragging Vagus and me with them. Malomira tried to protest our capture, but he could hardly move or speak. He just lay down on the ground, defeated and unable to do anything.

Desires

It was a peaceful nightfall in the Upper World. The stars shone in the night sky, a warm, gentle breeze graced the land, and a long, mellow note sounded from a horn being blown. The horn was blown by an angel flying across the sky and towards the Caelum Palatium. The dinosaurs fell asleep in their families. The bigger dinosaurs laid to sleep in the valley, while the smaller species rested in the forest. In the Caelum Palatium, all the immortals went to sleep. The angels tucked in their wings behind their backs and slept in hammocks on the rooftop.

Mother, Father, and Son were still awake, as the almighty gods can't and don't need to sleep. Father and Son strolled across the valley, overseeing the peaceful atmosphere across Heaven, while Mother was strolling with a Maiasaura in the forest. They encountered a family of Maiasaurs, which caught the attention of the dinosaur that was accompanying Mother. It lightly bellowed at Mother, and she laid her hand on its flat beak.

"Go, my bonitherta," Mother said gently while stroking the Maiasaura. "Your kind needs you, my sweet. Rest your eyes, and rest with the loves that surround you."

Mother kissed the Maiasaura on the top of its nose and the Maiasaura gently licked Mother's cheek and Mother then lovingly embraced it. The Maiasaura walked along to its family and laid right next to the alpha female of the group. Mother looked on with a loving smile. She was an all-loving being who had a loving spirit to all that surrounded her, including all the dinosaurs.

Hominem was fast asleep in his bed with Mulieris. They both lay holding each other's hands and their calves were linked with each other. While Hominem was fast asleep, Mulieris, meanwhile, was having trouble sleeping. She shook her head with her eyes closed, forcing herself to sleep. Eventually, she gave up and opened her eyes before letting go of Hominem's hand and sitting up. She turned to her left and looked down at Hominem, who was still sleeping peacefully and didn't notice Mulieris letting go of him.

"Forgive me, my love," Mulieris said with sorrow as she kissed Hominem on the cheek, who again didn't notice.

Mulieris got up from her bed, but her heart was pounding as she knew that Mother, Father and Son were awake and would be suspicious of her being awake during the night. Before she got out through the doorway, she looked both to her left and right, as she was cautious of who may spot her at that moment. She eventually snuck out through the doorway, treading lightly and constantly looking around as she went along. She reached the main staircase of the Caelum Palatium. She stood for a moment and looked around once more to see if there was anyone who was still awake as she feared getting caught.

Mulieris darted down the stairs elegantly, careful not to make a sound. As soon as she reached the bottom of the stairs, Mulieris moved to her left and put her back up against the wall, while walking towards the front door of the Caelum Palatium. Mulieris looked in all directions while walking, still wary of who may see her. She walked quickly but carefully so that she wouldn't make a sound. Mulieris eventually reached the front door, but before she could move outside, she once more looked in all directions, especially as Mother, Father, and Son were outside. As soon as she saw that they weren't anywhere in sight, Mulieris sprinted through the front door and to the valley. Her heart pounded rapidly as she ran, panting quietly so that she wouldn't make any noise. As she ran through the valley, she was extra careful not to bump into or awake any of the sleeping dinosaurs that were around her.

She eventually reached the forest and stopped suddenly when she saw Father and Son strolling along in the distance. She quickly darted to her left through some trees, to make sure that she couldn't be seen. She jumped into an evergreen fir bush, which formed a large gap between the trees. It was twice her height and had the width and length of half a football pitch. Mulieris huddled herself up and cried. She was still careful not to make too much noise and grab the attention of anyone. There was a waterfall of tears coming from Mulieris' eyes. She spent a long time sobbing in distress, as she had hidden desires which were forbidden, and neither Father nor Mother could ever know about them. Not only was Mulieris distressed, she was confused and had no idea who to confide in. She just kept on crying. Eventually, her tears subsided, although her sadness remained. She got onto her knees and looked down.

"Sapillien, if you hear me, I ask for your guidance," she said quietly while sniffling.

She looked up for a moment, anticipating a reaction. There was nothing but the cool, gentle breeze blowing at her. Mulieris got down on her knees once again, and she was tearful once again. Her face tensed up.

"Oh please, spirits, help me. I am lost. I cannot confide in my dear Hominem. Please. I beg you. Help," Mulieris pleaded tearfully. She looked up once again and again — no response from anyone or anything.

Mulieris then carried on crying, feeling lost and confused. She was not sure of what she could do and what her next step would be. She was too sad to think ahead and she just kept crying.

"I know your desires," a mysterious voice said.

The voice startled Mulieris as she looked up suddenly, and then stood up, looking around in all directions. Her tears started to dry as she became alert.

"Please, to whom I speak, come forward. I need you," Mulieris pleaded quietly, bearing in mind that Father, Mother, and Son could be somewhere nearby her.

"Mulieris, my sweet," the voice said again. "You need not despair, sweet child."

"Who are you?" Mulieris asked. "I'm in need of your guidance. Please help."

A warmer breeze blew towards her, and Mulieris became startled by the sudden change in temperature. She took a couple of steps back in shock. She started to accommodate herself to the change of temperature, and then saw a vague, shadowy figure emerge from the distance. Mulieris squinted in order to figure out who the figure was. The shadowy figure eventually neared, and then slowly revealed itself to be Femos. Her form up in heaven was the same as the figure she had back in the Underworld, which startled Mulieris as she had never seen anything like her before.

"Spirit, what are you?" Mulieris asked, intrigued and terrified.

"I am a mere representation of what you desire," Femos said in her hissing, menacing voice. "You are lost, child."

"Yes," Mulieris said, accustoming herself to Femos' appearance. "I fear I have sinned against Father of all. What must I do, spirit?"

"You are confined, imprisoned here," Femos said as she put her hand out to gently touch Mulieris' face. "You want freedom, don't you? You want to see what's outside, don't you?"

"How do you…" Mulieris started to ask, but then realized that as a spirit, Femos knew her doubts and anxieties. "Mother and Father can never know. I am frightened of myself."

"Embrace it, child," Femos advised. "You are only discovering your true self, and where your true destiny lies."

Mulieris became sceptical of Femos. She knew that the spirits of the forest knew what was in her heart, but she never knew that they would encourage her to act impulsively. Was Femos a genuine spirit of the heavens?

"Why do you speak of such defiance?" Mulieris asked suspiciously. "You know I have sin in my heart?"

"Mulieris, my sweet," Femos said, "what good is life when you're living as a saint for all your existence? An eternity of nothing. You're ageless, but not boundless. What is this constant ceaselessness?"

"But I cannot betray them," Mulieris argued, tearful again. "What of Mother and Father? My love, Hominem? I can't defy the loves of my life, I won't!"

"I am not demanding defiance," Femos said softly. "I'm just merely offering you a path to what you're looking for. You cannot deny what is in your heart."

"You believe that I will easily surrender the bliss I have here?" Mulieris asked defiantly. "Your foul wisdom will not influence me. You will not tempt me into the darkness. Just begone with you, foul creature!"

Mulieris lunged at Femos, but she just went through her. Mulieris then immediately huddled up once again and cried some more. Femos, however, didn't leave just like Mulieris requested, nor was she affected by Mulieris' attempted attack. She watched over Mulieris crying with a smirk on her face.

"I know what enrages you so," Femos said in a taunting manner. "You know what I say is what you feel. You cannot escape your true desires, and therefore you cannot escape me. Nobody can see me but you, my beauty. Mother and Father will discover what is really in you, and you will no longer taste any happiness or merriment."

Mulieris was still in tears and was hesitant to respond. She knew that Femos was right and she was scared of herself, and what impulsive measures she would take to satisfy her needs.

"What do you suggest I do?" Mulieris asked, surrendering herself to Femos. Her smirk widened.

"We take a journey, my fair Mulieris," Femos suggested.

"How?" Mulieris asked.

"There are means of escape from here," Femos said. "The celuti are not far from here. I've seen the wanderer himself transport on these majestic beasts."

Mulieris looked in the direction of the valley, as she knew that Femos was referring to the skywhales.

"Mother and Father will see, and they will know," Mulieris said with great anxiety. "There will be grave consequences. I can't spirit, I can't."

"Must you continue with your chronic boredom?" Femos asked cheekily. "Without adventure, there is no purpose to an everlasting existence."

"No!" Mulieris said assertively. "I won't fall foul to temptation, so leave me be!"

"Don't despair, my pretty," Femos said. "Your conscience will reveal your destiny to you."

Femos then proceeded to kiss Mulieris. After they kissed, Femos disappeared. Mulieris remained in her huddled position, unsure of what to do. Rather than deciding her next move, she instead took some time to really acknowledge and analyse her encounter with Femos. She had never encountered a spirit or any being like Femos, therefore she was still in shock and put herself in abeyance for a moment.

Mulieris eventually got out of the bush and just like before, looked in all directions to see if Father, Mother, and Son were in sight. When she saw that there was no sight of them, she sprinted through the forest and into the valley. She was so decisive in the way that she ran, darting straight across the valley and through the patch of various plants.

From a distance, behind Mulieris, Son looked onwards at her running, then rushed off into the forest in order to find and alert Mother and Father. He found Mother and Father in the forest and halted before them.

"Son?" Father asked urgently.

"I saw her, Father," Son said, also urgently. "Mulieris. She's running away."

Mother gasped in shock and horror, while Father's face was stern.

"Where is she going?" Mother said worryingly.

A high-pitched bellowing sound was heard from beyond the valley. It was then followed up by a low-pitched bellowing sound. Mother, Father and Son became even more alert.

"The celuti. Go!" Father said with the utmost urgency as he quickly rushed out of the forest, along with Mother and Son.

Meanwhile, the skywhale gracefully approached Mulieris and she jumped. The skywhale then flew; riding the skywhales presented new sensations to Mulieris. She had never felt such turbulence before. She was scared at first, just as I had been.

The skywhale eventually reached the dark cave, and Mulieris found herself in unfamiliar territory, outside of the Upper World. It was too late for her to turn back to the Upper World, especially as Mother, Father, Son and all of the Upper World would know that she'd crossed her boundaries. Mulieris tried not to think that thought, and instead focused on what was around her now. She noticed the water at the base of the cave, and the glowing spiralling rocks that were all around her. She had never seen anything like them, and she was still getting used to riding the skywhale.

Mulieris then got past the cave and reached the realms of outer space. Again, Mulieris focused on the new sights around her. Just like me, she had no trouble breathing in outer space, even though she was not as powerful as the deities above. She knew what she was doing was forbidden, but she gasped at the sight of the multicoloured nebulas. She was stunned by all these new sights, such as the shining stars and different sized planets, which were also in various colours. This was the excitement and adventure that Mulieris had wanted, and she was no longer worried about what she was doing being wrong. She was preoccupied with embracing the new sights and sensations around her. She briefly screamed with excitement and then laughed with enjoyment. She was now used to riding the skywhale, and no longer worried about falling off.

She let out another excitable scream before giant clouds emerged above her. As Mulieris had never been into space, she had no idea that these emerging clouds were an unusual sight. Dark yellow lightning bolts struck from the clouds, but the bolts didn't strike anywhere near Mulieris or the skywhale. That did not, however, stop Mulieris from being startled. Her gasping became gasps of terror.

"Mulieris!" Father's voice sounded from the clouds.

Mulieris was even more frightened now that Father seemed to be communicating to her in space. The skywhale, not affected by the clouds and lightning, turned back in the direction of the Upper World, and Mulieris' heart stopped. She was dreading going back to the Upper World and confronting the gods that rule the world above the stars. The skywhale reached the dark cave, and the sight of glowing spiralling rocks didn't fascinate Mulieris like before. The journey back was very sombre, and the sense of adventure that she had evaporated.

Eventually, the skywhale reached the waterfall of the Upper World, and waiting on the cliff was Father, Son, Mother, Hominem and angels wearing suits of armour. The skywhale dropped her off at the clifftop, and Mulieris reluctantly stepped off in front of those waiting for her. She got on her knees and sobbed uncontrollably.

"Mulieris, what have you done?" Father asked assertively. "Explain yourself!"

"Father, please," Mulieris pleaded tearfully. "I have nothing but sorrow in my heart. Please, Father."

"Why, my love?" Hominem asked as a defeated man, believing that Mulieris no longer loved him.

"Hominem, please. I'm sorry. I just..." Mulieris sobbed.

"We've given you eternal life, a sanctuary where you can be free," Mother said as she felt betrayed. "Why repay us this way?"

"Oh, Mother, please," Mulieris said, once again tearfully. "I beg your forgiveness, Mother. Please, feel my sorrow."

Mother and Father felt no sympathy whatsoever towards her, no matter how much she cried and begged for mercy. The angel guards ruthlessly grabbed hold of Mulieris, and Hominem looked on without a word to say in her defence.

"You have defied me after all I've given you," Father said, as he started to get angry. "I've given you paradise, and in return I get defiance."

"Father, please..." Mulieris pleaded.

"I have stated to you the commandments you must follow," Father said assertively. "If you betray those commandments, you will be imprisoned, and sentenced to expulsion into the world of death."

Mulieris pleaded for mercy but Mother and Father weren't interested. Hominem was saddened and shocked but didn't protest. He just looked on in horror.

"Take her in," Father ordered the angels as they grabbed Mulieris tightly by the arms and she walked along with them. She made no attempt to escape them. She was too sad to do anything and she just surrendered herself to them.

Righteousness

Vagus and I were still wrapped up in the yellow vines. We sat down on wooden chairs in King Deorege's bedroom. I was nervous, and considering that I had abilities to heal, I tried to see if I had the ability to unwrap myself from the vines. I tried to focus my mind but nothing happened, although it was much more difficult for me this time as the yellow vines were wrapped so tightly around me.

"It's okay, Terra," Vagus said calmly to try and reassure me, though it was hard to be reassured while being so tightly bound. "There's been many a time in my travels when I have found myself on the brink of death."

"What are they going to do to me?" I asked nervously. "Will they kill me?"

"I've never known any resident of Aurelia capable of killing an immortal," Vagus said, which somehow didn't calm me down.

"Did you bring anything to help get us out of this?" I asked. "Like a knife or something?"

"I'm afraid not, Terra," Vagus answered. "I never bring weapons with me."

"Isn't that, like, dumb?" I asked. "What if you ended up somewhere dangerous?"

"I trust, Terra," Vagus said. "I trust that there is good in all worlds, even in Aurelia."

"Maybe there was good at one time," I said. "Now it's being ruled by a maniac."

Vagus didn't say anything. He just put his head down, lost for words.

The door opened and two lizard-like creatures entered. They had eight legs tucked inside their bodies with a frill around the neck and a crest on the top of the head. Their skin was plated all over, giving it a rough texture. They approached Vagus and I, making barking sounds at us. Vagus flinched a little and just as I was about to scream, the door opened again, with a slam this time, and in came King Deorege and Gemilin. King Deorege was wearing his usual royal attire, while Gemilin wore a skimpy, low-cut green dress.

"Ah, Vagus, Terra, so glad the polifara have brought you to my attention," King Deorege said menacingly as he and Gemilin approached Vagus. The creatures approached King Deorege and he petted them both. "You're a strange breed, Vagus. Did you know that? A wanderer of worlds you are, and we see now this includes the forbidden lands."

Vagus didn't respond to his taunting. I didn't say anything either, even though I had some choice words to say to him. Gemilin stared at me, and licked her lips, which was so strange and troubling.

"Do you like my loyal companions?" King Deorege asked Vagus, then turned to me. "They have become the family to us. They both compensate for the brother we never had. They would never rebel against their master, unlike you. I almost admire your defiance."

"Bastard!" I said, which brought a glare from King Deorege and Gemilin.

"I had to," Vagus said, "for the sake of Aurelia, we had to."

"You saw him, didn't you?" King Deorege said, grinding his teeth. The creatures growled. "He spoke to you, didn't he?"

"Why?" I asked, full of fear and anger. "Why'd you outcast him? Couldn't you forgive him? He's your brother, you twisted freak!"

"Foolish child!" Gemilin screamed in a high-pitched voice which startled me.

"Calm, sister," King Deorege said as he touched Gemilin's arm and kissed her neck, which stunned and repulsed both Vagus and I. "My dear Terra, there is only so much betrayal a man can take. When a heart is broken, a man's good will is lost, and all sense of righteousness is lost."

King Deorege and Gemilin embraced each other before kissing passionately, making me sick once again. I didn't throw up though.

"So, you have succumbed to madness?" Vagus asked. "After what Malomira and Incurtea…"

"DON'T YOU EVER SPEAK THEIR NAMES!"
King Deorege screamed.

King Deorege walked right up in front of Vagus and punched him really hard in the face. The jewels in King Deorege's hand made the blow even more significant as Vagus' nose and jaw was broken and blood came pouring down his face. I looked on in horror as Vagus groaned with pain, and I also felt repulsed by the giant, lizard-like creatures. Were they going to eat me? I wasn't sure what they were going to do. I had never witnessed someone being so violent before, even though I had seen violence in movies. Gemilin was aroused by this and King Deorege kissed her neck, and then she grabbed his buttocks with passion. They kissed each other passionately once more.

"It seems that madness is now in my blood," King Deorege said with a smirk. "Righteousness is no more. Gemilin is what makes my heart beat now. She is my love."

King Deorege and Gemilin kissed before Gemilin walked up behind me and massaged my shoulders. The lizard-like creatures continued licking me.

"My sweet Terra," Gemilin said, as she started to massage my neck. "Never have I seen such beauty, such elegance, and so eternal."

Gemilin was so creepy that I could never accept a compliment from her. It was actually more of an insult to me. Gemilin then started to kiss my neck. King

Deorege looked on in satisfaction before laying his hand on Vagus' shoulder.

"Have you ever been heartbroken? Have you ever been betrayed?" King Deorege asked Vagus. He didn't reply as he was still in pain from being beaten. "The day I witnessed my brother's hand on my wife's bosom, the good life I strived to live was over. I have always abided by Father's law, and followed every commandment, to serve Aurelia like the noble king I strive to be. You see, Vagus, there is only so much good you can do for all around you, and when you are betrayed like I was, every sense in your body goes away."

Vagus tried to speak, but he was in too much pain to do so. All he was capable of doing was coughing out blood. The creatures then stood beside King Deorege, with one on his left and one on his right.

"Curiosity, Vagus, is a dangerous thing," King Deorege said, with Gemilin nodding her head in agreement. "There are forbidden lands that are dangerous and could get you killed. Was it worth the journey, Vagus? And to bring the sweet Terra alongside you?"

"You cannot kill her," Vagus said defiantly, spluttering blood as he spoke. "She is immortal. She is Mother's daughter."

"Of course, Terra is all powerful," King Deorege acknowledged as he paced up and down his bedroom. "Why would we think of slaughtering her anyway? She is the key to eternal beauty and eternal living. We are indeed honoured to have Terra in our company. We have our own use for her."

Gemilin started to untangle me from the vines. Why would she be setting me free? As soon as I was free, a light red glow came from Gemilin's body, which had an unusual, herbal scent. The glow moved towards me and as soon as I inhaled that scent, I felt dizzy and woozy and fell down on the floor.

"What's happening?" I asked, feeling queasy and intoxicated.

"Terra, you need not fear," Gemilin said as she got down next to me, but then I didn't see Gemilin.

I saw Laura.

I had always felt comfortable when I saw Laura with me, especially at the parties I went to back on Earth, but in the back of my mind, I had to tell myself that it wasn't Laura and I didn't know why I saw her. It couldn't be her.

"What is she?" Vagus asked in a broken voice.

"Extraordinary," King Deorege said as he was aroused by Gemilin. "She is a nympho of a sibling, and she truly bestows a spell upon you. The women in our family bear special genes that give them something more. A lust and desire."

Gemilin, similarly to King Deorege, had no regard to whether her deed was right or wrong. She was a sinful, seductive woman.

"Have you ever been in love, Terra?" Gemilin asked me.

I knew the answer to that, and it was with Laura. When I saw Laura asking me that, a rush of feelings came to me. They were a mixture of joy and fear, even though it wasn't actually Laura speaking to me. I wasn't sure if she was a witch or something, but I was just so caught up with seeing Laura in front of me.

"Let her go," Vagus pleaded with a cough.

"She is a thing of beauty, isn't she?" King Deorege asked Vagus.

Vagus didn't respond. The bleeding down his face had stopped, but he was still in too much pain to put together a sentence. He just groaned in pain and disgust.

"Gemilin and I, we are so alike," King Deorege said. "Of course, we are of the same blood, but both of us have lost all sense of righteousness. We no longer have any reason to be righteous again."

"What will you tell the people of Aurelia?" Vagus asked.

"What did you tell them?" King Deorege said bluntly. "Did you speak with someone of your forbidden journey?"

Vagus didn't respond.

"Who!" King Deorege asked. "I suggest you answer, Vagus. When you are in my world, you will obey and respect my authority."

Vagus still didn't answer.

"It was Ohlakan, wasn't it?" King Deorege said. "The two of you are close. I've seen you both speak.

You share with him your travels. Now I wonder if secrets are shared."

Vagus was about to reply but didn't want to jeopardize Ohlakan's safety. King Deorege walked over to his lizard-like pets, who were stood in front of his bed, and stood between the two of them. They looked at King Deorege, and after he nodded in Vagus' direction, the creatures charged at Vagus and bit off the vines, as well as mauling him in the process. Vagus wailed as the creatures bit him and slashed him. I watched in horror, but then Gemilin touched my cheek so I looked at her, but that was because I saw her as Laura.

"It's okay," I heard Laura say. "You'll always be safe when you're with me."

They were the words I had always wanted Laura to say, and that was how I felt when I was with her.

Eventually, the creatures freed themselves from Vagus, and he rolled around on the floor in extreme pain. His clothes were torn and covered in blood, though he was in a stable condition. The creatures walked out of the door, and two of the polifara, wearing black clothing like before, walked in and grabbed Vagus' arms.

"My trusted guards here will see to you now," King Deorege said. "I will tend to you later and decide what to do with you."

"They will know, Aurelia will know," Vagus said defiantly, but his voice was broken and weak.

King Deorege gave Vagus one last stare before he said to the polifara, "Take him."

The polifara dragged Vagus out of the door, and then King Deorege walked right up to me. There was still blood on the floor where Vagus had been.

"Forgive my hostile nature, Terra," King Deorege said softly as he stroked my hair. "When you are a ruler, you must always assert your authority, by any means necessary."

I wanted to cry but couldn't. Maybe it was because I kept seeing Laura next to me. I had never cried in front of Laura. She had seen me being upset before, like at the anniversary party, but I had never been tearful in front of her. King Deorege continued to stroke my hair and Gemilin stroked my back.

"You speak of this Laura," Gemilin said to me. "Do you love Laura?"

I didn't answer. I didn't think I'd said her name out loud. Maybe I said it unknowingly while I was hallucinating.

"Why don't you spend the night here in the Opraso?" King Deorege asked. "You've been through quite an ordeal, and you need to rest. There is someone who really wants to meet you."

I was terrified about what King Deorege and Gemilin would do to me, and terrified about this person who really wanted to meet me. Any friend of theirs had got to be twisted like them.

"I want to go home," I said weakly.

"Terra, my dear, we will take good care of you," Gemilin said as she embraced me.

"Please, Terra, it will be for your own good to remain here," King Deorege said. "We will speak about this soon."

I didn't want to argue back with King Deorege as he was clearly a volatile, twisted man. I eventually stood up and Gemilin escorted me out of the door and upstairs to the guest bedroom. I was too weak to escape, especially as I was still seeing Gemilin as Laura.

King Deorege, meanwhile, went out of the door and went down the stairs and through the corridor. He then went through the main coronation room and out of the front door. He stepped onto the green and pondered for a moment.

The green was vast and empty, and looked much bigger without anybody on it. King Deorege headed to his right and walked along a path which was covered in blue dust. He came across a wide hut that was made of red sticks and multicoloured leaves. They were strongly tied together, making it very difficult to break. He saw Ohlakan outside of the hut, strolling along and enjoying the night breeze. Ohlakan then saw King Deorege.

"Why, Your Majesty," Ohlakan said, surprised, as he went to approach King Deorege. "So unusual to see you at this hour. Uhla is asleep now, so I'm just…"

"Yes, Ohlakan," King Deorege said bluntly. "You are good friends with Vagus, aren't you?"

"Um… yes, Your Majesty," Ohlakan answered hesitantly. "Why do you enquire, sire?"

"This is just a pleasant colloquy," King Deorege said warmly, although he was cold inside. "I presume you had an exchange with him after his visit to the Opraso?"

"Why… yes, sire," Ohlakan said, hesitantly once again.

"I see," King Deorege said bluntly. "May I ask the subject of the conversation?"

Ohlakan remembered the secret he promised to keep for Vagus and had to be mindful before answering King Deorege.

"Nothing of great interest, sire," Ohlakan replied.

"Hmm, not any secrets, maybe?" King Deorege asked as he walked closer to Ohlakan. "Any plans for after my introduction?"

Ohlakan hesitated and felt pressured. He couldn't lie to King Deorege, nor could he betray Vagus. He eventually replied, "No, sire."

"I see," King Deorege said, as he could tell that Ohlakan was not being honest. He then pulled out some dark red berries from his pocket and asked, "Would you care for a refreshment?"

"Refreshment, sire?" Ohlakan asked, surprised that King Deorege was offering food.

"Have you not been offered refreshment before?" King Deorege asked with a laugh. "Please, take these. I grew them myself."

"Uh, thank you, sire," Ohlakan said as King Deorege gave him the berries.

Ohlakan ate the berries that King Deorege offered him. Ohlakan murmured with satisfaction as the berries tasted so sweet, satisfying every taste bud.

"Thank you, sire," Ohlakan said gratefully.

King Deorege didn't respond. He just stared at Ohlakan.

"Sire?" Ohlakan asked, wondering why King Deorege was staring at him.

Then Ohlakan collapsed to the ground, aching from everywhere. His whole body felt heavy and he couldn't pick himself up. All he could do was stay on the ground in pain. Ohlakan's arm started changing, it grew hard and he was unable to move it. The sensation spread to his entire body. Ohlakan *literally* became a statue.

King Deorege rushed to the lawn, where he saw four members of the polifara. He whistled to them, and they came along and approached the statue of Ohlakan.

"Take him," King Deorege ordered, and the polifara all dragged Ohlakan along the lawn and carried him to the corridor of the Opraso, where the other statues were.

It turned out the statues weren't tributes of those who disappeared from Aurelia.

They *were* those who disappeared from Aurelia.

The Visit

Edward Cox sat on the sofa cross-legged with a glass of scotch in his hand. He was tense and took long gaps between sips. Sandra entered the living room wearing a silver evening gown. She sat beside Edward and put her right arm around him and put her left hand on his chest. They both briefly kissed.

"She'll be fine," Sandra said softly. "Marsha has resources. She will help us."

"I know, honey," Edward sighed. "But you can't help but be worried about the disappearance of your daughter."

"Oh, I know, honey, I know," Sandra said, stroking Edward's chest. "I hate this feeling of not knowing so much. It pains that me that I can only see Terra in my dreams."

Sandra laid her head on Edward's shoulder, and Edward lovingly kissed her forehead.

"I remember the day when I discovered I couldn't have children," Sandra said, almost tearfully. "Do you remember? That day at the hospital? My heart just stopped. Like I had no purpose."

"But we got through it, remember?" Edward said. "I just knew something good would happen. And then Terra came along."

"She was…" Sandra sighed as she wiped the tears from her eyes. "She was the greatest thing to happen to us. She was a miracle. A miracle child."

"I know, honey," Edward said with a smile as he kissed Sandra's forehead and had another sip from his glass of scotch. "This is just a strange situation. That's what I keep telling myself."

"Terra was a miracle child, wasn't she?" Sandra said. "Just when we had given up hope, she came to us. Can't believe how lucky we were."

"I always believed that the greatest thing you could give is life," Edward said. "And that is my purpose here on Earth. To give life and to prolong life for the greater good."

Edward and Sandra stood up and embraced for a moment, with only a few tears coming out of their eyes. They both took deep breaths in and out, just letting the evening pass by. The buzzer of their apartment sounded. Christopher emerged from the kitchen and made his way to the doorway.

"May I ask who's calling?" Christopher asked.

"My name is Alan Donovan and I'm here about the disappearance of Terra Cox."

The mention of my name made Edward and Sandra's hearts jump, as they had been eagerly waiting for more information regarding her. Christopher invited

Alan up to the apartment. Edward and Sandra sat back down on the sofa as Alan arrived and approached them. He wore a suit with a black overcoat.

"Mr and Mrs Cox, hi." Alan greeted the both of them and shook their hands. "My name is Alan Donovan. I work with Marsha Bergsson."

"Hi, pleased to meet you," Edward said.

"Likewise," Sandra said.

Alan sat on the sofa adjacent to Edward and Sandra.

"May I give you a drink, sir?" Christopher asked.

"Nothing for me, thank you," Alan answered, then Christopher went back to the kitchen. "Anyway, I'm here because I have a development on Terra."

"How is she? Is she alive?" Edward asked eagerly.

"We still don't know how or where she is," Alan said. "However, there is something I want to show you."

Alan reached into his jacket pocket and took out a circular tablet. It wasn't a HoriTab like pretty much every other person had. It was a special, advanced tablet that only government officials had. It wasn't made by Horizon, but Yuji Industria in Japan, who made weapons and technology only available to government officials worldwide.

He opened up the 'photos' tab and a holographic image appeared from the tablet. Alan used his finger to swipe and browse through the photos. He eventually found a photo of me in the alleyway with Father Thomas. Edward and Sandra were in shock and had their mouths wide open with disbelief. The symbol around Father Thomas' neck, however, was familiar to Edward as this was worn by people who had previously protested his Type I project.

"This was taken the day before Terra disappeared — Thursday November 22nd, by a member of the RBPD," Alan said. "His name is Thomas O'Brien. We've arrested him and his wife Claire on suspicion of kidnapping."

"They did this?" Edward asked with a broken voice.

"Well, we couldn't prove that, so they've been released," Alan said. "As you can see in this image, he has this strange symbol around his neck. I've been in his house and he has other possessions with this symbol on them."

"What does this symbol mean?" Sandra asked, referring to the cross that Father Thomas was wearing.

"I honestly have no idea," Alan said. "It looks to me like some sort of cult. I've asked Thomas about what it means, and he tells me it's the symbol of 'our lord', whatever that means."

Edward sat stroking his chin. He and Sandra still didn't have the answers they were looking for, but Edward still held a grudge towards Father Thomas and Claire.

"He's innocent, right?" Edward asked.

"Yeah, they haven't done anything," Alan answered. "He confirmed that he did meet Terra before she was due in school and she was round his house that evening."

Edward smacked his hand on the table in frustration.

"Why was she there? What did they do?" Edward interrogated.

"They told me that Terra came round for something called a prayer meeting," Alan said, who, along with many other people in the world at that time, was unfamiliar with the concept of religion. "It sounded very suspicious to me, but he told me that it was completely innocent."

"I don't know, it just sounds wrong to me," Sandra said. "I just can't help but feel they did something to her."

"Those people make me sick," Edward said. "The whole damned thing is a cult. I'm sorry, but I just can't believe they are innocent."

"Look, Edward, we spoke with Thomas and his wife," Alan said, "and they have done nothing wrong. I wish I knew where Terra was as much as the both of you do, but I don't, and we can't explain why we don't know where Terra is. But we will not lay this case to rest."

Edward couldn't just let it go. Even though Father Thomas and Claire were innocent, he was angry and suspicious that they may have influenced me in a way that may have put her in danger. Lots of possibilities were circling round Edward's head and he couldn't think straight.

"Let me see them," Edward said. "What's their address?"

"Uh, Edward, I can't do that," Alan said, taken aback by Edward's request. "I just can't give out his details like that."

"I need to speak with them, please," Edward insisted. "I still have that feeling. I really must go and speak with them."

"Look, I really must advise against it," Alan said. "Believe me, Edward, you will end up doing something you regret. Just take my word for it."

Edward found it hard to accept Alan's advice and he clenched his fist in frustration. Alan got up and shook Sandra and Edward's hands.

"Look, I will be in touch if there are any new developments," Alan said as he began to bid farewell. "Don't be too hasty, Edward. Let us do the investigating, okay?"

Both Edward and Sandra said goodbye to Alan as he made his way to the door and left the apartment.

"Oh god, I hate this," Sandra said as she stroked her forehead. "Those people are just…"

"I know, honey, I know," Edward said. "Do you really think those radicals are innocent?"

"I don't know," Sandra said pessimistically. "But maybe we should just leave it to them. What can we do?"

Sandra got up from the sofa, while Edward stayed sitting, just staring ahead.

"You coming to bed, honey?" Sandra asked, as she placed both her hands on Edward's shoulders.

"In a moment, honey," Edward said as he turned back to her. "You go on ahead. It's been rough for the both of us."

Edward kissed Sandra goodnight and she went upstairs to the bedroom. Meanwhile, Edward reached for his HoriTab and opened up the directory app. A hologram appeared from the tablet.

Edward thought 'search', and then the magnifying glass icon, with 'search' written next to it, flashed and a typing bar emerged, and then Edward thought 'Thomas O'Brien'.

Options for Thomas O'Brien appeared on the directory. Edward browsed through the results, and when he pressed one of the options on the hologram with his finger, a photo, a phone number, and an address appeared. Edward browsed through the search results before he eventually found Father Thomas' photo and address.

"Gotcha," Edward said, satisfied with himself. He closed the app, which caused the hologram to disappear, and put the HoriTab down as he got up and thought about going straight up to bed, but then went into the kitchen instead. He got out a medium-sized glass from the cupboard and a bottle of whisky from the fridge and poured it into the glass, filling it up to the top. Edward had never been much of a drinker. He did love to have a drink at the parties he would go to, but he wasn't one to get intoxicated. Sandra had once told me that ever since they had fostered me, Edward had cut down on alcohol. That night, however, since I had been missing for so long, Edward drank more than he had in a long time, finishing his glass of whisky on the sofa, on the brink of crying.

***

Edward's car parked outside Father Thomas' and Claire's home on Jefferson Avenue. Edward was intoxicated and had so much fury in him. He sat in his car carefully planning his approach. He was holding a flask full of vodka, drinking from it while thinking. He had trouble thinking straight; he felt that Thomas and Claire had seduced me into joining their cult. He was plagued with so many thoughts, and he was so indecisive.

He got out of his car and walked over to the front door. He had trouble walking at first, as he was drunk, but managed to maintain his balance eventually. Before he pressed the buzzer by the door, Edward frantically breathed in and out. All he could try to focus his mind on was his approach. Edward was normally very decisive, so for him to be indecisive was very rare. After Edward pressed the buzzer, the door partly opened and Father Thomas emerged from behind, seemingly shocked to see Edward.

"Y-You don't know m-m-me, but I..." Edward stuttered, as he tried to get a sentence together for a man he despised. The alcohol was preventing him from speaking properly, as well as the expression on Father Thomas' face, but he tried to compose himself.

"I know who you are," Father Thomas said. "You're the man who tries to compete with our natural order."

Father Thomas opened the door fully, inviting Edward into his house. Edward made his way into the house and looked around in fascination at the cross symbols that were hung up on the walls and copies of the Bible which were laid out on the table. Claire and Kate were also present, sitting on armchairs. Claire was reading the Bible while Kate was on her HoriTab. Claire looked up and took off her reading glasses in shock to see Edward, while Kate, who was also surprised to see Edward, blinked frequently.

"Edward Cox, I didn't expect to see you," Claire said.

"Right," Edward said, unsure how to respond to that. Father Thomas, Claire, and Kate thought he would follow that up with something, but Edward didn't. Edward was visibly drunk, and Thomas, Claire, and Kate wanted to mention something, but didn't as Edward was also clearly hurting.

"Well, in case you haven't acquainted yourself with who we are, I am Father Thomas, this is my wife Claire, and daughter Kate," Father Thomas introduced.

"F-*Father* Thomas? What kind of title is that?" Edward scoffed mockingly, and Father Thomas ignored Edward ridiculing him.

"Edward, I first and foremost want to offer you my sincere sorrow about Terra's disappearance," Father Thomas said. "I have a daughter myself, so I understand the anguish that you must be going through."

"Well, I do appreciate that," Edward said, as he started to be more composed. "But she was here the day before she disappeared."

"As you may or may not know, Claire and I were arrested on suspicion of Terra's disappearance," Father Thomas said, mortified. "We had to spend the night in a police station, and have our faith put under such scrutiny. We've told the detective what needed to be told from our point of view."

"Why was my daughter here?" Edward asked assertively.

"Terra decided to come here for a prayer meeting that we were holding," Father Thomas said.

"You must know that coming here was Terra's choice," Claire said.

"I'm sorry, but I find it hard to believe that Terra would just *decide* to come here," Edward said. "Why would Terra come to a place like this?"

"Well, she did," Father Thomas insisted. "She's a very smart girl. She can decide for herself."

"I'm her father, I know what a smart girl she is," Edward said scornfully. "You *don't* know my daughter, so do yourself a favour and stop pretending that you *know* Terra."

"Terra can make her own choices and she chose to attend our prayer meeting," Father Thomas said, almost assertively, but he was not one to get angry and feel hate towards someone.

"You really expect me to believe that my daughter would associate herself with crazy, delusional people like yourself?" Edward ridiculed. "I'm sorry, but she knows better than that, and I don't know what you did to her, but…"

"We did not do anything to Terra!" Father Thomas said assertively, while trying to keep calm and not turning to anger. "You just can't accept that maybe Terra doesn't think the same as you do. After all, she is your *foster* daughter."

"I love Terra like a real father should!" Edward said angrily. "I don't know what you've done, but how dare you influence my daughter, you sick son of a bitch!"

"Don't you dare curse in our home!" Claire argued back, but Edward laughed in response. Kate was startled by the conflict taking place.

"Why not?" Edward asked daringly. "What kind of insane laws are you putting up? Is this part of your cult, huh?"

"You can't stand the idea that not everyone wants to compete with God like you do," Father Thomas said. "You said yourself that you want to become your own maker. You want to challenge he who created Earth.

232

There are some like us who wish not to violate the natural order."

"Do you hate humanity?" Edward asked. "Why do you stifle the progress that we are making? We have made strides to become a more dominant species, and somehow our infinite possibilities are an offense to you. What kind of example are you setting for your daughter? How could you confuse her with this crazed world of yours?"

"Edward, I feel your pain, but don't you dare tell me how to raise my child," Father Thomas said.

"Okay, I have to ask you this, have you been drinking?" Claire asked.

"No. I mean, not much," Edward said, unable to give a straight, decisive answer. "I mean, just some scotch and some vodka…"

"Okay, then maybe it's best that you leave," Father Thomas said. "You're drunk, and I understand the pain you're in, but please leave before you do something you'll regret."

"Oh, you'd like that, wouldn't you?" Edward challenged.

"Uh, sir," Kate said to Edward. "I actually agree with the values that my mom and dad have taught me. They haven't just taught me about God and the Bible, but also community and…"

"Oh, bullshit!" Edward said, which stunned Kate. "You're as fucked up as your mom and dad!"

"Don't speak to my daughter like that!" Father Thomas said. "Is our faith a joke to you? Do you consider the idea of worshipping a god somewhat crazed?"

"I do, but when my daughter is involved, then like any father, I get very concerned," Edward said. "Terra is lost, all because of this cult of yours."

"Again, I think you better leave, Edward," Father Thomas said sternly. "I think you have…"

As Father Thomas walked right up to Edward in an effort to get him to leave, Edward punched Father Thomas in the face. He fell down on the floor, and Claire rushed to him. Kate looked on in shock and started to cry.

"What have you done with my daughter, you sick son of a bitch!" Edward asked angrily.

Father Thomas and Claire didn't answer. Edward was not a violent man, but he was someone who wasn't afraid of getting what he needed or wanted by any means necessary. There was blood coming out of Father Thomas' nose, and Claire rushed to get a tissue from the table. Edward glared at Father Thomas, who looked back in pain rather than in anger. Edward was still angry with both Father Thomas and Claire, but he then conceded that he was not going to get the answers he wanted from either of them. Edward stormed out of the house, slamming the front door behind him. After Edward left, Claire cried as well as Kate, visibly distressed by what had happened.

Edward put his thumb on the thumbprint of his aerocar and the door automatically opened. He stepped into his car and rather than drive away, he sat for a moment in order to review what had happened back in the house. He took several deep breaths in and out, trying to calm himself down. He also thought about whether he should have another drink to try and comfort himself. But then he thought about whether having another drink would affect the drive back home, even though aerocars drove automatically. Eventually, he decided against having another drink and pressed the phone icon on the control wheel and thought 'call Anton Monroe', and then a dial tone sounded and the phone call was made.

"Edward," Anton's voice said as a hologram of him appeared from the control wheel, looking directly at Edward. "What happened?"

"I was there, Anton," Edward said. "The crazy people's home, I was there. They did something to Terra, I just know…"

"Woah, slow down, Edward," Anton said calmly. "Those are the crazy people with those… symbols, right? The ones who've been protesting our work for years?"

"Yeah, that's them," Edward said, and then burst into tears. "I just hate them, Anton, I really do."

"You did something, didn't you?" Anton asked, knowing that Edward was full of regret. "What did you do?"

"Well, I may have hit the guy," Edward said reluctantly, still crying. "I was angry, Anton. Terra is missing and I just know that they are behind all of this."

"Listen, Edward," Anton said, "you did the right thing. You have every right to be angry. I know how much you love Terra. You shouldn't feel guilt, Edward."

"I know, but I just…" Edward said, filled with regret. "Also, I said something to the daughter too."

"What did you say?" Anton asked.

"I told her…" Edward said, once again reluctantly, full of regret. "I told her that she is as fucked up as her dad."

Anton shook his head but could see that Edward was in pain, and he knew that Edward was not a violent man.

"Edward, you're a loving, caring man," Anton said, trying to reassure him. "You would do anything to ensure Terra's safety. You are just the type of father she needs."

Edward took a deep breath. He was angry deep down but trying to keep a calm exterior.

"Look, maybe you can come to my house sometime and we can talk more about this, okay?" Anton suggested. "Also, have you been drinking?"

"Yeah, maybe," Edward said. "I only had a bit, not much. I'll be going now, Anton."

"All right, bye now, and do be careful," Anton said. The hologram disappeared.

Edward took another couple of deep breaths before he started the car and it drove Edward back home.

Incarnation

Mulieris sat in the corner of the Caelem Palatium dungeon with her head down. The dungeon wasn't as beautiful as everywhere else in the palace. It was a dark, gloomy place with hardly any light. The walls, floor and ceiling were all made of stone, and the door was guarded by a Deinonychus that stood upright, maintaining its focus, though it was only Mulieris who was inside. The Deinonychus stared at Mulieris, condemning her for what she had done.

Then there were scratches heard from the door. The Deinonychus pushed the door open, and there was another Deinonychus, who communicated with it. Then the other Deinonychus made way for Hominem to enter the dungeon, and then the door closed. Mulieris was elated with the entrance of Hominem, and she rushed to embrace him. Hominem was conflicted, however. He was happy to see Mulieris, but he was upset with her for going beyond the Upper World on the skywhale and betraying Mother and Father.

"Oh, Hominem," Mulieris said tearfully. "This place is… oh, I can't find the word."

Hominem hesitated to speak, careful not to upset Mulieris any more than she was. After Mulieris and Hominem embraced, Hominem kept his head down.

"My love?" Mulieris said, addressing Hominem's silence.

"Why?" Hominem asked with a broken voice while his head was still down.

Mulieris hesitated, before she eventually said, "Hominem, please, I don't want to…"

"Why!" Hominem asked, more assertively this time. That brought out a brief roar from the Deinonychus, who sensed the commotion within.

"I…" Mulieris began hesitantly, as she struggled to bring herself to explain her actions. "I was tempted."

"Tempted," Hominem said; that was what he hadn't wanted to hear. "We went to see Quercus Alba for guidance. He explained that it was forbidden to go beyond the Upper World and…"

"I know, Hominem," Mulieris said. "I remember."

"So why did you do it then?" Hominem asked assertively.

Mulieris sat back in the corner and cried, with her hands on her face. Hominem usually rushed to Mulieris' side any time she was sad or under distress. He just stood still, however, even though he still didn't like seeing Mulieris distressed. Hominem wanted his anger at Mulieris to subside, but it was too hard for him. Mulieris hadn't just betrayed him, she'd betrayed everyone from the Upper World, particularly Mother and Father.

"You knew that it was wrong, and you did it," Hominem said. "Was the Upper World not enough? Was I not enough?"

"How could you ask such a thing?" Mulieris asked. "You and everything here are more than enough for me."

"I wish I could believe you," Hominem said.

"Please, my love, please believe me," Mulieris begged.

"I didn't think you could hurt me," Hominem said, with tears starting to emerge. "I didn't think you could hurt anyone. I always thought you were good and innocent. Mother and Father thought so too. You don't know how much my heart aches."

"Oh, I do," Mulieris said. "My heart aches too, my sweet Hominem. I never want to cause anyone pain. It hurts more to cause pain than to receive it."

"What was so wrong with the Upper World that you had to venture out?" Hominem asked. "Why?"

"I told you, I was tempted," Mulieris said, crying once again. "Please, Hominem, I don't wish to discuss this."

"What else do we have to talk about?" Hominem asked. "I cannot stop thinking about what has happened. I just don't know what to think."

"What do you mean, Hominem?"

"About everything. I thought we were made to be together forever, to live in the Upper World for all eternity, but that wasn't good enough for you. You knew what the commandments were, Father explained them to us, and we accepted. The celuti were not made for us. We were made to remain, not to venture. You have sinned, Mulieris, and you should feel nothing but guilt and shame."

"How could you say that?"

"How could you do what you did? What foul thing tempted you to ride the celuti?"

Mulieris didn't answer. She just sat with her head down, hurt by being berated by Hominem, the man she loved.

"The spirit was right," Mulieris said.

"What spirit?" Hominem asked eagerly. "Was it Sapillien?"

"No, somebody wiser," Mulieris said.

"Who could that possibly be?" Hominem asked, incensed that she thought there was a spirit out there wiser than Sapillien, the wisest of the forest spirits.

"She didn't have a name," Mulieris answered. "She was hideous, but she was right. I am imprisoned here. I will always be confined here."

"No, you're not," Hominem said. "Whatever foul thing you spoke to, she's lying. No wise spirit would ever tell you that, not even Sapillien."

"And how would you know that?" Mulieris asked, challenging Hominem. "Have you spoken with her?"

"No, my love, but…" Hominem answered hesitantly, as he was surprised by Mulieris' change of attitude.

"Precisely, Hominem," Mulieris said, starting to get assertive like Hominem. "Nobody can seek Sapillien. You told me that. You would not know what Sapillien would say. There is no freedom in the Upper World!"

"Take that back," Hominem ordered. "Don't you dare say that."

"I just wanted to explore, to gain knowledge," Mulieris said. "I wanted to experience a new world, meet new people. What is so sinful about that? Could I not educate myself?"

"You wouldn't know what to do with it," Hominem argued. "You are prone to temptation, which is why you must remain here with me. Mother and Father intend to keep us safe."

"Safe? Confinement isn't safe! Keeping me prisoner isn't safe! How dare you support this repression."

"I'm telling you this because I still love you! I'm hurt and angry, but my heart can't help but love you. I hope you will learn, my love, and one day you will be free with me."

"If you can't understand my need for curiosity, adventure and independence, you are no love of mine. You can never be."

Hominem was deeply hurt. Mulieris was now on her feet, confronting Hominem, who was in complete disbelief. He didn't know how to respond, as Mulieris appeared to be a completely different person to him.

"What demon could have possibly possessed you?" Hominem asked. "That was no spirit you spoke with, it was a foul, ill demon who has corrupted you."

"If a desire for independence makes me a demon in your eyes, then I sympathize with you," Mulieris said. "Do you have any desires, Hominem? Don't you wish to think and do for yourself?"

"I know better," Hominem answered. "I know better than to have such thoughts."

"Then enjoy your life as prisoner," Mulieris said. "I don't want to continue this life any more. Get away from me, Hominem."

"Mulieris, no," Hominem said. "You're possessed. You can't be the…"

"Get away!" Mulieris screamed; the Deinonychus roared in response to try and calm her down.

Hominem was completely stunned. He had never seen Mulieris so angry. She didn't apologize to him, but instead just glared at him. Hominem walked towards the door, and the Deinonychus let him out. Mulieris retreated back to the corner of the room. She cried once again, but only for a short while. Her love for Hominem had slowly evaporated.

She no longer had regret for what she had done.

She no longer loved Hominem.

She no longer loved Mother and Father.

***

Hominem walked out of the Caelem Palatium and sat down on a step in the village, crying. Mulieris was no longer the woman he loved. He was devastated. It felt like Mulieris had died. What had happened to the sweet, innocent woman who would love him forever? What had happened to the woman who would abide by the Upper World? Hominem didn't know what to think any more. It was like his whole life was a lie.

Hominem then got up and walked out of the village and into the valley. He saw Son walking with a Polacanthus. As soon as Son made eye contact with him, Hominem approached him.

"That night, you told them, didn't you?" Hominem asked.

"What night?" Son asked. "Are you all right?"

"Of course, I'm not," Hominem said. "Didn't you see Mulieris get imprisoned?"

"I know, I'm so sorry," Son said. "She did disobey Mother and Father and…"

"Did you tell them?" Hominem interrogated Son. "That night when you saw Mulieris and I speaking with Quercus Alba, did you tell Mother and Father? After you had sworn to keep our conversation secret?"

"I had to tell them," Son said. "Mother and Father had the right to know about Mulieris and her desires."

"Why?" Hominem asked. "Why did you have to involve them?"

"Because we don't want another war," Son said. "We have trusted before, and our trust has been broken before, and we don't want to risk it happening again."

"She wouldn't have broken your trust," Hominem said. "She's not evil."

"We have thought so about the outcasted before," Son said. "I understand your undying love for Mulieris, but she did something wrong and had to be punished."

"She's possessed," Hominem said. "She said she spoke with someone that night."

"Who?" Son asked.

"She didn't say her name," Hominem said. "She said that it was a spirit, a female spirit, of some kind. It wasn't Sapillien, but she said that she was wiser."

"Wiser than Sapillien?" Son asked. "She's become wicked. What kind of spirit would guide her to do such things?"

"She just needs help," Hominem said. "She's become corrupted somehow and she needs the help of Mother and Father."

"We can't help her," Son said. "We've done everything for her. We've given the both of you, food, shelter, love, and she has betrayed our trust."

"You betrayed us," Hominem said, challenging Son. "We came to you with a secret and now because of you, my dear Mulieris lies in captivity."

"I wish to discuss this no more," Son said, as he started to walk away with the Polacanthus. "What had to be done has been done."

Hominem was angry and felt betrayed by Son. Even though Mulieris had grown to despise Hominem, he was so convinced that she must have been cursed or something. Whatever may have happened to her, Hominem wanted help for her and hoped that she could go back to being the woman that he loved.

Then a Tyrannosaurus let out an almighty roar as it emerged from the forest, which startled Hominem and caught the attention of Son. A Parasaurolophus stopped drinking from the valley and bellowed. The Tyrannosaurus and Parasaurolophus seemed distressed, as they moved frantically. Then the dinosaurs in the valley all stomped and made loud noises. The angels emerged from the village, alerted by the loud noises that the dinosaurs were making, and Mother and Father rushed out of the Caelem Palatium and onto the valley. Mother approached the Tyrannosaurus, a dinosaur that she had a close bond with.

"My trecarun, what is it?" Mother asked urgently.

The Tyrannosaurus kept roaring, but Mother's bond with the Tyrannosaurus was so deep that she could actually understand what it was saying.

"Terra. What about Terra?" Mother asked the Tyrannosaurus.

Then the Parasaurolophus made a series of loud noises. Just like with the Tyrannosaurus, Mother also understood the Parasaurolophus.

"Oh no," Mother said with great despair, then she approached Father and said, "That distress call from Aurelia...."

"Where Vagus went?" Father asked.

"Yes," Mother answered. "It wasn't a distress call at all. It was a trap!"

Everyone exclaimed in horror, and the dinosaurs let out noises of despair too. The Upper World got word that I was in danger, along with Vagus. The concern was mainly for me though, as Mother and Father had trusted Vagus. They didn't believe that he was a traitor, but he was too trusting and that had led to me being in great danger. Mother was so tearful that tears came out of her eyes like rain.

"You!" Father said to a couple of angels. "Get the celuti, send them to Aurelia and make sure they bring back Terra!"

The angels flew across the valley to approach the skywhales to order them to Aurelia and try to bring me back to the Upper World.

The Power of Terra

I was in Gemilin's bedroom, still under the spell that had put me under. I still kept seeing her as Laura, and I had a habit of inadvertently saying her name out loud. I was still so dizzy and faint and had trouble moving. I lay down on a purple fur rug. Gemilin was incredibly amused by what was happening to me, and she sat on her bed, watching with satisfaction.

"Tell me about Laura, Terra," Gemilin requested.

"I…" I began trying to speak but I was so sedated it was difficult to find the words. "I'd rather not."

"Tell me!" Gemilin raged as green flames emerged from her eyes, hair and fingernails. Were those flame weapons? Was she going to set me on fire? I had no idea, but as I was under her spell, there was not much I could do. "She's a friend, yes?"

"Yeah, she is," I answered breathily.

"That's nice," Gemilin said. "I was never a popular girl. I'm royal, yes, but royalty doesn't guarantee popularity. As I grew, I became more popular. I had friends. I even had lovers. Were you popular on Earth, Terra?"

"I don't know," I said, once again breathily. "I'd talk to other girls at school, but I'm not, like, close with them or anything. I guess Laura is my closest friend."

"You are quite fond of Laura, aren't you, Terra?" Gemilin asked, though I still kept picturing her as Laura, so it seemed like a weird question as it seemed to me that Laura was referring to herself in the third person.

"She just made me feel safe," I said. "At parties and stuff, I always felt more comfortable when she was around."

"Tell me about these parties, Terra," Gemilin said.

"My foster dad Edward is a scientist," I said. "He's pretty rich so I would go with him to these lavish events and stuff, and sometimes Laura would be there with me. I would often meet other rich people too, which was kind of awkward."

"Wow, Terra, you have such a wonderful life," Gemilin said as she got up from her bed and strolled around the room in a daze. "You are so, so privileged, and ever so beautiful. Tell me Terra, have you had any lovers?"

What kind of question was that to ask a fourteen-year-old? If I had a boyfriend, I'd never refer to him as a lover. I don't think I've heard anybody ever called that, except on these period dramas that I used to watch on Viewpoint. I just shook my head.

"Oh?" Gemilin said, seemingly shocked. "How could someone so fair, so pure, not attract those of the opposite sex?"

249

"Don't know, guess it just hasn't happened," I said. "I'm only fourteen."

"When you grow, Terra, men will travel worlds for you," Gemilin said. "You would be surprised about the sacrifices they would make just for you. Just to be near you. Tell me about Earth, Terra."

"Uh, what do you want to know?" I asked.

"Vagus has told me and my brother many tales of his travels," Gemilin said. "They don't worship Mother and Father, do they?"

"Not really," I said. "I think they used to, years ago."

"My, my, how could you live on a planet with such little faith?" Gemilin said. "It must be awfully depressing. You know, a friend of mine is also from your planet."

"Earth?" I asked.

"Yes," Gemilin said. "He has been dying to meet you, and he will be summoned before you."

I didn't know who this friend was, or how this person knew who I was, but he must have been a total nut job like Gemilin and King Deorege were. I just wished that I had the strength and the courage to escape, but I was struggling to move. I had tried getting up, but I just kept falling down. I had no balance. I was like a baby who was struggling to walk. Gemilin just stood by me, grinning as I was so out of my mind and out of strength.

Then I saw a statue at the corner of Gemilin's room. It looked familiar to me, but it wasn't one of the statues I had seen when I was walking through the corridor. It was of a centaur and it appeared to be lying down. Was it one of the centaurs that I had met? I wasn't sure. I just kept looking at it, to see if I could recognize it.

"Do you like my statue, Terra?" Gemilin asked. "It's another tribute to the fallen."

"You're lying," I argued, although my voice was weak.

"Oh, Terra, you're delusional," Gemilin teased. "This is to remember one of our dear friends from Aurelia. Such a tragedy that he has gone. It was so recent as well. Now we can gaze upon him and admire him for the majestic stallion he was."

So, I gazed at the statue to see if once again I could remember who it reminded me of. I looked at the hooves, but there was nothing distinguishable there. I looked at the body, but again, there was nothing that appeared significant to me.

I tried one more time to stand up. My arms and legs were like jelly, and barely had any strength due to the spell that I was under. I tried lifting myself up, but my arms kept shaking. I fell down once again, and Gemilin laughed.

"Silly girl," Gemilin said in a mischievous manner. "You need to rest, my pretty. You need to save your strength for when my friend arrives. He will help restore you."

I was only up a brief time to get a better look at the face of the statue. There were small horns at the top of the head and a beard. I tried thinking about whether or not that statue was of one of the centaurs I had met. After a while, I figured it out: it was Ohlakan. King Deorege and Gemilin must have murdered him, I thought. I was so sad about Ohlakan's death. I wanted to cry, but I was just so numb. Because of Gemilin's spell, it was like I couldn't feel anything, like my arms and legs, hence why I couldn't get up.

"You really are special, Terra," Gemilin said. "You know I am special too. You would be amazed at what I can do. You really admire that statue, don't you? Now that you can't move, I suppose that you're a statue too."

That insult made me think. What did Gemilin mean by 'a statue too'? Why did she refer to the statue as a person?

"Now I am going to refresh myself for bed," Gemilin said as she picked up a key from a bedside table and went towards the door. "Of course, you can't escape, Terra, but just to be sure, this door will be locked."

Gemilin went out of her bedroom and locked the door as she went to the bathroom. I was still under Gemilin's spell and had trouble getting up. Then I had a thought. Was Ohlakan a statue? That seemed like a crazy thought, but then again, Gemilin could do magic. Maybe she was capable of that? I then had another realization: I could heal. This may be a long shot, but could I bring statues to life? It seemed crazy, especially as I couldn't think straight when under Gemilin's spell, but if I was right, this may have been my only way out.

Unable to get up, I tried using my arm to drag myself across the floor to the statue. I had to try and get to it before Gemilin returned in case she got suspicious. I didn't know if it would work though, but I was at that point where I would have tried anything to get out of there. I grunted as I dragged across the floor, as I tried using whatever energy I had, which was not much. I tried not to grunt too loud so that I wouldn't attract suspicion. I was getting closer, but I had to get there before Gemilin got back.

I eventually reached the statue. I just hoped my theory was right. I tried to cast my mind back to what happened with the leaves at Vagus' house and with Deorege's flowers in the garden of the Opraso. I tried to focus, even though I was under enormous pressure.

I touched the statue, focusing my mind on bringing it to life.

Nothing.

Maybe I was crazy, or perhaps I wasn't doing it right.

Then I heard echoing footsteps. That must have been Gemilin returning to the bedroom.

I tried again. I focused my mind on bringing life to the statue of Ohlakan, believing that it was really Ohlakan in there.

I heard the key unlocking the door. I tried not to panic.

Then I heard a scream, but it was not coming from outside the bedroom. It was right in front of me.

It had worked! Ohlakan came back to life.

Gemilin opened the door with such urgency as she heard Ohlakan's voice, and when Gemilin entered the bedroom, Ohlakan charged towards her and knocked her down. I was finally free from Gemilin's spell. My strength came back, and I finally was able to stand up again.

"Ohlakan, thank goodness!" I said with such relief as I embraced him.

"What happened, Terra?" Ohlakan asked.

"You were a statue," I answered. "Gemilin and King Deorege, they did it. There was no monster. They must have done it to the others too."

"What?" Ohlakan said, outraged.

Gemilin had gotten up, and she was furious. Green flames started to emerge from her. Ohlakan charged towards her again, and once again, he knocked her down.

"There isn't time, Terra," Ohlakan said. "The king's men, they'll come after us."

"But we should free the others," I said. "We need to free everyone."

"Terra, I need to get you out of here," Ohlakan said. "There isn't time to rescue everyone."

"But they'll capture you again," I said, concerned for Ohlakan's safety.

"Terra, it's more important to get you to freedom," Ohlakan said.

I heard running footsteps from outside the bedroom. It must have been the polifara, as they must have heard Gemilin's scream, believing that something was wrong.

"Get on my back, Terra," Ohlakan said as he sat down. "I'll get you out of here. Don't worry about me, Vagus or anyone else. I'll try and do something."

I got on Ohlakan's back, trying to figure out how people rode horses in the past, and then he stood back up and charged out of the bedroom. The polifara came from the right of the corridor, so Ohlakan dashed towards the left. The polifara ran after us. I was so nervous. The polifara shot vines at us, but Ohlakan was able to outrun them, and the vines kept missing. My heart was racing, and nerves rushed throughout my body as Ohlakan kept galloping across the corridor.

Eventually, we made it outside the Opraso but the polifara kept chasing us. Ohlakan galloped across the lawn and into the forest, with the polifara still after us. As it was nightfall, Ohlakan had to be careful not to trip over any sticks or anything. I heard all kinds of screeching and howling in the forest. They were sounds that I had never heard before, which made me nervous. I was worried that they might attack me and Ohlakan, or stall us and let the polifara catch us.

Ohlakan and I made it out of the forest and we arrived at the spot where the skywhales dropped off Vagus and I.

"Why are we stopping?" I asked as Ohlakan came to a halt.

"The celuti arrives at this spot," Ohlakan said. "Vagus has told me of the skywhales. They will take you back to the Upper World."

I got down from Ohlakan's back. I looked up but couldn't see any skywhales. Then the polifara made it out of the forest, and my heart stopped as I froze with fear. Ohlakan didn't move either, so that he could protect me.

Then a gentle, deep noise came from above. Ohlakan and I looked up, as well as the polifara. The skywhale had arrived, to my relief. It swooped down from the air and used its tail to hit the polifara really hard, sending them back through the forest for a great distance. I embraced Ohlakan once more.

"Thank you," I said.

"Terra, you get back safe now," Ohlakan said. "Don't you worry about me. I will alert the others in Aurelia and I will fend off the palace."

I jumped onto the back of the skywhale. I was much more confident getting on the skywhale this time, especially as it had helped save me too. Once the skywhale flew away, I waved goodbye to Ohlakan, who then galloped away through the forest.

I was relieved to be free from the Opraso, but I feared for Ohlakan and Vagus, as well as the others. I hoped that they would be okay. I felt a mixture of relief and concern as I flew back to the Upper World.

Harvest of the Nasinata

Satan sat on his throne at the top of his tower. Women who were entirely made of flames were dancing in front of and around him. The women were giggling, but their facial and bodily features were not seen. He lusted for them, but behind the lust he felt a sadness and emptiness. The dance routine the women made of fire did was a very regular occurrence for Satan as long as he had lived in the Underworld, and the fire women didn't compare to the beauty he had witnessed in the Upper World.

Satan got up and the fire women stopped dancing. He approached them and stroked the tops of their heads, as he thanked the fire women for their dance and for entertaining him.

"I am most grateful for your flames of pleasure," Satan said to them gratefully, and then they bowed to Satan and their flames increased, allowing them to disappear. The flames touched Satan's torso, but he wasn't affected. He walked over to the edge of the tower, just admiring the view. Femos arrived at the top of the tower, and Satan turned to her.

"Ah, Femos," Satan said. "I am glad to be in the presence of a trusted one at last, now that Aurelia failed to do their deed and bring me Terra."

"I'm so sorry, sire," Femos said.

"It is not you who needs to be sorry," Satan said. "I asked for Terra and I got nothing."

Satan leaned on the wall of the balcony with his head down in disappointment. He then let out a scream of anguish.

"I have news, my Lord," Femos said.

"I can't bear any news of failures," Satan said, with his head still down. "Now I must think of a new plan to get the girl in my grasp."

"They're not news of failures, my Lord," Femos said. "I've used kausark. I entered the Upper World."

"Good," Satan said as he turned around. "I'm glad that you have mastered the technique. Tell me of your visit."

"I met the girl," Femos said. "She goes by the name of Mulieris."

"Mulieris, I see," Satan said. "Tell me of your encounter with her."

"She is lost, sire," Femos said. "She longs for escape; she desires to be free from the Upper World. She is tempted."

"Of course!" Satan said as he raised his arms with euphoria. "We now have another plan."

"Yes, sire," Femos said. "You've taught me kausark well. I am most grateful to you, my Lord."

"Please, my young apprentice, your thanks aren't necessary to me," Satan said. "It is I who should be thankful to you. She and Hominem, they are the key."

"Hominem, my Lord?" Femos asked.

"The love between them is so strong," Satan said. "And their love will be the key. If we can claim Mulieris, we can claim Hominem too. I've told you of the harvest, have I?"

"The nasinata, my Lord?" Femos asked.

"Yes, Femos, the seeds that will allow us to claim the souls we desire," Satan said. "We feast on the weakness they have. My time on Earth has taught me that all great plans require time and strategy. Their fall is our gain."

Femos and Satan shared a callous, sadistic smile, taking satisfaction at the prospect of souls succumbing to their evilness.

"Let us make our way to Boroju," Satan said. "Then we can watch our nasinata grow."

Femos nodded in agreement, and then Satan walked down the tower. Femos followed him. Satan and Femos reached the bottom of the tower, and strolled together through the village, and when passing by, the villagers all kneeled before him, worshipping their most fearful master.

"You all bow before me well." Satan gave a rare compliment to the villagers, but they thought nothing of it. They just continued kneeling before him without thinking any more or less of him. Satan was such a fearsome figure that any difference of opinion would have dangerous consequences. So, they kneeled and worshipped their lord in the same way that they always did.

Satan and Femos passed the village, with the former satisfied with the villagers' worship of him. They approached the river of red water, where Palia was waiting with his rowing boat.

"Ah, greetings to both of you," Palia said.

"Palia, my friend, could you take us to…" Femos said.

"No, Femos, we don't sail to Boroju," Satan said.

"Ah, Boroju, I know that place," Palia said. "They say that's the Hill of the Dead. Legend has it the spirits of the deceased gather there, and that it is their haven. All those guilty souls uniting and living."

"Yes, it is a beautiful place," Satan said. "You've not encountered Boroju, have you, Femos?"

"I've only heard stories, my Lord," Femos said. "This will be my first encounter of Boroju. How do we journey to this place?"

"We fly," Satan answered as he spread his wings, ready to fly. "Hold on to me, Femos, and then we will journey."

Femos put her arms around Satan's chest and then Satan started to flap his strong, sturdy wings. As a result, Satan flew above the ground, perfectly capable of carrying Femos. He flew towards a dark green mist, and a low groaning sound was heard.

"The deceased are singing their night's song," Satan said to Femos. "Such a beautiful sound, isn't it?"

Femos nodded with agreement. They flew through the mist, and there was a foul stench brewing through the mist. Femos kept coughing and gagging and held her nose, but Satan was unaffected. He just kept flying onwards. Beyond the mist was a very steep mountain. The indigo rocks were sharp and jagged, and some rocks had brown moss on them. On the mountain top, a large group of whitened spirits were floating, and the groaning sounds intensified.

Femos looked up, as she and Satan got closer to Boroju. Femos had never seen a clan of spirits before. The spirits saw Satan, and then they wailed as they hailed their master. Satan welcomed their response as he landed on Boroju, and Femos jumped onto the ground.

"This, Femos, is the land of the nasinata," Satan said, as his toes embraced the velvet, dusty surface. "You are now the second citizen of this world to enter Boroju."

"Can I see the nasinata?" Femos asked enthusiastically.

"Why of course, my young apprentice," Satan said. "Let us listen with appreciation to the spirits who salute us."

The spirits floated around Satan and Femos. Satan opened his arms as he embraced the spirits that surrounded him. He always enjoyed the admiration and fear that others showed towards him, and he always thrived on the attention that others gave him. Femos, meanwhile, had never been given so much attention, and she wasn't much of a public figure in the Underworld compared to Satan. The recognition she got from the spirits was alien to her.

"Now let us make our way to the wondrous crops," Satan said.

Satan and Femos walked past the floating spirits and then they came across ravens that had no eyes. They screeched in such a high pitch that Femos covered her ears, but Satan, as indestructible as an immortal would be, was not affected.

They approached a field full of small, round seeds that were as red as blood. The seeds were laid out and ripened in velvet soil. Satan dug his hand into the soil and picked up a handful of seeds.

"I present to you the nasinata," Satan said as he held up the seeds in front of Femos.

"These are the crops I present before Mulieris?" Femos asked.

"There lies deep magic within these fruits," Satan said. "Magic that will allow a living soul to give in to us."

"And they will abide with us," Femos said.

"Yes, Femos, once they become part of the Underworld, they will fight for our cause," Satan said enthusiastically.

The sound of bells rang on Boroju, and Satan crouched down, screaming and covering his ears in agony. The sight of Satan in pain was a rarity for Femos, but she knew the sound of bells was an Achilles' heel for Satan. The spirits in the distance wailed to the sound of bells ringing, but they weren't in any real agony like Satan was.

"It's the bells from the village," Femos said. "Nightfall must be coming."

The bells eventually stopped, and Satan stood back up, recovering from the agony of the bells sounding.

"Even for an eternity, I struggle to endure the bell chimes," Satan said.

"But why do the bells sound?" Femos asked. "Could you stop them, as king?"

"The strongest sense I grasp in the Underworld is pain," Satan said. "It is pain that makes you stronger, and to become ruler of all one must be strong."

"And when you become stronger, you won't feel pain?" Femos asked.

"Eventually, my young apprentice," Satan said. "There will come the day when all weakness is lost. The seeds will gain us more members to our army."

"She will come, my Lord," Femos said with confidence. "She will be tempted by the seeds."

"Yes, the poor, pitiful girl will succumb to us," Satan said. "Your news of Mulieris will keep our plan in motion. Her weakness will be our strength, and her demise will be our triumph!"

The Crisis of HORIZON Technologies

The disappearance of Terra Cox, foster daughter of Cox Industries CEO Edward Cox, last month has brought on a lot of criticism in the direction of HORIZON Technologies. CEO Don Williams has been under scrutiny after the nanotech clothing products she was wearing were unable to locate Terra after she disappeared. Parents have expressed concern over this and worry whether the product will work on their children.

Just last week, to compound the leading technology company's problems, Don Williams has been arrested for assault, with a trial to take place later this fall. Williams will be represented in court by high-profile attorney, Paul Dawson. HORIZON Technologies has been in the temporary stewardship of vice-president Megan Lockhart while the legal case against Williams goes on.

"We at HORIZON Technologies are very saddened by the circumstances that Don has found himself in," Lockhart said. "He has been an outstanding CEO for this company, and I know him as a wonderful kind man. I will do my very best to fill in for him while he is going through his legal battle and I hope we can look forward to welcoming Don back in the near future."

Don Williams founded HORIZON Technologies back in 2277 and the company has revolutionized technology by applying mind reading to their products such as phones, tablets and televisions. The nano-clothing products were another revolutionary product, but the disappearance of Terra Cox has caused major concern amongst parents and has caused HORIZON to lose shares in the stock market. Megan Lockhart now has a huge job to help HORIZON out of a very deep crisis.

A Reason

It was late at night and Sandra sat down on the couch waiting for Edward to come home. It was so late at night that Christopher had shut down for the night. He always stopped operating around eleven p.m., which was when everybody would usually be in bed. Edward was not someone to go out so late, but my disappearance was having such a bad effect on him that it had led to uncharacteristic behaviour from Edward. He always tried to set an example and be a good role model for me, like he would go to bed before midnight every night so that I would do the same. However, it was almost one a.m. and Sandra checked her HoriPhone frequently so that she could track Edward's location. She saw that Edward was almost home, and she began running through what she would say to him in her head. So many things ran through her mind as she had become upset with him, and she couldn't decide whether to talk calmly or shout and scream at him.

Edward eventually stumbled through to the living room, hysterically laughing while doing so. Sandra stood with her arms folded, scowling at Edward.

"Do you think this is funny?" Sandra asked.

"I don't know," Edward replied with laughter. "I mean, kinda, if you think about it."

"Well, I'm not laughing," Sandra said. "You have no idea how worried I was."

"Worried?" Edward asked, still laughing.

"Please, stop laughing!" Sandra said, with her voice starting to become assertive. "This is not like you, Edward, and this is making me very concerned."

"Please, people change," Edward said, dismissing Sandra's concerns. "Sure, maybe I wasn't like this before, but guess what, I've changed. I like this new me. I can finally have fun!"

"Fun?" Sandra asked, with her tone of voice still assertive.

"Yeah, toots, you know," Edward said, which made Sandra cringe. "I need to have fun again, Sandra. I need to be reborn."

"Edward, nobody has said 'toots' for well over three hundred years," Sandra said. "You're embarrassing yourself, Edward, and you're not really making any sense."

"Whatever, you're not the boss of me," Edward answered back. "I own me, and I own my own company. I am a god!"

"Edward, you're being ridiculous," Sandra said. "I mean, if Terra saw you…"

"Don't!" Edward snapped in a sudden change of tone. He then went to sit down on the couch. "Don't say her name."

"Are you just going to pretend that she doesn't exist?" Sandra asked as she approached Edward.

"She doesn't exist any more," Edward said, close to tears. "She's gone, Sandra. She's never coming back."

"Edward, they're still searching for her and the very best people are on it. We just have to be patient, okay?"

"Sandra, I don't think I have the patience. If it's Terra, then I want her found now."

"This situation is difficult on all of us, but all we can do now is have faith."

"Have faith?" Edward then asked scornfully. "You sound just like *him*!"

"Who?" Sandra asked.

"You know, Thomas O... something," Edward said. "You know, some stupid Irish name."

Sandra was stunned, and in fear of what the answer might be, she asked, "You didn't go over and see him, did you?"

Like Sandra, Edward paused for a moment, and quietly answered, "I had to."

Sandra gasped, although Edward's response was pretty vague. Sandra, again fearing what the answer could be, asked, "What did you do?"

"I..." Edward took a deep breath and hesitated before he said, "I attacked him. I just punched him in the face, and I also cursed in his home, which I know is no big deal, but you know what those people are like; they make a big deal of everything."

"Edward, how could you?" Sandra asked, incensed. "You heard what Alan said; Thomas O'Brien had nothing to do with Terra going missing."

"Come on, Sandra, you don't really believe that, do you?" Edward asked.

"Actually, I do, because Alan is a professional detective, personally recommended to us by Marsha Bergsson," Sandra said, sounding assertive once again. "What reason does he have to protect them?"

"None," Edward said, and stopped speaking for a while as he knew subconsciously that Sandra was probably right. Then he said, "But he must know people. Maybe it wasn't Thomas himself, but he has associates, right? Those people would be insane and dangerous enough to kidnap Terra or worse."

"Edward, stop!" Sandra commanded. "Do you know how crazy you're sounding right now?"

"Crazy?" Edward asked angrily as he stood up, though he had trouble with his balance at first because of his drunken state. "I'm trying to find Terra, Sandra."

"No, you're just coming up with these crazy theories that just don't make any sense," Sandra argued. "If Mr O'Brien had associates who were under suspicion, they'd be in custody by now. Alan Donovan is not a bad detective as you're making him out to be."

"Well, where is Terra then?" Edward asked. "Because I sure don't see her here."

"Edward, I honestly don't know what to tell you," Sandra said reluctantly.

"Uh-huh, exactly!" Edward said. "Alan Donovan has failed at his job!"

"Edward, the search has barely lasted two weeks," Sandra said. "Nobody has failed at their jobs; all we can do is just give it some more time."

"Then maybe... *we* failed," Edward said reluctantly.

"What do you mean *we* failed?" Sandra asked.

Edward took a deep breath before he said, "Well, maybe there was a reason why we couldn't have children."

"What are you talking about?" Sandra asked. "We had Terra, didn't we?"

"No, I mean biologically," Edward said. "Like maybe there was a reason why we weren't able to naturally have children. A reason why you were unable to give birth."

Sandra awkwardly let out a burst of laughter, which offended Edward.

"Edward, that has to be the dumbest thing I've ever heard," Sandra said. "Do you seriously believe that my natural cycle determines what kind of parent I would be?"

"Don't laugh at me, Sandra," Edward said. "I'm trying to make a point."

"Just go to bed, Edward," Sandra said. "You're drunk. You need to get some rest."

"Hey, don't send me away!" Edward insisted. "I've never been clearer. Maybe Terra ran away from us. I don't know. I'm still trying to come up with all these theories."

"Edward, stop! The liquor is making you insane," Sandra said.

"No, I'm serious!" Edward shouted as he slapped Sandra around the face.

Sandra covered her struck cheek and Edward walked back, horrified at what he had done. Both were in shock at what had just happened. Sandra cried, and all Edward could do was look on. He didn't know what to say. Would an apology be enough for hitting Sandra? Edward and Sandra had had arguments before, but there was nothing that had been as intense as this.

"Sandra, I'm…" Edward started to say, although he was not sure of what to say.

"Edward, please leave," Sandra said while she was crying.

Edward became even more surprised because Sandra had never asked him to leave the apartment before, but a moment later, he knew that he couldn't have blamed her. He had hit her. Edward had never hit a woman before, and he had never felt so guilty and disgusted with himself.

"Please, let me…" Edward tried to say, but Sandra shook her head, disinterested in what Edward had to say.

"Just go," Sandra said tearfully as she went up to her bedroom. Edward sat on the couch, still trying to understand what he had done in his drunken state.

Anton's aerocar parked in his usual spot, opposite the front door of his mansion. Anton got out of his aerocar and then helped Edward out, who was still drunk. Anton also got out a bag that Edward had brought along with him. It was a see-through suitcase containing Edward's clothes and other things of his. Anton opened the front door and walked in, while Edward stumbled behind.

"Thanks again for letting me stay here," Edward said.

"Please, don't worry about it," Anton said. "Andrew is shut off for the night, so I'll show you into the guest room."

"Great, thanks," Edward said. "By the way, don't suppose I could have another drink?"

"Oh no," Anton said. "I think it's best you stay off the liquor for a while."

"Oh, come on, I just want another glass," Edward said.

"No, Edward, no more alcohol for you," Anton persisted.

Edward then went into Anton's kitchen to help himself to another drink, but Anton quickly followed him. There was a struggle between the two of them as Edward craved another drink, as if he wasn't drunk enough already, but Anton was not going to let him have another drop. Eventually, Edward pushed Anton to the ground and he thudded against the kitchen table; a glass fell to the ground, breaking into so many pieces.

Thankfully, as glasses were able to do back then, the pieces automatically put themselves back together, although the cracks were shown. The cracks would've disappeared soon enough. Edward took a couple of steps back, just as he had when he'd struck Sandra, horrified by what he had done.

"Anton, I'm…" Edward spoke tearfully.

"Edward, it's okay," Anton said as he got back up.

"No, I'm truly sorry," Edward said.

"Edward, seriously, it's fine. I'm okay. Don't worry about it," Anton said as he then embraced Edward. "I know this is a very horrible situation for you."

Edward nodded in agreement while taking out his handkerchief from his jacket pocket to wipe away the tears from his eyes. Edward then asked, "Are you sure you're okay?"

"Trust me, I've been alive for over a hundred years and I've survived worse than this," Anton said with a smile, which drew a laugh from the two of them. "And do you know how I survived so much for so long?" Anton pointed at Edward, which drew another smile from Edward, but it was an awkward one. Edward didn't know how to react to any kind of flattery, especially after what he had done to Sandra. "Come, Edward, let's talk this out on the couch."

Edward and Anton then made their way to the living room, where there was only light at the end of the room where the couch and armchairs were. Edward sat on the couch, and after he poured a glass of water from a glass jug on one of the shelves, Anton sat next to him, giving the water to Edward.

"Edward, I gotta ask," Anton said. "When you went to Thomas O... What was his last name?"

"Uh, I think it's O'Brien or O'Reilly," Edward tried to remember. "I don't know, some Irish name."

"I'll call him Thomas Irish," Anton said, which drew another laugh from both of them. "Anyway, when you went to his place and when you punched him, you were drunk, weren't you?"

Edward nodded. "I also cursed in his home."

"Oh, that's nothing," Anton said. "I know it's a big deal to him and his family, but it's not something to be so remorseful for."

"I guess," Edward said. "I just had a feeling that they had something to do with Terra missing. I know they were out on bail after being arrested, but it's just... did I tell you how Thomas encountered Terra?"

"Don't think you did," Anton said. "What did he do?"

"He asked her to go to his house," Edward said.

"For some religious thing, right?" Anton asked.

"Yeah, some kind of gathering," Edward said. "One of the G-75s saw him with her. He wasn't arrested then as it didn't look like he was actually doing Terra any harm."

"But he approached her because she's your daughter," Anton said. "Okay, your foster daughter, but still, this is a guy who's always been against your work. I can imagine why you would have been suspicious."

"If the police mention Terra to me, I worry," Edward said.

"That's just parental instincts," Anton said. "Of course, you and Sandra were meant to have kids. Just because Sandra was unable to reproduce doesn't mean you guys would ever be bad parents. You knew what you said to Sandra was bullshit, right?"

"Yeah, I guess it was," Edward said. "You believe me about Thomas, right? He must have been involved, right?"

"I can't tell you," Anton said. "I don't know him or whatever happened to Terra. I remember congress actually campaigned to make religion illegal. That was back in 2292, a year after…"

"I got shot. Yeah, I remember that," Edward said. "I mean, the bullet only grazed me. Hey, let me ask you something; if the bullet actually hit me and if I died, do you think then that religion would've been made illegal?"

"Edward, the last thing I want to do is imagine you dead," Anton said. "I do understand your question, though. If that shooting had resulted in a fatality, maybe that campaign would've got more momentum, certainly from the media anyway. Unfortunately nobody can establish a direct link between religion and acts of terrorism, so religion couldn't just be declared illegal, otherwise this country would be seen as some kind of fascist state. Politics is complicated. There is no simple way to explain why certain decisions regarding this country and our society take place, especially with someone who is as wasted as you."

"Anton, come on, I'm not that bad," Edward said. "I only had…"

"Okay, okay," Anton said. "Anyway, there's a lot to consider if a president decided to ban something, like religion for instance. Members of congress argued that such a ban would contradict the libertarian foundations of this country. There is never a simple explanation in politics, but maintaining some of our history and tradition is important, especially if the world isn't what it used to be. We all know that religion in this country has gone down. What we have done with science has made people believe in what *is* instead of propaganda."

"Right." Edward said, unable to form a response to what Anton said. His drunken and grieving state prevented him from debating what Anton said. "Anyway, the night before Terra disappeared, we actually had an argument. It was about when she met Thomas."

"Didn't know you guys had an argument," Anton said. "I hope it wasn't serious."

"Yeah, Terra wouldn't open up about what happened on her way to school and what the G-75 saw. Sandra and I were so worried and all we wanted was for Terra to be okay."

"I can understand that."

"So, I raised my voice at Terra, asking her what happened. She was upset and went up to her room. I had never raised my voice at Terra before. She was always such a good girl. Then she told me that she was going over to Laura's place to study, which wasn't true, but I didn't know that at the time. Terra had never lied to me before. Maybe there's something else Terra had never told me."

"Again, I can't answer that."

"Part of me thinks that this is my fault. If I had never shouted at her, maybe she'd still be here."

"Edward, you can't blame yourself for this. Nobody could've known that this was going to happen, and I know you did all you could to protect her."

"Terra was also upset that we couldn't tell her who her real parents are. When we adopted her, we had no information on her birth family. The orphanage we adopted her from, a religious place, said that she was special."

"Of course, she's a great kid."

"No, not like that. They said that she was divine, miraculous and that she wasn't just full of life, she *was* life."

"Wow, that's pretty powerful."

"It sounds crazy, right? It's crazy saying it."

"I guess because you're drunk it would sound crazy, but no, all kids would be praised in that way. They're the most precious thing any human can have."

"Yeah, I get that."

"So, shall I show you to your room?" Anton said as he saw Edward yawning and stretching. Edward nodded, so they both got up off the couch. "You really need some rest, Edward. It's been a rough night, as I guess every night has been without Terra."

"Hey, uh, thanks for listening, Anton," Edward said.

"Don't worry about it," Anton said. "Also, let me suggest something: take some time off work. This whole thing isn't doing you any good and I think you could do with a sabbatical."

"I don't know," Edward said.

He had been so devoted to his job, the idea of him taking time off work was something he had never thought about. I had never spent a lot of time with him as he was often so busy working. I spent more time with Sandra, who would look after me while Edward was working.

"Look, you read about the Don Williams thing, right?" Anton said. "It's badly affecting the company, and I don't want something like that happening to Cox Industries. Take a sabbatical. I'm sure Natasha can run things while you're taking your time off."

"I guess I could do that," Edward said. "She is an amazing vice-president."

"Of course," Anton agreed. "Now, come on, let's get you to bed."

Anton and Edward walked up the stairs and Anton turned on the lights in the spare room, which was opposite Anton's bedroom. They said good night to each other, and they went into their separate rooms.

A Deal

King Deorege and Gemilin were sat on the bed in Deorege's room, both with their heads down in shame. Anton was there too, looking down on them.

"Once again, I know we have failed you, my Lord," Deorege said.

"You underestimated the girl and what she can do," Anton said. "Terra is the bearer of life. I mean, that's what they call her, but she is more powerful than you can imagine."

"Please, my Lord, I beg your forgiveness," Gemilin said with remorse.

"If I may say so," Deorege said, "if you had made yourself present from the very second we had Terra in our quarters, then…"

"Oh, so this is *my* fault, huh?" Anton asked back sharply, as he was close to reaching outrage. "Blaming your incompetence on me is a pretty low point for you guys. I don't know what other excuses you useless morons have got, but if you *seriously* expect an apology from me because I'm supposed to just show up in an instant like some fucking genie, then you're gonna be disappointed. I have other things to do, you know. I also have important business to take care of in other places.

At least I can handle my affairs and get things done, okay. I don't know how you people manage things over here, but maybe you can try being more responsible and more efficient. Do you think you can handle that?"

"Yes, I'm so sorry, your lordship," Gemilin grovelled. "If I may ask, sire, what is a genie?"

"It doesn't matter," Anton said. "The point is that I just want you to do as I had asked."

"Of course, sire," Deorege said as he grovelled too. "I do hope you can forgive us, my lord."

"Okay, don't call me 'my Lord' or any kind of royal bullshit," Anton said. "It's just weird. Just call me Anton, all right? Looking at how you two have messed up, I can see why we don't have royalty on Earth any more."

"What will you do now, Master?" Deorege asked.

"Okay, again, please don't call me stuff like that, it's really weird," Anton said. "Don't worry about me. I have a plan, however complex it might be; it's what must now be done. What did you do with the man, or thing, that helped her escape?"

Deorege and Gemilin stood up and Anton followed them as they walked out of the bedroom and along the corridor, where they stopped at a statue of Ohlakan.

"Not a bad piece of work," Anton said. "I do appreciate good artwork. How many more of these things are there?"

"Many," Deorege said. "These are our treasures. Unfortunately, there are certain subjects of the Aurelian population that are treasonous, so what you see in front of you is a new sense of worth that we have found for them."

"Interesting," Anton said.

"Do you like our treasures, Anton?" Gemilin asked.

"I do," Anton said, as he laid his eyes on a pair of emerald gauntlets hanging on the wall. "May I try something?"

Anton picked up the gauntlets and put them on his hands. He then punched the head of the statue of Ohlakan with rage, sending it flying off his body. Deorege and Gemilin stepped back with fear as Anton kept thrashing the statue of Ohlakan, and then he eventually picked up the pieces and threw them across the corridor. Deorege and Gemilin looked on at the broken statue, and then Anton took hold of the gauntlets and sat on the floor, trying to catch his breath from brutally breaking the statue of Ohlakan.

"Are you... okay?" Deorege asked awkwardly.

"I'm fine," Anton said as he was still trying to catch his breath, having put so much force and energy into breaking the statue. "I'm sorry that you had to see that, but as you can see, I hate traitors as much as you do."

Deorege nodded his head in agreement.

"You said that Terra didn't come here alone, right?" Anton said.

"We've taken her companion prisoner," Gemilin said. "Another traitor by the name of Vagus."

"Right," Anton said. "I've never met this Vagus before. He's a traveller, right?"

"Yes," Deorege said. "As my dear sister has said, we've taken him prisoner."

"I'd like to meet him," Anton said.

Deorege hesitated before he said, "Of course."

Deorege and Gemilin escorted Anton along the corridor and they reached a spiral stairway going upwards. They all went upstairs and reached a wooden door covered in vines and leaves. Deorege opened the door to a small room and they saw Vagus in the corner, covered in blood, his clothes reduced to rags. There was nothing in the room. Just a stony floor and walls with a window looking out at Aurelia. The view was of the mountains and wasn't as beautiful as the other end of Aurelia.

"Give us a moment," Anton said to Deorege and Gemilin. They closed the door behind them and waited outside.

Anton approached Vagus, which scared Vagus initially as while he had been kept prisoner, he had been so isolated that he was not used to any kind of company other than seeing Deorege or Gemilin.

"You don't know me, but I'm a traveller like you," Anton said. "I have to tell you that you look like shit."

Vagus didn't respond. He just stayed sat in the corner with his head down.

"So, the king and his sister, they're pretty weird, right?" Anton said.

"That's one phrase," Vagus said. "There's many I could use to describe them."

"Of course," Anton said. "I now see why we don't have royalty on Earth."

Again, Vagus didn't respond. He wasn't in the mood for humour as Anton seemed to be light-hearted about the situation.

"You have to admire the view from here," Anton said as he looked out of the window.

"The only thing I see is immorality," Vagus said. "I knew something was wrong with this place. Now I see what I have suspected all this time."

"Right, you mean because of the siblings…" Anton said.

"Yes," Vagus interrupted as he didn't want to think about Deorege and Gemilin as lovers any more. He was sickened after seeing them kiss and imagining what else they could have done.

"That's pretty messed up," Anton said. "You've been to Earth, right?" Vagus nodded, before Anton got close to Vagus and asked, "What do you know about a Thomas O'Brien?"

Vagus looked up, stunned. How could Anton have known about Father Thomas? What did he want with him?

"Shall I take that stunned silence as a yes?" Anton asked.

Vagus, still stunned, eventually answered, "I'm afraid I don't."

Anton's face then looked incensed, and he punched Vagus so hard in the face that a tooth was knocked out. Blood then poured out of his nose.

"You know, I've been to so many worlds, and you have no idea how many ways that I have been lied to," Anton said. "So, Vagus, you must have been through a lot of pain already. Am I going to have to inflict some more on you?"

Vagus didn't say anything. He didn't want to betray Father Thomas, especially when it seemed to him that Anton wanted to harm him. Anton decided to pace up and down the room instead of beating Vagus again.

"You know, I'm actually a good guy," Anton said. "I have friends on Earth who are concerned for Terra's disappearance. They love her very much and they are so worried for her. I'm sure you would be if you had kids too, right?"

Again, Vagus did not reply.

"I know Terra was at Thomas' house the night she disappeared," Anton said. "I'm guessing that he lives out in the suburbs, the poorer area. You were there too, right?"

Vagus remained silent, and his silence indicated to Anton that he was there that night as Anton had suggested. Anton became enraged again and kicked Vagus once in the face, and once Vagus was lying down on the ground in pain, Anton proceeded to kick his stomach.

"You're not going to tell me where Terra is now, are you?"

Vagus coughed after Anton had kicked him, and once he caught his breath, he said, "I don't know. She was here."

"Now, that was honesty," Anton said. "That wasn't hard, was it?"

Vagus just kept coughing, struggling to get up, and then Anton left the room, closing the door behind him. Deorege and Gemilin were there, and they escorted Anton down the stairs.

"What did you speak with Vagus about?" Deorege asked.

"I needed some answers about Terra," Anton said. "I must now take my leave."

"Farewell then, good sir," Gemilin said.

"Our apologies again for not detaining Terra for you," Deorege said.

"Don't worry about it," Anton said as he embraced them. "I'll see to it that you are compensated for your efforts," he said and then walked out of the Opraso.

***

Back in the cave in the mountains in Aurelia, Malomira was crying. He had been greatly depressed since Vagus and me had been captured. They were the only two people to have understood him and the horrifying truth about Deorege and Gemilin, and Malomira's betrayal.

He was desperate to find out the fate of his two children from the affair he had with Incurtea. Malomira couldn't come out of the cave though, because of how disfigured he was. He would have scared the citizens of Aurelia, therefore nobody would have believed his side of the story. Malomira was in a constant state of sorrow. It seemed that nothing could cure him of the deep depression that he was going through.

Then Malomira heard a sound that he very rarely heard — footsteps — and they were getting louder as they drew closer. A man emerged, and this scared Malomira, who had been so deprived of company for a long time, other than the company he had with me and Vagus. Malomira cowered away, all the way to the back of the cave.

"Hello? Who's there?" Malomira asked in a panic.

"Relax," the man said, who turned out to be Anton, as he approached him in a calming manner. "I'm a good guy."

"Who are you?" Malomira asked, still panicking.

"Let's just say that I'm your soulmate," Anton said, which made Malomira uncomfortable. "Not in that way; I'm straight, believe me. What I meant is that I'm someone who is just like you."

"How do you mean?" Malomira asked as he started to calm down.

"I'm a man betrayed by someone I thought I could trust," Anton said. "Unfortunately, it turned out that this trust was misplaced. Does that sound familiar?"

Malomira was starting to warm to Anton. How could he have understood what Malomira had been going through, especially as he said that he had been in Malomira's situation himself?

"It all started years ago," Malomira said. "He caught me with his wife, my beloved Incurtea."

"So, you had an affair?" Anton asked.

"It wasn't just an affair," Malomira said. "We were in love. Our love was forbidden, yes, but it was so perfect and true. My brother could never have loved her like I could."

"So, your brother did this to you?" Anton said in reference to Malomira's disfigurement.

"Yes," Malomira answered tearfully. "He killed my beloved, took away our two children and left me here in exile."

"I didn't realize that you had kids," Anton said. "Whatever happened to them?"

"I don't know," Malomira said even more tearfully. "I don't know if they're dead or alive. I'd give anything to see them again or find out where they are."

"I bet. I can't blame you," Anton said. "I really wish I could help you there. I really do. There may be another way I could help you though."

"Help me?" Malomira said, sceptical of Anton's proposal. Malomira had given up on any hope that he could ever be helped. "How?"

"There might be a way I can restore you back to your previous form," Anton said, as he reached into his pocket and got out a flask. "You see, I like to think of myself as a bit of a culinary visionary. I know the plants here have certain effects, so I thought that maybe I would mix them with certain ingredients from my world."

"Oh?" Malomira said, intrigued as Anton handed the flask to him. "What is this?"

"I haven't given it a name yet," Anton said. "Maybe let's call this salvation."

Malomira was unsure about the drink in the flask, but he had nothing to lose, so he took a swig out of the flask, and gagged immediately. The taste was so bitter and sour. Anton then tipped the flask back into Malomira's mouth, ensuring that he would drink the whole flask. Anton then took the flask back once it was empty, but Malomira kept gagging and coughing from the drink.

Eventually, Malomira started to feel a burning sensation coming from his face. He felt his cheeks, and they were so hot. The burning feeling grew, and it began to feel painful for Malomira. There was a red glow coming from Malomira's face. Anton didn't react; he just looked on as Malomira put his hands to his face. He was in such pain and agony, so much so that he didn't notice the shape of his face changing. His face was much less wide and didn't carry as much weight as a moment before. In fact, his face had been restored back to what it was before he was disfigured by his brother. Malomira had to keep feeling his face as he couldn't believe that the shape was different. There weren't any puddles or anything that would have shown Malomira's reflection, so Anton took a pocket-sized mirror out of his jacket and handed it to him.

Malomira couldn't believe his reflection. His face was back to normal. He gazed into the mirror for a few seconds, as he found it so hard to believe. It was a dream come true for him to have himself back to his true form. Yet it was a reality. Malomira laughed and cried with delight.

"Was this the best drink you ever had?" Anton asked, who shared a smile with Malomira.

"This…" Malomira was lost for words. He was still so overjoyed. "My face, it's… I will forever be in your debt."

"It's the least I can do," Anton said. "After all, I want you to do me a favour."

"Anything," Malomira said enthusiastically. "What do you need me to do?"

Anton reached into his jacket pocket and got out a HoriGun. HoriGuns had a lot of different functions. They were firearms that could shoot electricity to shock and paralyze the target, or a laser beam that could kill. They were incredibly advanced weapons, especially as there was a small screen at the front allowing the user to choose their target. They were mainly owned by the US government. Anton handed the gun to Malomira.

"You've never seen one of those before, have you?" Anton said. "Look at the picture on the front and aim. If you tap on the picture, you'll find the answer you'll be looking for."

Malomira held the gun, and Anton guided his hand to make him aim for a vacant spot in the cave. Malomira pulled the trigger and a laser beam shot out of the gun, causing a minor explosion at where Malomira was aiming. Malomira was amazed. There were no firearms in Aurelia, so the gun was new to him and he couldn't believe the impact that the blast made.

"Is this… magic?" Malomira asked.

"You could say that," Anton said. "In my world, we have a lot of devices like this which you could say are magic. But no, it's just advanced. More advanced than anything this world has to offer. I mean, you pretty much have just swords, shields and shit like that, right?"

"Can I have this?" Malomira asked.

"Oh, of course," Anton said. "Let me just give you a tutorial, and then I want you to do something for me."

"What do you want me to do?" Malomira asked.

"I want you to do what you've always wanted to do," Anton said. "I want you to end your brother's rule here and take his place."

Anton reached out his hand and Malomira kissed it, agreeing to Anton's request, excited about the prospect of finally seeking revenge against his brother who had betrayed him in the worst possible way.

Perfection

As soon as I arrived back at the Upper World, I got off the skywhale and Mother rushed to embrace me. I embraced her back. It was a real relief to be away from those freaks in Aurelia. Father and a Tyrannosaurus were there too, and then the Tyrannosaurus bowed down to me. I stroked its snout and it moaned with satisfaction. It brought a smile out of me, as I always thought that it would be vicious and dangerous, but it wasn't a monster. It was just an animal, even if it was a big animal, like me, and everyone and every other creature around me and around other worlds too.

"Terra," Mother began to speak. "I know you have suffered much. I didn't know why Aurelia really called for you. Vagus has been a trusted ally."

"It wasn't Vagus' fault," I insisted.

"No, of course not," Mother agreed. "Vagus would never betray us, but he has been betrayed before, and even now he's been deceived once again."

"So, shouldn't we go and help him?" I asked.

"Vagus is not our responsibility," Father said. "That is not contempt. You are our responsibility, Terra, and we will always do what we must to protect you. We cannot interfere with the will of other worlds, unless one

293

of our own needs help. It is up to other forces to save Vagus now."

I was disappointed but I understood. Well, kind of. I mean, if they had that kind of power, I guess the Type I wouldn't have happened on Earth.

"So why was I really wanted on Aurelia?" I asked.

"It was a trap," Father said. "We don't know who set it exactly, but the intentions of your visit were different to what we had believed them to be."

"Why would they trap me?" I asked.

"You have a special power, Terra," Mother said. "There are outside forces, evil forces, that will do whatever they can to obtain it somehow."

"Is that why Deorege and Gemilin tried to trap me?" I asked.

"Perhaps it was them, or perhaps it was someone else," Mother said. "We wish we could know for certain who did this, but what matters right now, Terra, is that you're safe."

Mother and I embraced again, although I was still curious about why exactly Vagus and I were enticed to Aurelia. Did someone else put Deorege and Gemilin up to it? I didn't know and I didn't think there was any way of knowing at that moment, but all I could do was trust that Mother and Father would protect me. I was also worried for Vagus. Would Deorege and Gemilin kill him? I wasn't sure, but there wasn't much that I could do. I wished that they could've helped Vagus too, but he wasn't an inhabitant of the Upper World, just a visitor, and a kind visitor too. Should I have tried to save Vagus with Ohlakan when I had the chance? I was then starting to feel guilty, but I tried to not let it consume me. Maybe Vagus was already dead by the time I escaped, but I wasn't sure. I really hoped that he was still alive. Maybe that was all I could have done, just hope.

***

Back in the dungeon, Mulieris sat in the corner, looking up, wondering if she would ever get out. Nobody had mentioned if and when she would be released. She just knew that she was going to be in there for a long time and that neither Son, Father or Mother would come and speak to her and see if she was rehabilitated. Mulieris just kept thinking of Hominem and the hurt that she had caused him. He was so distraught and betrayed when he visited her, and that guilt stayed with Mulieris. As long as she was in the dungeon, that guilt was trapped inside with her. A Deinonychus was stood guarding the door. It stared at her with such intensity, always on the alert for the slightest movement.

Then a hissing sound was heard by both Mulieris and the Deinonychus. Mulieris sat up and stared in the direction of the sound, and then the Deinonychus bent its knees and looked ready to pounce. A spiral of ash and dust then emerged and the hissing sound became a long, exhalated breath. The Deinonychus started to snarl, as a shadow emerged within the spiral, and then the breathing started saying "Mulieris". This made Mulieris stand up, and she was completely on edge. She wasn't sure what the spiral and shadow was and was so stunned that she couldn't bring herself to ask or to look away from the figure. The Deinonychus was still poised to attack the shadow, whatever it was. The shadow stepped forward, and then appeared to blow a kiss at the Deinonychus. The creature then stepped back and yelped out in pain. The Deinonychus seemed to be struggling to breathe, and then it vomited on the floor. It then lost balance, unable to stand upright and looked like it was going to fall over. Eventually, the Deinonychus fell with its face in its vomit, stopped moving and its body fell, lifeless.

The figure stepped out of the spiral and it turned out to be Femos. Mulieris wasn't sure how to feel about Femos' arrival. She was certainly surprised, but she didn't know whether it was a good surprise or bad surprise. She was just so enthralled with Femos' arrival that she couldn't process it and couldn't decide how she should feel about it.

"Oh, you poor thing," Femos said as she approached Mulieris. "Incarcerated for being free. This is such a cruel world, isn't it?"

"What have you come for?" Mulieris asked.

"For you, my precious one," Femos said as she sat down and put her arms around Mulieris. "How could freedom make you prisoner? Look at you, in a dungeon just for wanting what should be your right."

"Mother and Father know what's best," Mulieris said defiantly. "They know this world, this life, is best for me."

"But do *you* know what's best for you?" Femos asked.

"I…" Mulieris struggled to answer that question. She was conflicted. She was so used to meeting the needs of Hominem and being under the instructions of Mother and Father that she never once thought of herself. Mother and Father were protecting her and Hominem, of course, but she didn't know that.

If only she had known in that moment.

"So why is Mulieris in jail?" I asked Mother.

"She's locked up for betraying the laws of the Upper World," Mother answered.

"What do you mean?" I asked, still curious.

"Mulieris is a spirited woman," Mother said. "Her heart is warm and loving and is bound with Hominem, but her mind is curious."

"Isn't it good to be curious?" I asked. "Is it so wrong to want to know so much? I mean, I wanted to learn so much at school."

"Terra, to learn is a wonderful thing," Mother said. "You must understand that Father and I care deeply for the ones we create. Every rule and regulation in place for everyone here, including Mulieris, is to protect them. Mulieris is curious and there are things outside of this world that she doesn't understand, and that she *mustn't* understand."

"Like what?" I asked. "Are they things that I know of already?"

"I'm sure you have learnt of war and temptation in your world," Mother said to me, to which I nodded. "Mulieris' mind is not just curious, but delicate too. If she knew of those many horrible things, what if she surrendered to them?"

"So, did Mulieris try to escape or something?"

"She rode one of the celuti out of here. If she had got far, she could've been exposed to such terrible things. She is in the dungeon, and that is for her protection."

"Will she be released?"

"One day, hopefully. We will assess her and hopefully she will be reunited with Hominem again. We don't wish to imprison her forever. Our wish is that all our creations, like Mulieris, will have learnt what they did wrong and vow never to repeat the mistakes that they made. There is no flawless mortal, Terra. Can one ever truly create perfection?"

"I guess…" I began to say, but then I thought about it. What was truly perfect? I wasn't sure. Maybe perfection only existed in our minds, like only we define what is perfect. "I guess we can view something as perfect but not everyone else will. Maybe perfection is subjective, like through our own perspective."

"Every mind is unique, Terra," Mother said. "Even if you agree with another on occasion, you will always form your own mindset and your own perspective."

What was my idea of perfection? Perhaps being with Laura, but in the Upper World, my true home. New York was fine too. I had lived there all my life. Even if I hadn't been with my real parents, I loved being with Edward and Sandra too. They did care for me, after all, and I should be grateful for that.

Suddenly, I heard the Tyrannosaurus roar out of distress.

Mother and I jumped, as maybe it was alerting us to something serious.

Mother and I ran to the Tyrannosaurus as it was clearly in despair. Then the Parasaurolophus bellowed, and then other dinosaurs made distressing sounds. Mother's face was one of sheer terror, as if something awful was happening.

"What's going on, Mother?" I asked.

Mother, whose facial expression was still horrified, replied, "Terra, come with me."

Mother grabbed my hand and she ran and pulled me through into the forest, gathering speed. All the dinosaurs were panicking and were making loud, frantic sounds. I didn't know exactly what was going on, but I sensed that it wasn't good.

We then approached Quercus Alba, who was also confused and ridden with anxiety just like I was.

"Mother," Quercus Alba said. "I sense your despair."

"Quercus Alba, please protect Terra," Mother said. "There is a presence here, and it cannot reach Terra."

"Of course, Mother," Quercus Alba said as he closed his eyes and then he forced the growth of tree branches from the ground. Mother and I stood back as the sticks grew up to my height, forming some kind of shelter.

"Mother, what's going on?" I asked.

"Terra, please stay in there," Mother said. "I will come for you, please just keep yourself safe."

"It's okay, Terra," Quercus Alba said. "My branches will shelter you from this. Mother will return for you."

I got inside the shelter and then more branches grew in front on me, to form a door to hide me from whatever the threat was, little did I know about it at the time.

The dinosaurs in the valley were visibly in a panic, with many roaring in despair, running around in different directions and some waving their tails, lashing onto the ground. Mother frantically ran towards the Caelum Palatium, as did other angels from the village too. She saw Father outside of the Caelum Palatium and she ran up to him.

"I sense a presence, Father," Mother said to him.

"I don't know what it is, Mother," Father said.

"Is it from the Underworld?" Mother asked. Father paused as if to think about the answer. "Is it Terra they want?"

"I cannot be sure," Father said. "They might be after someone."

Hominem then ran up to Mother and Father.

"Mother, Father, where is Mulieris?" Hominem asked, breathless.

"She's still in the dungeon, Hominem," Father said.

"Father, the presence! Is it after Mulieris?" Mother asked, which then brought alarm and realization upon Father and Hominem.

"My sweet, you must have hopes and dreams, don't you?" Femos asked Mulieris as they were sat down against the wall together, closely next to each other.

"I want to see," Mulieris said.

"See?" Femos asked. "But you can see, can't you, girl? You're not blind, are you?"

"No, that's not what I mean," Mulieris said. "When you see the same thing for all your life, then it just makes sight meaningless. When you're stuck in one place, with the same people, then all your senses are so mundane."

"That was why you rode the celuti, wasn't it?" Femos said.

Mulieris nodded and then she started to cry, through a combination of frustration and guilt. "But I don't want to hurt them, and I don't want to hurt

301

Hominem. I love Hominem, he's good to me. Mother and Father are good to me."

"They are so good to you that you wish to escape?" Femos asked.

"It's not…" Mulieris said tearfully. "It's not… No! I mean…"

Mulieris wasn't sure how to answer the question. She was so conflicted that she couldn't decide whether she wanted to remain in the Upper World or leave it. Her heart yearned for a chance to explore a new world, somewhere outside of the Upper World, but her heart also bore the love of Hominem, Mother, Father, and the Upper World. The indecision that Femos was feeding Mulieris was insufferable. Mulieris had a dilemma that tore into her.

If she stayed in the Upper World, she would be doing what was best for everyone else.

If she left the Upper World, she would be doing what was best for her.

"An opportunity awaits you, my child," Femos said.

"What kind of opportunity?" Mulieris asked.

"I can take you to new places," Femos said. "Just like those you desire."

"New places?" Mulieris asked with great intrigue.

Femos presented a handful of nasinata seeds to Mulieris. The seeds were glowing, still as red as blood. Mulieris gasped in amazement as she stared at the glowing seeds.

"What are they?" Mulieris asked.

"These beauties before you will take you to wherever your heart desires," Femos said. "They will taste sweeter than you can imagine."

"Really? How?" Mulieris asked.

"The taste within those seeds is the start," Femos said. "It's the start of a new beginning."

Then the sounds of footsteps came from outside the door. Mulieris panicked, but Femos remained calm.

"Come on, dear girl," Femos said. "Those seeds will take you to the freedoms you seek. If you don't eat them, then you are doomed to be prisoner forever."

Mulieris' heart was beating rapidly and then there was a thumping sound coming from the door. She had to make a very difficult choice. Eat the seeds and leave the Upper World, or not eat them and continue living her safe life in the Upper World, free of the risk that leaving the Upper World would bring. It appeared that there was an attempt to break the door down, so it seemed that Mulieris didn't have much time to make her choice.

The thumping sound from the other side of the dungeon door was a Pachycephalosaurus using the bony tip of its head to try and break down the door. It kept running and charging towards the door. However, the door wouldn't budge. It was made from solid stone and it was locked. A Deinonychus was also trying to break the door down too, also running and charging towards it. Still nothing.

"Go, my aurussae!" Mother urged as she stood alongside Father and an anxious, panicky Hominem.

"Oh, Mulieris!" Hominem said with anguish. "I wish I could've done more to protect you."

"Stay calm, Hominem," Father said with his arm around Hominem's shoulder. "We'll get to her. I promise."

Hominem wished he could believe Father. His fear and doubt paralyzed him. He stared at the Pachycephalosaurus and Deinonychus trying to break the door down. He couldn't look away. He was petrified for Mulieris and fearing the worst.

Then Pachycephalosaurus barged into the door and it became unstuck.

Hominem ran straight through.

Mulieris was dead.

She had eaten the nasinata seeds and her spirit had been extracted from her body and sent into the Underworld with Femos.

Hominem screamed with horror, while Mother and Father gasped in shock as they also saw the lifeless body of the Deinonychus that was guarding Mulieris. The other Deinonychus screeched in despair as it saw its fellow dinosaur was dead.

Hominem rushed over to Mulieris, having no idea that she had died. He tried to wake her, but it was no good. Her body was lifeless. He screamed again and was inconsolable as he then sat in the corner of the room, crying. He had no idea what happened or how she died. Mother went over to Hominem, who was crying uncontrollably. She sat next to him and put her arm around him. Hominem didn't react. He was clearly traumatized and shaken.

"Hominem, I don't know what happened," Mother said. Hominem didn't reply or look at her. He just tucked his head down onto his knees, not wanting to engage with anybody.

"Lucifer must have done this," Father said. "That spirit that Mulieris saw, that must have been his doing, somehow. I don't know how, but we must call upon the Krygurra to reinforce our security."

"Can we bring back Mulieris?" Hominem asked Father. "Is there a way?"

"Hominem, my child, we cannot reverse death," Father said. "We must never corrupt nature's laws, however cruel they may be."

"But she was murdered," Hominem said. "We must do something."

"What's done is done," Mother said. "We have never wished death or cruelty on Mulieris or you, Hominem. Reversing death is forbidden."

"But why, Mother?" Hominem asked tearfully.

"Nature, my child," Mother said. "Resurrection would corrupt everything we've created and would cause destruction. I know it's hard to understand but reversing and forcing nature will only bring carnage and anarchy. I hope you will understand, Hominem."

Son entered the room. He knew of what had happened so wasn't really shocked when he saw the Deinonychus and Mulieris dead. He approached Hominem.

"Hominem, I'm sorry about what has happened," Son said. "You know that I cared about Mulieris deeply and I feel your horror, my friend."

Hominem then looked up at Son and his tears started to dry up, but his eyes were then filled with rage. Hominem started to tremble and then he got up.

"You cared for Mulieris?" Hominem asked. "We trusted you with a secret."

"He only did this to protect you both," Father said in Son's defence. Son nodded with agreement.

"Mulieris would have still been alive if you had just kept our secret," Hominem said, trying to control his temper.

"Please, Hominem, I care about you both." Son said. "Mother, Father and I only did what was best. I'm as sad as you are, Hominem, please trust me. We will call the Krygurra for help and we will work for the safety of the Upper World."

"Trust you?" Hominem said, as his resentment grew. A fire was starting to brew within him. He clenched his fists in anger and glared at Son with fury in his eyes.

Then Hominem charged towards Son, knocking him over. He then threw punches at Son's face and kicked him in the stomach. Hominem had never fought anybody before, so his fighting style seemed very amateurish. It took everyone by surprise, as Hominem was normally peaceful, as he was with Mulieris.

The Deinonychus then charged at Hominem, trying to protect Son. Hominem then punched the Deinonychus in the nose, and then it slashed across Hominem's stomach, ripping his toga, leaving bloodied scars. Hominem was undeterred however, as he barged into the Deinonychus, knocking it over, and then he went for Son again.

"Enough!" Father shouted as he stretched out his arm, and then a strong gust of wind blew Hominem away and knocked him over against the wall. Son was in pain, with blood trickling down the side of his face. The Deinonychus then got up and snarled at Hominem, ready to attack him. Mother then glanced at the Deinonychus, and gave it a stern look, causing the dinosaur to back down.

Father then marched furiously towards Hominem. "We only wanted to protect you, and Mulieris too. This is how you repay us!"

"She's dead," Hominem said, as tears emerged. "Mulieris is dead!"

"We can see that she's perished!" Father shouted, as he then started to cry too. "We all loved Mulieris. She wanted a life of peace, and you start causing a war!"

Mother then walked up to Hominem, with her face still stern. "What you did was against everything our

Mulieris lived for," Mother said. "What will she think of your act of war?"

Hominem just looked down, and just repeated tearfully, "She's dead."

"I thought you were a good child," Father said, still welling up but still furious. "We provided you with the best life you and Mulieris could live. Of course, we would never wish any of you two to cease. Now when I look at you, I see Lucifer!"

Those words were damning for Father to say, and anybody to hear. Hominem tried to calm down. He wanted to beat Son again but knew that he couldn't. He had no choice but to stand down and face the severe punishment coming his way.

"We will need three Terrungu to watch you," Father said. "If you consider yourself still worthy of the Upper World, you will remain in the dungeon before we command your release. If you object, then you will be cast into the Underworld like Lucifer."

Hominem didn't argue. He knew he couldn't win and couldn't go against him. Two more Deinonychus entered the room and they stood on either side of the door. The other Deinonychus just stood by him. Father, Mother and Son, who eventually managed to get up while being in pain, left the dungeon, leaving Hominem alone with the three dinosaurs.

Outcasts

Meanwhile, back in Aurelia, four polifara guards dragged Vagus to King Deorege's bedroom, where Deorege and Gemilin were waiting. They were both sat on the bed, close beside each other. Vagus' clothes were ripped, and his face was covered with bruises and scars. The polifara dropped Vagus in front of Deorege and Gemilin. Vagus grunted in pain as he thudded onto the floor. The polifara then left the room.

Deorege then got up off the bed and approached Vagus.

"Well, Vagus, I suppose we are now to find a new use for you," Deorege said.

Vagus didn't respond. He continued to stay down in pain.

"We are still full of sorrow that your friend Terra has gone," Gemilin said.

"She escaped," Vagus said. "She had to."

"Of course, you would stand up for Terra, wouldn't you?" Deorege said. "A special, beautiful girl she is too. The things that she could do, she truly is Mother's daughter."

"You lied," Vagus said. "You tricked me."

"But how else are we to stand before Terra?" Gemilin said. "We were ordered to bring her here to Aurelia."

"Ordered?" Vagus asked as he stood up, struggling to do so because of the pain and trying to maintain his balance.

"By a friend of ours," Deorege said. "A traveller, just like you."

Vagus gasped in shock and then said, "He... he..." Vagus struggled to put the words together, as the person they were referring to was Anton, who wanted information about Thomas O'Brien. Vagus then said, "He wanted information."

"Yes, he was quite anxious to meet you," Deorege said. "He was indeed very curious about a friend of yours. Being a traveller, you must have friends in all sorts of places, mustn't you?"

Vagus didn't reply.

"Now what to do with you?" Deorege said. "A man of your wisdom could be so useful."

"You are a treasure, like your friend Ohlakan," Gemilin said. "You would make a great monument, just like Ohlakan was."

"Was?" Vagus asked, worried about Gemilin speaking about Ohlakan in the past tense.

"Ah, we forgot to mention," Deorege said. "I regret to inform you that your dear friend Ohlakan has sadly perished."

Vagus then knelt on the floor with his head in his hands, devastated. Vagus had endured so much pain but hearing that Ohlakan had died was such a huge blow to him. Tears started to roll down Vagus' bloodied face as he grieved for his friend Ohlakan. Vagus then let out a scream, but only briefly. Vagus was normally very calm and collected, but he had never experienced this amount of pain before, both physical and psychological.

"Yes, you see our friend, Master Anton, was rather careless," Gemilin said. "He has a bit of a temper, you see. You know that, don't you? Anyway, he was rather clumsy when he encountered Ohlakan and that lead to your dear friend's death."

Vagus fell into a deep silence. He was too devastated to respond.

"You must be wracked with grief right now," Deorege said. "Ohlakan was a dear citizen of Aurelia, and a dear friend of yours too. He will be missed by all of us." Deorege then bent down and put both his hands on either side of Vagus' face. "Now, what better way to honour Ohlakan than to reacquaint the two of you."

Then gunshots were heard from outside the room, which grabbed everyone's attention, especially Deorege and Gemilin as they never had any guns in Aurelia and the sound of gunshots was very strange to them. Deorege immediately stood upright and rushed to his bedside table, where he picked up a dagger and held it out, ready to use.

"What demon is this?" Gemilin asked.

Deorege didn't answer. He was still stunned and prepared to attack whatever unforeseen opponent this was.

Then the door swung open and Malomira emerged, still with his face restored, drawing a gasp from everyone. Deorege stepped back in disbelief, seeing his brother return from exile. Malomira held the gun that was given to him by Anton, pointing it at Deorege.

"No, your face, I…" Deorege said in disbelief.

"Do you know how many years I've waited to see you again?" Malomira asked. "And with my face restored, I would have treasured this reunion."

"How, brother?" Deorege asked.

"A friend from another world helped me," Malomira said. "Never found out his name, but he was like me, cast out from the world he knew."

"Is it him, my Deorege?" Gemilin asked, referring to Anton. "The demon who asked for Terra?"

Deorege then thought about it and came to the realization that Anton had betrayed him. "Because we failed to deliver Terra to him," Deorege said. "This must be our punishment."

"Where is Terra?" Malomira asked. "Did you kill her?"

"No, she got away," Vagus said. "She's safe now."

"Oh, Vagus, what have they done to you?" Malomira said. "I will help aid your recovery."

"Brother, what is this weapon you carry?" Gemilin asked.

"It's called a gun," Malomira said. "It's very effective, as I defeated your no-faced guards. Do you recognize it, Vagus?"

"Yes," Vagus said. "It's very dangerous, Malomira, so be careful."

"Vagus, these people are going to kill you," Malomira said. "They were family to me once, but the day you poisoned my face and made me an outcast was when you were no longer brother and sister to me."

"Please, brother, we beg for mercy," Gemilin said. "We beg for your forgiveness."

Malomira laughed. "Where was your mercy?" he asked. "And where was your forgiveness when you did those things to me?"

"Brother, we were fools, both of us," Deorege said. "Now, brother, please put the weapon down. Don't be a fool, now."

Malomira hesitated and rejected their pleas as he then shot Gemilin in the stomach.

"Sister!" Deorege cried as he rushed to Gemilin. She screamed in pain and she collapsed onto the floor, as blood was spilling from her midriff. Malomira then shot her in the chest. Deorege held Gemilin, but she was slowly dying. Deorege cried as he saw Gemilin losing life. He kissed her forehead and then on the lips, still crying.

"Were you in *love*?" Malomira asked with disgust. "Or did your morality die with my beloved Incurtea?"

"She was my beloved!" Deorege screamed at Malomira as he then stood back up. "You took her from me! And now you take away my Gemilin, our sister!"

"She is no sister any more!" Malomira shouted. "And you are no longer my brother!"

"But why, brother?" Deorege asked. "Why Incurtea? Why nobody else?"

"I was in love!" Malomira said. "Not that you would understand love, you vile specimen. Casting aside your own brother, and my children. What have you done with them?"

"We banished them, but I know not of their present surroundings," Deorege said. "We didn't kill them."

"But why banish them?" Malomira said. "They're children, innocent, defenceless children. How could you have abandoned them?"

"Because I saw you and Incurtea in them," Deorege said. "All they did was remind me of the pain and heartbreak I went through. I couldn't even look at them, and I'm sorry, brother, but I couldn't."

"Your humanity has ceased since that day," Malomira said. "You are no brother of mine. You are no man."

"And yet you slay our sister," Deorege said. "You betrayed your own brother with his wife. And you plan to kill me too? Where is your humanity?"

"Maybe I have no humanity left," Malomira said. "I never dreamt the day that I would be able to return, with your polifara at your protection. Now I hold this gun in my hand, I now think of what I'd do to you if we reacquaint ourselves."

"And what do you plan to do, brother?" Deorege said. "You have our sister's death on your conscious, and you plan to have mine, don't you? I have failed you, brother. All those years of idolizing my older brother have been in vain. We are both sinners, brother. My heart broke so much I sought solace in our sister, then we were in love. We couldn't help ourselves, brother. When you and Incurtea betrayed me, I lost myself. I lost all sense of right and wrong. I trusted Gemilin, my younger sister, and she was there for me when I needed someone. Now you've killed our sister, I don't fear death. Malomira, you have my permission to do what you will. In death, I will reunite with Incurtea and Gemilin."

Malomira then shot Deorege in the head. He walked up to his corpse and then bent down to get a look at his dead face. He felt a satisfaction at getting a closer look at his brother's dead body. He then turned to Vagus, who had looked onwards at their conflict and was relieved but also saddened, as he was a very peaceful person and never took any pleasure at witnessing the suffering of others.

"My friend, are you okay?" Malomira asked Vagus as he approached him.

"I..." Vagus coughed and then said, "I'm sorry you did that."

"Why must you apologize? Malomira asked. "My brother and sister are both traitors. You saw what became of me, because of what Deorege did?"

"Of course, and I know the pain you felt," Vagus said. "To be made an outcast by your family must have been dreadful."

"Yes, very dreadful," Malomira said. "You and Terra weren't repulsed by me, by what I became, and I will be grateful for that, as I am grateful for Terra's safety."

"Of course," Vagus said.

"You must rest, Vagus," Malomira said. "I will find you medicine to aid your healing."

"Thank you, Malomira," Vagus said.

Then a purple male centaur came into the room, one who Vagus had never met. The centaur had furry skin but a very scaly tail.

"What happened?" the centaur asked.

"Who are you?" Malomira asked.

"My name is Harisa," the centaur said. "His Majesty Deorege came to see me and…"

"He made you prisoner, didn't he?" Malomira said.

"I couldn't remember what happened," Harisa said. "Not for a long time."

"Were you a statue?" Vagus asked.

"I don't know," Harisa said. "I saw statues changing, like back to their live selves, I think."

"It was her magic," Malomira said. "Gemilin must have done this, and Deorege too. She is dead now, so whatever magic she has done to the people is no more."

"Malomira, is that you?" Harisa asked, and Malomira nodded. "His Majesty Deorege deemed you to be dead."

"Of course, he did," Malomira said. "My brother is something of a deceiver and a traitor. He is not the man they all think he is."

"Is that His Royal Highness?" Harisa asked, looking at Deorege's dead body.

Malomira had another long look at the dead body, and then realized that he was king now that Deorege was dead. "Yes, your king is no more. I am now in line for the throne of Aurelia."

"Oh, then forgive my presence, Your Highness," Harisa said.

"Please, your presence is welcome here," Malomira said. "Now, Harisa, please help my friend Vagus to bed. The second room on the right of the corridor. He's been hurt and needs rest, and please gather the citizens of Aurelia. I wish for the announcement of my reign."

"Yes, sire," Harisa said as he approached Vagus and safely lifted him and carried him to the bedroom.

Malomira sat down on the bed and reflected for a moment. He reflected back to when he had been cast out and made to live in the cave; how he went through years of loneliness, and how he might never see his children again. His children then dominated his mind and he kept imagining the worst happening to them.

"They're dead," Malomira said to himself before crying. "My little ones are dead."

Then a polifara guard entered, who hadn't been met by Malomira when he entered the Opraso.

"Prince Malomira, we believed you to be dead," the guard said.

"Is that what they all think?" Malomira asked.

"Yes, sire," the guard said. "Deorege announced your death to his royal subjects."

"I suppose I am dead in some way," Malomira said. "It was not just my brother and sister who betrayed me, but the people too. I've lost everything now. I have no family left."

"I'm sorry for your losses, sire," the guard said.

"Are there more of you?" Malomira asked.

"Yes, Your Highness," the guard said.

"Then we must talk about some new regulations for this place."

"In Aurelia, sire?"

"Yes. Now be on your way, I must visit my friend Vagus."

"Very well, sire."

The guard left the room and Malomira then also left the room and went into the bedroom that Vagus was in. He was sat up in his bed, resting. Vagus had been sleeping on a floor while prisoner at the Opraso, so it was the first time that he actually felt comfortable since being a prisoner.

"I hope you will be well rested," Malomira said to him.

"Thank you," Vagus said. "What will you do now that you're king?"

"I've come to a realization," Malomira said. "I have no family left. You're the only friend I have left."

"Thank you, Malomira," Vagus said. "I'm sure the people of Aurelia will grow to like you."

"Will they?" Malomira asked. "Where were they when I needed them? When I was outcast? Betrayed by my own brother? They believed I was some sort of monster and believed every lie my brother spoke of me."

"Deorege was king," Vagus said. "The people would always believe the word of royalty."

"Even if those words were lies and deceit," Malomira said. "My children were banished from the kingdom, and they never took it upon themselves to help them. They must be dead now. They let my children perish."

"Of course, they didn't," Vagus said. "That's such a foolish thought. There are good people in Aurelia."

"And you believed that my brother and sister were good people?" Malomira asked. "The way they held you prisoner, the things they did to you and to others, do you believe they deserved to die?"

"Malomira, I hate to see conflict and I hate to see death," Vagus said. "I believe in forgiving the mistakes of others. I am grateful to you, but I don't take any pride in seeing the suffering of others, no matter how evil they have become."

"Vagus, you're speaking like a fool. Every year I spent up in that cave, alone, unable to clear my name, I was haunted and powerless. I have power now."

"Malomira, I think you should put down that gun before you harm someone."

"This gun is my key to power and superior to every weapon on Aurelia. I will get respect. I will command respect."

"Malomira, please think about what you are doing."

"Vagus, you need to rest here. I must address my people."

"Malomira, stop!"

Malomira ignored the warnings from Vagus and left the room. Vagus was clearly concerned about Malomira's intentions. Malomira had so much resentment brewing in him, and as Vagus was worried that as long as he held onto his gun, the consequences of Malomira's hatred could turn deadly. However, as Vagus was still in pain from the torture he had been through, he couldn't run after him straight away. He tried, but he found himself hurting whenever he tried to move too fast.

Malomira then entered the kingdom, where a mixture of centaurs, including Harisa, and humans with elf-like ears were present. Polifara guards were also there in corners of the room, monitoring everyone's behaviour.

"Sire, is it true that the king is dead?" a human asked.

"It is true that King Deorege and Princess Gemilin are dead," Malomira said. "Therefore I, Malomira, brother of Deorege, am now your new king!"

"But we thought you were dead," the human said again.

"Deorege spoke many lies," Malomira said. "The rumours of my death were false. I am alive before your eyes."

"But, sire, how is it that our great king perished?" another human asked.

"*Great* king?" Malomira sneered. "I don't care for your definition of the word great. My brother was a traitor who banished me and murdered the woman I love and embarked upon a love affair with our sister Gemilin. And you all call Deorege a great king?"

There were gasps of shock, and some people also said "never", not believing Malomira at first.

"If I may speak," Harisa said as he stepped forward. "The king and his sister turned me and fellow citizens into statues. We knew not of how we became statues, but the curse ended when Malomira saved me. Their deaths have made some of us live again."

Then everyone in the kingdom applauded Malomira.

"So, it was you that killed the king and the princess?" another human asked Malomira.

"Indeed, it was," Malomira said proudly. "Now if I may ask, where were you? Why did you all fall for the lies that my brother told? Deorege murdered Incurtea, your queen, and you all did nothing. My face was scarred, and I was banished by my brother, and not a word about it was spoken. My children were also abandoned. My sweet, innocent children were discarded by the people who claim to be my family. They're probably dead now. I have no family left. My life was torn apart while you all stood back and worshipped the man who had ruined me and destroyed the people I loved most."

"But, sire, we knew not of what happened," Harisa said. "Please, spare these good people of any blame. You have my gratitude and our sympathies."

"Your gratitude and sympathies won't bring back my children," Malomira said. "They will not restore my family."

"Please, Your Majesty, I wish we knew what happened to you," Harisa said. "His Highness said the beast came and took you and Incurtea and…"

"Of course, the beast," Malomira said. "I suppose I was that beast. My brother made me that beast of which you speak. You pitiful fools fell for his lies and prolong my suffering!"

"Please, stop!" Vagus said as he limped into the kingdom. "Malomira, please don't hurt these fine people."

"*Fine* people," Malomira sneered. "These *fine* people worshipped my corrupted brother who made me suffer, and made you suffer. They are all accomplices!"

"No, they are not!" Vagus said. "You are just angry, and I understand that, but violence against these people won't bring your children back. Please, Malomira, this is just irrational and this anger of yours won't compensate for the suffering that you've been through."

"But my children," Malomira said, bursting into tears. "I hadn't seen them in so long and doubt that I will ever see them again. With no family left, I am the one who is truly dead."

"No, Malomira, you're a king now," Vagus said encouragingly. "These people need a true king, and that power must give you some purpose."

"Vagus, when you recover, please help find my children," Malomira requested.

"Malomira, there is no way that I can," Vagus said. "I wish I could help, but…"

"Why not?" Malomira asked with some anger. "You're a wanderer of worlds, aren't you? Where must they be?"

"Please, I don't wish for hatred," Vagus said with caution. "It is not in my position to find your missing children."

"So, you're prepared to do nothing?" Malomira said. "Will someone prepare themselves to find my children? Not for their king?"

"Please, Your Majesty, we are all in deep sorrow for your losses," Harisa said. "We peaceful folk would help if we could, but how can we? We know not of what they look like, and is killing your brother and sister the best example for your children?"

This drew fury from Malomira and he immediately pulled the trigger on his gun and shot Harisa in the head, killing him instantly. This drew screams of horror from the crowd and they ran away, out of the Opraso. Vagus then tried to take the gun from Malomira but couldn't.

"You need rest, Vagus!" Malomira said. "I wish not to hurt you."

Malomira then signalled for the polifara to come on over, and they did so.

"Take Vagus back to the bedroom," Malomira ordered. "He needs all the rest he can get."

"Malomira, stop!" Vagus said in protest.

"Vagus, I'm trying to help you," Malomira said. "You're injured, so guards, please be gentle with him. Carry him back and lock him in the bedroom."

Two polifara guards carried Vagus back to the bedroom. Vagus tried to struggle free, but he was too injured to succeed. The polifara placed him gently onto his bed and then locked the door behind him. With the kingdom empty, Malomira then marched back to Deorege's bedroom, and then he changed out of his ragged clothes that he had worn up in the mountains, and put on Deorege's royal attire, including the crown, and then looked in the mirror, drawing a callous smile to himself.

***

Back in New York, Father Thomas had another prayer meeting in his home. Claire was there, and some other people that I saw when I had been there before, but Kate wasn't there.

"I was lost when my husband died," a middle-aged woman in the group said. "He was a devoted man, did anything for me, and we were so happily in love. But when he was made redundant from his job in favour of a G-54, we struggled for money and food. He became ill and, well, because we were low on money, he…"

"It's okay," Claire said as the woman became tearful and unable to finish her sentence. "It's very brave of you to tell your story. You're doing very well."

"So anyway, after he died," the woman began again, "I was alone, I got depressed and, I'm not gonna lie, I even thought about suicide. I know Christianity had been long gone, but a neighbour and I got talking one day, and he told me about this verse from Corinthians. You know, the verse which begins with 'Blessed be the God and Father of our Lord Jesus Christ, the Father of mercies and God of all comfort'. That was when I started reading more of these verses and it really helped me when I really needed it. Sounds stupid, I know."

"No, of course not," Thomas said softly, which drew a sigh of relief from the woman. "There is nothing stupid about having faith in our Lord, especially when we face adversity and we are left in the darkness."

"But wait a minute, doesn't the Bible also say, 'Even the darkness is not dark to you; the night is bright as the day, for darkness is as light with you'?" another man in the group asked.

But this man wasn't exactly a stranger, although he was a stranger to the group.

It was Anton Monroe.

Anton was dressed in plain clothes; he wore beige trousers and a blue shirt underneath a dark red hooded sweater.

"From the book of Psalms, yes," Thomas answered. "That is another passage that has helped many people in their time of need. It teaches us to embrace the darkness that comes our way and that we must stay strong for when we do find ourselves in darkness. Right, well thanks everybody for another warming meet-up, and we'll look forward to another gathering next week."

Everybody got up from their chairs, with the attendees each saying goodbye to Thomas and Claire. Then eventually Anton approached Thomas and Claire.

"Hey, would it be okay if I can just stay and talk to you about the group?" Anton asked. "I didn't get a chance to speak to you guys during the break. Just for ten minutes?"

"Uh, sure," Thomas said. "Slightly unorthodox as we prefer to speak more with our group members during the break, but sure, we can talk to you more about the group."

Eventually, all the other group members left. Anton then picked up his chair and sat opposite Thomas and Claire.

"So, how did you find your first time here?" Thomas asked.

"Very interesting, actually," Anton said. "I too lost somebody long ago, so I was particularly taken with that last woman's story. What was her name again?"

"Veronica," Claire answered.

"Yeah, her," Anton said. "Anyway, it did bring back those painful experiences for me, but like her, the Bible helped me find myself again."

"Well, great," Claire said. "I'm glad that you managed to find comfort in our Lord. It's Anton, right?"

Anton nodded.

"So, were there any other verses you found inspiring?" Thomas asked.

"I also found God's teachings on growth to be useful," Anton said. "Like the verse which says, 'But grow in the grace and knowledge of our Lord and Saviour Jesus Christ. To him be the glory both now and to the day of eternity'."

"Yes, that is a very powerful passage," Thomas said.

"It did get me thinking though," Anton said. "Like, we shouldn't fear the growth of a person, especially if that growth is making that person better."

"Absolutely," Thomas said.

"So, take Edward Cox for example," Anton said. "I know you guys see Edward and everything he's done as an abomination, but his growth as a scientist and the growth of everything he's done has contributed to the greater good, so we shouldn't fear his Type operation, but we should embrace it."

"Do you know Edward Cox?" Thomas said, as he and Claire started to grow suspicious of Anton.

Anton took a deep breath before he answered, "All right, I confess, I am a friend of Edward's. I didn't want to say anything because I didn't want to upset you guys."

"Okay, I get it," Thomas said. "Did you know that Edward came over here recently?"

"Yes, I heard he did," Anton said. "And I know he attacked you, which was unacceptable of him."

"Well, I'm glad you understand that," Claire said.

"Edward's not normally like that," Anton said. "He's a good guy really; he's just going through a hard time right now because, as I'm sure you must have heard, Terra is missing."

"No, I do understand that," Thomas said.

"He should never have hit you though," Anton said. "That was wrong of him, but he's not in a good way. This is just a really horrible situation."

"Oh, I can imagine," Thomas said. "We do understand the anguish that Edward is going through. I know we'd be feeling the same thing if this happened to us."

"How many kids do you have?" Anton asked.

"Uh, we have one daughter, Kate," Claire said. "She's seventeen years old now."

"She not here?" Anton asked.

"No, she's staying with my sister," Claire said.

"Does she ever come to these meetings?" Anton asked.

"Sometimes," Thomas said. "We don't normally have young people here; we've had a few kids join us in the past, and Terra was one of them."

"Yeah, I heard she came over here," Anton said. "I mean, I heard it from Edward. I've actually never met Terra myself, but I've known Edward for a long time, and he says that she's a very bright, intelligent girl. How did she find this group?"

"Well, she found it very interesting," Thomas said. "She got on with Kate and hopefully we'll see her again."

"Well, we *all* hope that we see Terra again," Anton said as Thomas and Claire nodded in agreement. "I know Edward and a lot of the guys in the upper classes don't really think much of religion, but I've always had an interest in God. My former girlfriend, Mary, was a Christian. We met while we were at university in Scotland. She taught me a lot about God and the teachings of the Bible. Sadly, she got sick and died, but I always remember everything she taught me about religion. Not everybody understands the concept of faith these days, but there are still some folk, like myself, who have some understanding. Do you guys ever have that chicken or the egg argument?"

"What do you mean?" Claire asked.

"You know that question of what came first, the chicken or the egg?" Anton said.

"Uh no, not really," Claire said.

"Anyway, I'm sorry about the passing of Mary," Thomas said. "My grandfather was a pastor at St Thomas' Church in Michigan. It was actually the last known church in North America. I was named after the church. My parents were also devout Christians, taught me about the Bible. Churches were never around since Claire and I were born, so we learnt more about God and Christianity in secret Bible study sessions. That was where Claire and I met actually. We both had an interest in religion and that has kept us together for so many years now."

"That's really romantic actually," Anton said. "I guess Christianity is a beautiful thing if it could help you guys fall in love."

"Yes, I suppose it is," Claire said.

"Anyway, a lot of folk like myself felt persecuted by our interest in God," Thomas said. "Now that religion is equated to insanity, it's hard for people like Claire and I to engage anywhere. We're not rich, but we're not the kind of people that crave money. There are more important things than capitalism, like community and understanding. That Bible study group in high school was one of the best times of our lives. We felt part of something, and we felt appreciated for just being ourselves. That's what I want these gatherings to be; a place where nobody can feel afraid of being who they really are."

"Of course, I totally understand that," Anton said. "I guess Christianity is now some kind of a socialist movement, the sort of thing that a Democrat would do. It's sad that now, here in this world, you good people are seen as outcasts."

"I guess that's one way of putting it, sure," Claire said.

"I guess that faith can be a sign of submission," Anton said. "I mean, look at the ten commandments and the seven sins. You guys might say they're there to help us become better people, but are they there to help us or to dictate to us? I guess one way of looking at those commandments are that they're threatening our humanity, our freedom. I'm surprised they haven't tried telling us how to vote yet."

"I can assure you, the Bible doesn't dictate to anybody," Thomas said. "Those commandments are there to help us become better people, as you suggested before, and live more accomplished lives."

"You see, I actually disagree," Anton said. "As human beings, we're not perfect in God's eyes, so why should we strive for perfection? The only laws we abide by are the ones put into place by the United States of America. Power is such an aphrodisiac and people like Edward work so hard to achieve power, but our way of becoming more prominent in our society is to sometimes contradict the commandments put into place by God. It doesn't mean we're evil of course. I know Edward works hard to provide for his wife and Terra, and I'm sure you guys work hard at what you do to provide for your daughter. In order to become better people in our own eyes, not God's, we don't abide by a particular faith that may wrap us up in guilt. Why should we feel guilty for becoming more powerful? Power can't be a sin, can it? All we want to do is help our fellow men and to make our society and our country a better place to live in. Why is that so wrong?"

"I think you really misunderstand our faith," Thomas said. "We're not demonizing power; we just ask that people think about whether prominence and wealth is really that important. There is more to life than fame and fortune. We're not rich, and the people who come here aren't rich either, but we're not bothered by this. We just want to survive in this world and to be loved and respected by our family and friends. Family and friendship are also very important to us. You,

Edward, and your kind of people might choose to obsess over money and other materialistic things, but our reason for living isn't to obtain as much money as possible, but it's to help our fellow men and be kind to one another. I guess we all have a different meaning to life."

"I guess we do," Anton said. "Well, thank you guys for telling me more about these meetings, and thanks for letting me stay a bit longer."

"You're welcome, Anton," Thomas said. "Have a safe journey home, and hopefully we'll see you at the next meeting."

"Possibly," Anton said as he shook their hands and then walked towards the door. Anton then turned round as soon as he reached the door. "Actually, can I let you guys in on a secret?"

"Uh, sure," Thomas said.

"I have this genetic condition," Anton said. "Let me show you guys."

Anton walked up to Thomas and Claire and presented his hands in front of them. He then asked them, "Do you guys notice anything?"

Thomas and Claire looked closely at Anton's hands, unsure of what it was he wanted to show them. They noticed that Anton's skin was really smooth, almost like the skin of a teenager.

"No fingerprints," Anton told them. "It's very rare amongst people, but it's like I'm an outcast too, just like you guys. In fact, it's almost like I don't even exist."

Anton quickly reached into his sweater pocket and got out a gun and immediately shot Thomas in the head and a scream was only very briefly heard from Claire as she was also shot in the head. They both lay dead next to each other in a puddle of blood. Anton then knelt beside the dead bodies, mindful to not kneel in their blood.

"Technically, I guess this is murder," Anton said to the bodies. "Technically, they'll call it murder, but really, this is transition. This world, this society, is no longer the world for you. Your tributes will say that you've gone to a better place, and they'll actually be true. Now you will be reunited with your people. They who value what used to be, when having faith was a blessing instead of a curse. I think you will both be truly happier in death than you have been in life. You were right about one thing though; we do have a different meaning to life. We can ask 'What is the meaning of life?' and we can expect all kinds of different answers every time, but we all have different purposes and living has many different uses to us. Maybe we should accept that we're all creatures of sin and the ten commandments don't help us like you think they do. They restrict us and dictate to us, and therefore we're not really living. Your spirits may never thank me and may wish vengeance on me, but please understand that

I'm doing you both a favour. For people like you, life is a curse, and death is a blessing."

Anton then stood up and calmly made his way out of Father Thomas' home.

The Prophecy

Hominem was sat against the wall in the dungeon, supervised by three Deinonychus. Two of the dinosaurs stood at each side of the door, while the other was right beside Hominem. He just sat down, still traumatized by Mulieris' death.

Mother then entered the dungeon and the Deinonychus all bowed before her. Hominem stayed sat down and didn't even look at her. He was completely unmoved by Mother's presence.

"Never in an eternity did I ever expect to see you here," Mother said. "And never did I expect you to resort to conflict."

"I trusted him," Hominem said, still looking away from Mother. "He betrayed me."

"Son only acted in everyone's best interests," Mother said. "Including you, Hominem. Son cares about you, even still, and he cared about Mulieris too."

"Did he?" Hominem asked sarcastically, still angry with Son.

"I know you're angry, Hominem," Mother said. "We all know you're angry. We are all sad about Mulieris' death. You are not alone, Hominem, but if your solution to the grievance you bear is to attack, then you will be alone, and you will remain a prisoner here."

"What good is freedom now?" Hominem said. "Without my Mulieris, what good is anything now?"

"The good will come, Hominem," Mother said. "The lives we have made are to experience the good that is out there. There will be pain, Hominem, I cannot deceive you, but the pleasure will come, Hominem. Please trust me."

"The way Son wanted my trust?" Hominem asked, as he started getting angry. "Why must I trust anyone any more? The concept of trust is a lie."

"Trust is a sacred bond, Hominem," Mother said. "A bond that I share with everyone in this world."

"Did Son have that bond?" Hominem asked, still getting angry. "Did Son ever trust in me?"

Hominem then burst into tears. Mother went over to comfort him, but Hominem shunned Mother.

"No, don't," Hominem said. "I cannot trust any more. Without Mulieris, I cannot love any more."

"Then I will leave you, Hominem," Mother said. "If you wish for my company again, I will come, as will Father and as will Son."

Hominem didn't respond. He just remained sat down, staring blankly away from Mother. She then left the dungeon.

Mother then came up to see me in the palace bedroom. I was sat up in the bed, as I was trying to deal with everything that had taken place. I had heard about Mulieris' death and Hominem's imprisonment but wasn't sure why Hominem attacked Son and how exactly Mulieris died. I had a lot of questions, and was hopeful that Mother could answer them, as I was finding it so hard to process everything. Mother then sat beside me on the bed.

"I hope you are finding yourself in comfort, little one," Mother said.

"Yes, Mother," I said. "But what happened, Mother? How did Mulieris die?"

"We don't know precisely, Terra," Mother said as she put her arm around me. "All we know is that it was a disturbance, some kind of intrusion."

"Was it Lucifer?" I asked.

"It's a possibility, Terra," Mother said.

"Does that mean that I'm not safe, here?" I asked, growing anxious.

"Terra, you know that Father and I will protect you with every last breath in our bodies," Mother said. "There was a time when you wouldn't have been safe here. That's why we placed you on Earth. The Underworld have attempted many assaults on our world, but our defences will be stronger this time, Terra. I swear to you."

"Okay, I believe you," I said. "Wouldn't I be safer on Earth?"

"After what happened in Aurelia, there is no other world that can promise your safety," Mother said. "We brought you here when the time was right for your return. Do you miss Earth, Terra?"

"No, I do like it here," I said, but almost reluctantly as I didn't want to hurt Mother's feelings. I did miss New York, but only a little. I missed Edward, Sandra, and Laura, but the Upper World was my true home, the one I had been looking for. If I returned to Earth, how would I explain where I had been? If I told him that my real mother and father were gods and I had been to another planet, he would have thought that I was crazy. I also thought about what could happen to Father Thomas and Claire, and if Edward or anyone would have hurt them. I didn't know of their murder back on Earth. I thought long and hard of what to say next. "It's just, you know, I had been living on Earth and I had a close bond with my foster parents. I mean, kind of close, like I never told them about what I can do, like my healing and stuff."

"Yes, many on Earth would not understand your capabilities," Mother said. "We understand completely what you can do. You are special, little one. Were they good to you on Earth?"

"Oh yeah, they were," I said. "They were never horrible to me or anything, but I've been looking for my real home for so long and I'm so happy that I've found you, but I…"

"What, child?" Mother asked.

"I just never knew that I was ever in danger," I said. "I mean, I was okay on Earth. I mean, I thought I was,

339

but that was because I never knew about the Underworld and Lucifer and that I was targeted. I guess there's so much that I'm learning about myself, like maybe I had no idea who I really was and what destiny I really had."

"I know it's all so much for you, Terra," Mother said. "Believe me, Terra, this is where you belong. I know in your heart Earth was your home, but you've been searching for us your whole life, even if we were not what you anticipated."

"I never imagined that I was royalty. We don't really have royalty on Earth."

"I know this is all new to you, Terra, but this is what has awaited you. I hope you will become accustomed to this lifestyle. We all love you, Terra."

Mother kissed me on my forehead and then embraced me. She said "good night" to me, and then I said it back, and then rested my head on the pillow, slowly drifting off to sleep.

Mother headed into the forest. The valley was quiet, with the dinosaurs resting under the clear night sky, with others resting in various parts of the forest. The adult dinosaurs rested around their young in protective positions, concerned about what had recently taken place in the Upper World. Mother then approached Quercus Alba, who was joined by Father.

"Father, do you have news?" Mother asked.

"A prophecy was told by the Krygurra," Father said.

"What is of this prophecy?" Mother asked.

"The prophecy tells of a saviour," Quercus Alba said. "A boy who comes to save us all."

"A boy, they say?" Father asked.

"This is a very delicate time for our world, and murmurs from Sapillien and the spirits call for a saviour," Quercus Alba said. "The Krygurra speak of one. A boy, not of this world."

"What world does he hail from?" Father asked.

"He is of Earth, Father," Quercus Alba said. "Just like Terra, though they have not met."

"Are the Krygurra sure of this?" Mother asked.

"Mulamma is the wisest of all prophets, Father," Quercus Alba said. "He is sure of this foretelling. A trusted source, he be."

"What does Mulamma know of any other spirits?" Father asked. "Mulieris said she saw one, but it was not of this world. Are there any intruding forces at present?"

"We've been at war since Lucifer's banishment," Quercus Alba said. "The Underworld will always launch assaults on us, and we must be prepared. This saviour might be the solution we seek."

"Did they speak more of this saviour?" Father asked. "Will he be brought to us?"

"In time, he will come," Quercus Alba said. "He is young, they say, but the strength he bears will save us all, as Mulamma speaks. He will need training before he fulfils the destiny he has, and Mulamma plans for his training before his potential will be reached."

"What is his name?" Mother asked.

"Michael," Quercus Alba said.